I picked up the phone. I'd start with my brother.

I dialed his number and the answer was almost immediate. A woman's voice said, "Provincetown Police Department, may I help you?"

"Hi, Jeanine. It's Alex. Is Sonny handy?" She thought so and would ring his office. My brother Sonny is known more officially as Detective Lieutenant Edward J. Peres of the Provincetown Police Department. He's a good cop, and will someday make a good chief. Right now he was my big brother sounding oily, like he wanted something.

"Hey, Alex! Thanks for calling. I know you've got a busy day. Really appreciate it. How's Fargo?"

"Yes, I do, Fargo is fine, what do you want?" I sipped my tea, careful of spills.

"Gee, Alex, it's good to talk to you, too. Nothing big. Trish just bought a little runabout up in Eastham. My SUV can pull it okay, but there's no boat trailer available. I thought maybe you could borrow Mary Sloan's. I know she owes you a favor or two. It would save Trish renting one. We'd like to get it in the water this weekend."

"No. I thought it would be simpler if you handled it. Why?" Simpler for him, maybe. "I don't know. When I got home, I had three phone messages. Yours, one from Mary Sloan and one from John Frost *about* Mary Sloan. That's an awful lot of Mary for one day."

I could sense him shrugging at the phone. "No idea. But I'm sure it's not about the boat . . . just coincidence."

He was wrong. It would be an event-filled summer, but you couldn't really say any of it was coincidental.

Visit

Bella Books

at

BellaBooks.com

or call our toll-free number

1-800-729-4992

The Weekend Visitor

Jessica Thomas

Bella
BOOKS

2006

Printed in the United States of America on acid-free paper
First Edition

Editor: Cindy Cresap
Cover designer: Stephanie Solomon-Lopez

ISBN 1-59493-054-6

To Carol and John, who've proved to me that families needn't be near to be wonderfully close!

And to my editor, Cindy Cresap, who caught a Hail Mary pass—and made a touchdown.

About the Author

Jessica Thomas is a native of Chattanooga, Tennessee, where she attended Girls' Preparatory School. She later graduated cum laude from Bard College, Annandale-on-Hudson, New York, with a bachelor's degree in literature.

After an early retirement, Miss Thomas spent a bit of time doing some rather dull freelance assignments and ghostwriting two totally depressing self-help books, always swearing someday that she would write something that was just plain fun. When her friend, Marian Pressler "gave" her Alex and Fargo, Jessica took them immediately to heart and ran right to her keyboard.

Miss Thomas makes her home in Connecticut with her almost-cocker spaniel, Woofer. Her hobbies include gardening, reading, and animal protection activities.

Chapter 1

The minute I got home, my partner let me know in no uncertain terms that I was in deep trouble. Having been alone in the house for about five hours, he was threatening to report me for cruel and unusual punishment. He'd had food, water, toys and air conditioning, but he hadn't had *me*, and he hadn't had *out*. He was complaining loudly as he now ran around the backyard, keening, nose an inch above the ground, checking what trespassing squirrels and cats might have taken advantage of his imprisonment to frolic on his lawn.

Oh, in case you haven't met, my partner is Fargo, a ninety-pound black Labrador retriever who has never quite grasped the meaning of the phrase, "You can't go with me." But he has other, more positive qualities. He has a sleek, muscular body, a beautiful deep bell of a bark and a heart the size of New Jersey. He is ever (well, nearly ever) by my side—alert and businesslike—and only a fool would raise a hand in my direction.

1

There is one minor fault we keep strictly *entre nous*. When confronted by an upsetting situation, like the time the little cocker spaniel bitch found his attentions too intrusive and bit his ear, or the time a duck hunter fired off both barrels when we were nearby on the beach, Fargo forgets he is not a twenty-pound puppy and leaps into the safety of my arms. This results in my landing flat on my back with Fargo on top of me and both of us highly embarrassed. So I have learned to do a fast sidestep as I grab his collar and yell, "No, Fargo, no attack, boy!" He has no idea what this means, but I think it impresses anyone nearby.

Anyway, he loves me and I love him. I don't comment on his penchant for rolling in strange dead things on the beach. And he has never, *ever* asked me if I am really going to wear that shirt out of the house. Great unions have been built on less.

My telephone message machine wasn't in the best humor, either. Its bleary little red eye was going *blink-blink-blink* pause *blink-blink-blink*, telling me I had three messages waiting-waiting-waiting. I was not in a conversational mood. I was tired. I was hot. I still had a lot to do today. You know how it goes. Feast or famine. Today was feast.

Early this morning I'd flown from Provincetown to Boston to testify in court for an insurance company that pays me to check out possible fraudulent injury claims. Me? I'm Alex Peres. My real first name is Alexandra, but unless you are a close relative at least fifty years in age, you will be wise to call me Alex. I'm a Private Investigator retained by several insurance companies to look after their interests in Provincetown. Tourist towns are always happy hunting grounds for those who feel a fortuitous slip or a fall or a nudge by a slowly moving car is a great way to fill the family coffers while enjoying a bit of sun and sea. I try to separate the likely claims from the absurd.

From time to time, I also check out a potential employee for a local business, trace down an heir, look for runaways whose parents think, or at least hope, their kid may have headed here, and when *my* coffers are low, I do my least favorite work: I investigate

2

a spouse who is thought to be grazing in forbidden pastures. I've even looked into a murder or two, but unfortunately have never been the kind of slick TV sleuth who can toss off the third martini, cuddle up to a statuesque blonde and say, "Your place or mine, kiddo?" and not have the fourth martini poured in my ear.

This morning's insurance case had been pretty simple. A few weeks back, a woman had taken a fall over a tricycle left on the walkway of the B&B where she had been staying here in Provincetown. She was carted, groaning, to our nearby clinic, where doctors found nothing obviously wrong but would not commit themselves regarding a back injury. She hobbled around town for a couple of days, walking laboriously with a cane. But late one evening, she and her husband headed quietly for a local club, where I took several very clear photos of them enjoying a rather athletic *salsa*. I presented the date-stamped photos in court this morning. And once again, justice triumphed! Or at least fraud lost.

That chore complete, I hied it back to Logan Airport, where my friend Cassie was waiting. Cassie is president, pilot, mechanic and receptionist of Outer Cape Charter, whose fleet includes a small twin-engine Beechcraft . . . period. She is a consummate pilot, a pal to cherish, and I'd have taken off for Timbuktu with her in a heartbeat. When I needed to get somewhere in a hurry she was always there, and charged me airline—not charter—rates, so I could legitimately pass the expenses along to my clients.

Back at Ptown Airport, we parted quickly, without our usual coffee or beer. We both had to be spiffed up and shining at the same place in about two hours: namely, Fishermen's Bank.

The bank was having a dual celebration late this afternoon. For one thing it had just finished a lavish and long overdue interior redecoration of its 1870's building, including, of course, its two main conference rooms. The larger would feature original art by several of Ptown's most accomplished painters. The smaller would be hung with no less than seven of my black-and-white photos! Nature photography has long been a hobby, avocation, second career . . . whatever . . . for me. My work appears in several local

3

galleries and brings in a fair amount of money. But this . . . this was not only a helluva sale, but also an honor.

The second half of Fishermen's gala was to mark the opening of their Financial Services Center, of which the Chief Financial Planner was my lover, Cindy. So I figured I'd better get my tail down there before too long because, one, I'd do well to make nice with the Board of Directors and, two, Cindy would kill me if I didn't show up.

But before I headed for the shower, I punched the play button on the answering machine. When the tape finished playing, I was less thrilled than ever and was thoroughly confused as well. The first call was from my brother, Sonny. He wanted to ask me a small favor regarding Mary Sloan. The second call was from John Frost, a local attorney who sent most of his investigatory work my way. He wanted to see me regarding a possible case that had been referred to him by Mary Sloan. The third was from Mary Sloan, who wanted me to call her regarding an important matter.

I don't know Mary Sloan very well, and I don't like her very well, either. She's a rather small woman with curly, sandy hair, still this side of forty, but not by much. She works for the phone company, apparently a valued, long-time installation/repair person, and she lives down in the east end of town in a small, immaculately kept house with a small, immaculately kept yard and an immaculately kept tan SUV. As far as I knew, the SUV got briefly dirty twice a year . . . when she put her immaculately kept boat into the water, and when she took it out again.

For these two tasks, Mary needed help. She called on various people, seemingly at random, not with a request for aid, but a statement of when and where you were to appear. You'd figure that, after the wet, messy chore was completed, Mary would invite you back for coffee or a drink or, if you were walking, at least give you a ride home. Not so. A stingy word of thanks about did it, and you were left to squish your way home, or to the nearest bar, or first aid station, as you saw fit.

I'd been her victim last fall. We finally got her boat out of the water and onto the trailer, just as it started to pour rain. Reluctantly, Mary gave me a ride downtown, where she said she had a dental appointment, and left me to walk home in the rain, nursing a badly scraped shin. The spring before my misadventure, she'd abandoned a friend of mine who'd stepped in a hole and hurt his ankle while getting her boat *into* the water. Poor Wolf had had to hobble to the nearest phone and get his lover to come rescue him. Another time, one of the local cops had fallen casualty by helping push Mary's vehicle when she got it stuck in the sand. They got it rolling. She roared away trailing rooster feathers of water and sand and leaving Mitch standing in eight inches of water, looking as if he'd been sprayed with stucco.

This general attitude may have been why Mary seemed terminally single. She wasn't bad looking, and she fell in love easily. The minute the affair was consummated, she wanted the other woman to move right in and start their life together. Unfortunately, when the move was consummated, the new lover usually found most of her belongings exiled to Mary's garage because "there just wasn't room" in the house, and discovered her weekends devoted to housecleaning, which found Mary dusting and "picking up," while the lover mopped the kitchen and cleaned the bathroom.

One of her recent exes had cornered me in the Wharf Rat Bar shortly after their breakup. It was a dismal day and Dee was fertilizing her depression with a heavy treatment of scotch. With every sip she felt compelled to tell me more about their short-lived romance. She knew it would go no further.

That's both an advantage and a disadvantage to being a private investigator. People know a PI may have big ears, but they also know you won't be in business long if you have a big mouth. So you become the vault for many strange confessions, most of which you'd rather not hear and try to forget, but occasionally for information that is, or later becomes, quite valuable. I had no reason to think Dee's screed was of any potential value, but I couldn't shut her up, either, so I had simply let the words flow.

Actually, I only remembered one small section of the monologue, and that because it struck me funny. According to Dee, Mary was not especially physically motivated, but was extremely *romantically* motivated—at least verbally. Dee said it was like being trapped in an old movie rerun with breathy comments like, "Take me, my darling, I'm yours," "You fill me with mad desire," "Do what you will, I am helpless in your arms," and other remarks that would have sent me scampering down the street, still pulling on my clothes.

Now I didn't say any of this information was nice. But it comprised my mental file on Mary Sloan, and you can understand it did not brighten my day that Mary had appeared, as it were, three times on my horizon.

A shower didn't give me any inspiration. Nor did putting on makeup and getting dressed in my "other" good summer outfit. I donned the navy slacks and white blouse. I'd add the blue-and-white striped blazer when I got to the bank. For now, I walked into the kitchen, wishing for a beer and settling for iced tea. My partner approached, looking sad. He knew that the "good" clothes probably meant he wasn't invited. Again.

I looked into those intelligent, warm brown eyes and explained, "There's a party at the bank. I have to go." He gave half a tail wag. If there was a party, why was he being left behind? "It's business." *Yeah?* "Lots of people." *So?* "Forget it." *Sigh.*

"Now, Fargo, what do you think of the Mary Sloan tapes?" He slumped morosely to the floor, possibly because Mary was not one of his favorite people either. "I know," I said. "I'm not fond of her myself, but I wonder what on earth is going on." I sat at the table and lit a cigarette. It was my fifth of the day . . . all I allowed myself. If I had another one, I would lecture myself quite sternly. I checked my watch. I still had a little time.

I picked up the phone. I'd start with my brother.

I dialed his number and the answer was almost immediate. A woman's voice said, "Provincetown Police Department, may I help you?"

"Hi, Jeanine. It's Alex. Is Sonny handy?" She thought so and would ring his office. My brother Sonny is known more officially as Detective Lieutenant Edward J. Peres of the Provincetown Police Department. He's a good cop, and will someday make a good chief. Right now he was my big brother sounding oily, like he wanted something.

"Hey, Alex! Thanks for calling. I know you've got a busy day. Really appreciate it. How's Fargo?"

"Yes, I do, Fargo is fine, what do you want?" I sipped my tea, careful of spills.

"Gee, Alex, it's good to talk to you, too. Nothing big. Trish just bought a little runabout up in Eastham. My SUV can pull it okay, but there's no boat trailer available. I thought maybe you could borrow Mary Sloan's. I know she owes you a favor or two. It would save Trish renting one. We'd like to get it in the water this weekend."

I took a drag on number five and thought for a moment. Trish was Sonny's latest girlfriend. She was a nice young woman lawyer, and John Frost's assistant. And now she wanted a favor from Mary Sloan. All happenstance? "Sonny," I asked, "Have you already talked to Mary?"

"No. I thought it would be simpler if you handled it. Why?"

Simpler for him, maybe. "I don't know. When I got home, I had three phone messages. Yours, one from Mary Sloan and one from John Frost *about* Mary Sloan. That's an awful lot of Mary for one day."

I could sense him shrugging at the phone. "No idea. But I'm sure it's not about the boat . . . just coincidence."

He was wrong. It would be an event-filled summer, but you couldn't really say any of it was coincidental.

Chapter 2

I got one of the last spaces in the bank parking lot, which told me the party must be well underway. I walked through the little pocket park, past the fountain and approached the big, heavy double glass doors set between their towering guardians of granite pillars. A uniformed guard took my invitation and opened the door for me. How very Hollywood!

I walked inside to find my eyes drawn irresistibly upward by a giant, radiant crystal chandelier, reaching all the way to the third floor ceiling, its thousands of facets reflecting golden daggers off the tellers' brass grilles and the brass bars protecting the open vault, where I was certain one could still find small chests of escudos and louis d'or and golden guineas among the grimy canvas bags of current base metal coins and grubby paper bills.

The old steel and tile counters where customers could write checks or fill in slips had been exchanged for stands made from single pieces of polished marble that somehow looked light and airy and had bases that traced the upward sweep of the powerful marble support columns. The old bank had become a bright and welcoming place of business while retaining its dignified message that you were in a place where serious transactions took place, involving . . . *money*. It looked and felt and smelled like a bank, as opposed to so many banks today, which remind you of a somewhat sleazy real estate office. I loved it.

Brilliant crimson paths of carpeting led you wherever you wished to go. Right now, I wanted to go to a young woman some twenty feet away, bidding a smiling farewell to a middle-aged couple. The young woman had short, dark curly hair, never entirely under control, rich brown eyes and a slightly Mediterranean complexion that made her tan beautifully. Her wide mouth smiled easily and her nose just missed being Roman. She wore an off-white dress with a scooped neck and a slightly draped hemline. Except for a slim gold wristwatch, her only jewelry was a gold chain holding a fairly sizeable ruby that made her somehow an integral part of this elegant building, and which I recognized as belonging to my mother. Obviously it was on loan for the occasion.

As the couple moved away, I approached. Cindy turned to me and smiled, and I felt a warmth that was far more than physical. I touched my fingertips lightly to her cheek for a moment. "You are simply stunning."

She ran her hand along my jacket sleeve. "We make a stunning pair. Blue is definitely your color. I'm so glad you made it. I was afraid you might get tied up. But I saw Cassie come in a minute ago, so I figured you'd be along."

A waiter approached with a tray of filled champagne glasses. I took one gratefully. Cindy shook her head regretfully. "Later," she sighed, "Much later."

I laughed. "The price of glory. When do you think you'll get out of here? Do you want to go out to dinner or what?"

"I'll be lucky to be out by seven. You know these things drag on. By then I doubt if either one of us will want to go out. You must be tired already. Why don't you just get some takeout, and that way if you get hungry, you can eat."

"Okay." I was about to add that I'd wait dinner for her, when I saw my nemesis *du jour* approaching, already too close for me to make an escape, and bearing down on us with the all-cylinder dedication of a Hummer traversing deep mud. "Hello, Mary, how are you?"

For some reason, she shook my hand. "Hello, Alex." She turned with a slight bow. "And you must be Cindy?" Before Cindy could answer, Mary carried on. "I'm Mary Sloan and I'd like you both to meet Maureen Delaney."

Amid handshakes and hellos, I looked closely at the girl, for girl she was. I put her at about nineteen and wondered who on earth she could be. A young cousin? A niece? Surely not a lover? Although she would certainly make an attractive one. Red hair, blue eyes, creamy skin . . . Irish to the core. She had a sweet smile and seemed rather shy, yet when she shook hands, her clasp was warm and firm. And when she spoke, there was the slight, appealing lilt that confirmed my earlier thought.

As usual, Mary came right to the point. "Alex, did you get my call?" At my nod, she continued. "Good. When can we get together?"

I thought swiftly. I wanted to see, or at least talk to, John Frost before I talked to Mary. "Well, uh, I have an appointment in the morning. How about tomorrow afternoon?"

"Fine. I get off at three. I'll see you at my house a little after that." She turned to Cindy. "Now, Cindy, we need to talk to you about investments, especially one of those funds where you get a tax break on money saved for a child's college expenses, and also how we can set up a Roth plan when there's a company pension."

Cindy looked a little dazed, but swung manfully into her professional song and dance. She wasn't the only one confused. Why would Mary be interested in college plans? She had no children that I knew of, and if Maureen were indeed a relative Mary was helping through school, she would need money *now*, not ten or fifteen years from now. Before I could think further down these lines,

Mary turned to me and said, "So I'll see you tomorrow, right, Alex?"

I had been dismissed. I smiled weakly, muttered something and turned away, resisting a strong impulse to come to attention and salute. I found a waiter, traded my empty for a full glass and started upstairs toward the conference rooms to regroup. I was irritated at myself for being so spineless. It was Mary who was out of line, not me. This was a social occasion, not a time for intimate financial discussions. She might have advised Cindy she'd like to talk with her, but not started into details. And she had obviously embarrassed Maureen. I should have stepped on Mary's toes.

No, I shouldn't. I would then have embarrassed Cindy, who was at work, not play, this afternoon. It was her problem, not mine, and she would handle it graciously. Let it go. Face it, Mary was like a label in your shirt: either you don't know it's there, or it's driving you crazy. I walked into the small conference room and my mood immediately brightened.

Here the crimson carpet gave way to deep sumptuous gray, on which sat a large table with eight matching chairs, all in American cherry, matte finished in black and hand-rubbed to let the rich brown of the wood intermittently show through. The walls were a pale peach and adorned with several of my black-and-white photos, greatly enlarged and framed in cherry wood. Deeper peach draperies were pulled closed, and spotlights shown on each photograph. It was a spectacular room!

And the photos were mostly my favorites. There was one of Fargo, on his hind legs, front paws stretched up against the trunk of a small pine tree. Just above him was a head-down squirrel, nose not two inches from Fargo's . . . both laughing. Another favorite was a line of nine starlings, feathers bushed out and dripping wet, grumpily sitting out a heavy rain along a phone wire, and looking like Supreme Court Justices about to hand down an unpopular verdict. And there was one of a glass water tank filled with minnows, a homemade *Bait for Sale* sign askew on the tank's side. On the mesh top lay a very contented, very fat cat dozing in the sun.

The other pictures were more commercial. A flight of Canada

geese, a fog rolling in across the marsh, an old dog dozing beside an empty deck chair, a fishing boat, lines garlanded with rime, sparkling in the sun. They all looked great to me. Nature photography was my "second career," and it looked as if it were taking hold. I felt I had arrived.

I walked out onto the balcony and perused the scene below. Cindy had somehow gotten rid of Mary and Maureen and was now shaking hands with a young man I didn't know. The two Ms had progressed to a buffet table and were making a meal out of a bowl of iced shrimp. It looked tempting. I'd get there at some point. Maureen said something to Mary with a smile. Was Maureen gay? My gaydar, usually sharp, was not telling me anything.

I continued my visual sweep and spotted my mother talking to bank VP Choate Ellis. Mom looked particularly elegant in a lavender dress with a lavender, green and white short jacket. Ellis made some remark that made her reach out and touch his sleeve, laughing. He preened as she touched him, and I didn't blame him. She looked great when she laughed. Still slim and straight, she had good legs and square shoulders. Her wavy hair, once a true auburn, now had enough white in it to look reddish blonde. She was damn good looking for a woman in her fifties. I was told I was the spitting image of her when she had been in her early thirties. I hoped that luck held.

My glass was empty, so I made my way back down to waiter country and got a fresh one. I made my curtsies to various bank officials to thank them again for selecting my photos for display, in between snagging some broiled scallops with bacon from a tired-looking waitress. I managed a fast hello to my Mom and a brief stop at the shrimp shrine. I waved to Cassie, said hello to Vance and Charlie and suddenly realized I was beat.

Cindy was now surrounded by three earnest-looking young men, so I simply caught her eye, blew a kiss and left. I made a fast stop at the Chinese take-out. I figured egg rolls, shrimp with bacon, chicken with veggies and pork-fried rice ought to give us a nice variety.

At home, I let a sulky Fargo out while I changed into oh-so-welcome T-shirt and jeans and poured some iced tea. I saw Fargo walk over and look down the driveway. Then he looked at me, *Where was Cindy?* "Later," I called, "She'll be here later." I went out and flopped on a handy chaise and scratched Fargo's ears. "She had to work. But she will come soon, soon." He sighed and lay down, and I wondered again about Mary Sloan's companion. Obviously, friendships and love affairs were not limited to people of your own exact age. Everything I knew about Mary said she was a control freak. Maybe Maureen didn't mind that . . . very young, in a strange country. Maybe she was using Mary as a mother. And Mary was using her as a . . . what? My first, uncharitable thought was a maid. But maybe not. Maybe Maureen *was* a relative, or maybe Mary felt Maureen was a surrogate daughter. Maybe they were madly in love. Maybe it was none of my business.

I wondered what problem Mary had that required, first, a lawyer and then, probably, an investigator. That *would* be my business. But it would wait for tomorrow. In a few minutes I would go and cut up a salad to have with dinner. Right now, I would have a cigarette. I had the feeling it was number six for the day, so I lectured myself sternly and swore it would be the last. Probably.

It was still a little strange to me to consider two for dinner. When Cindy had moved up from Rhode Island to take the job with Fishermen's Bank, she had rented a diminutive cottage from my Aunt Mae. Cindy loved the little place, which overlooked a small pond and my aunt's extensive herb gardens. And when we finally became lovers, she saw no reason to give it up.

I say finally, because we knew each other and were friends for several months before we found our way to bed. I assure you it was worth the wait. It was simply a great departure for me. Usually, I fell madly in lust, fell immediately into bed and then fell into mild depression wondering what the hell I had gotten myself into.

This way I pretty well knew what I was into. And I liked it. I think.

Cindy could still come up with surprises. She had learned early

13

on that I was leery of commitments, and when we became lovers, she suggested that we not live together. Sometimes our schedules disagreed sharply. Sometimes I traveled a bit. Sometimes one of us would simply feel like being alone. We should have that option, she opined. It had nothing to do with monogamy and with loving each other.

It seemed to be working well. And I went happily in to chop up some greens. As I did this, Cindy came in the back door, carrying her shoes. "I think I am crippled for life." She gave me a sort of sideswipe kiss. "Shower. If I am not back in fifteen minutes, call 911."

I finished the salad, put the entrees in the microwave and set the table. Cindy timed it well and came through the kitchen door as the micro buzzed. She was barefoot and wearing only a terry robe. I held her close for a moment as she sighed, "Forgive me for not getting dressed. I simply couldn't face it."

"Let's eat," I said. "Then we can just collapse."

She looked in the cartons and began to fill her plate. "Oh, this all looks wonderful!"

We ate silently and fast for a few minutes and then slowed. "How did it go?" I asked.

"Great, I think. I know Choate Ellis was pleased, and he's the one who counts. So was his stone-faced brother. I actually saw him break a smile. Small, but it was there. And loads and loads of new people seemed interested in our Financial Planning Services. If even half of them follow through, I'm gonna be really busy."

"Great. Among them, I'm sure, will be Mary Sloan and friend."

"Oh, please! She's a walking emery board. Wherever you touch her, she rasps. Pass me my fortune cookie." I complied and she broke it open. "It says I will be very busy in my chosen work. Wonderful. Tell me something I don't know."

I followed suit with the other cookie and unfolded the little paper. "Oh, great. It says I will soon go on a trip. I hope that means to bed. I am beat."

We gave the kitchen a fast straighten-up and went to bed. We

14

both struggled to stay awake through an episode of *Law and Order.* Cindy was losing the battle. I leaned across her to turn off her bedside light and caused the top sheet to fall away from her breast. She had brought a glass of wine to bed, but hadn't finished it. It sat on her night table, and I caught a few drops of wine on the end of my finger and drizzled it on her breast. She opened one sleepy eye and smiled.

I dipped my head and licked the wine. Pretending to savor it, I smacked my lips and said, "A-aa-aah! Delightful little wine! A bit sassy and assertive, but—"

Somewhere, Cindy found a surge of energy. "*Sassy and assertive?*" she laughed. She sat up and pushed me away and I rolled onto my back. "You want sassy and assertive? *I'll* give you sassy and assertive."

And so she did.

Chapter 3

I felt a cold, wet nose nuzzling the back of my neck. Being a trained observer, I was pretty sure it was Fargo, not Cindy. I turned over softly and reached an arm out into the cool morning to stroke his silky cheek. His warm, bright eyes held a hopeful look, and his rudder tail gave little half-wags. Perhaps I am a pushover, but I find it very hard to resist those eyes.

Dogs are not allowed on the beach in the summer. It is against the law. I am the sister of a police officer. I am on friendly terms with most of Provincetown's finest. But I don't speed. I don't drive when I've been drinking much. I don't park in crosswalks or near fireplugs. I don't start fights in bars or shoplift or make loud noises late at night. I try to be very law-abiding, so that neither Sonny, nor his subordinates nor I might be placed in an embarrassing situation.

But I took Fargo to the beach. He understood many things, but he did not understand why he could not run and swim on a fresh and sunny early summer morning. And neither did I. So I broke that law three or four mornings a week, secure in the knowledge I would not be ticketed. We went to Race Point. It was barely six o'clock, and the beach was deserted except for a few surf fishermen, left over from the night. The surf itself was gentle, the air calm. It did not have the brittle snap of the fall, but a softer, enveloping touch, like a cool hand on a tired brow. The tide was out, and Fargo took off across the hard sand, low and fast, like a solid black cheetah, chasing some unseen prey for nearly a quarter of a mile. He made a sudden skidding turn and was in the water, all fifty-five degrees of it, splashing through it, swimming out, then back. Then trotting up to me for a pat and bringing with him the odor of ocean and wet dog. I found neither objectionable. Then again, he ran, joyous and enviably carefree.

I was armed with a plastic bag for poopie pick-up, being not entirely unmindful of our obligations to our biggest cash crop— the tourist. And if a passing patrol car noticed us, they did not make their presence known.

When we got home, Cindy was seated at the kitchen table with hot coffee and cold cereal. She was already dressed and presented her cheek for a chaste kiss. "I know where you two have been." She smiled. "I wait for the day I have to come and bail you out."

I poured a mug of coffee and sat opposite her. "Won't happen at least till the current crop of officers retire," I said smugly. "We're safe for now. How come you're wearing jeans and a shirt? Aren't you going to work?"

"It's dress-down Friday," she reminded me. "Thank God. I'm not up to another day like yesterday. Even sneakers hurt. What's your drill for the day?"

I lit cigarette one of the allotted five. The first one was always the best. Obviously it was bad for you. Nothing that tasted that great could be good for you. "I've got to catch up with John Frost this morning. Mary Sloan has retained him for some reason, and he wants me to investigate something connected with it. I've no idea what. Then around three, I have to see Mary herself. I can't imagine what on earth this is all about."

I got up and got more coffee. Cindy shook her head at the

carafe I had waved toward her. "Maybe," she said, "Mary came into some money. She was asking about all kinds of investments yesterday . . . or trying to, until I finally convinced her she was at a party, not a business conference. Well, change of subject—I have every hope of leaving that bank on time today. Why don't you come over to the cottage when you finish with Mary and we'll do something about dinner?"

"Fine. I shouldn't be long at Mary's, I imagine."

"Well, if you beat me home, take the chicken out of the freezer and light the grill." She stood, gave me a light kiss, Fargo a light pat and was off.

I turned to my coffee and cigarette. My thoughts jumped hither and yon. I mused fruitlessly over what John wanted. Maybe Cindy was right about an inheritance, but why would that involve me? You just took the money and ran. A problem at work? Harassment, maybe. Or with a neighbor? Mary wouldn't take kindly to any encroachment, real or perceived. Any way I looked at it, I was surprised Mary would spend the money on a lawyer and allow him to hire an investigator unless it was really important. Well, I'd find out shortly.

A couple of hours later, Fargo and I set off for our 10:30 appointment. We walked down Commercial Street toward the center of town, and we had lots of company. We already had a ground cover of tourists. Like weeds, they started popping up in May, grew thick in June, and completely overran us in July and August. Slowly, slowly they began to thin again in September and pretty well disappeared in November, depending on how the weather held up. Very few tourists were spotted for the following four months . . . and they were the purists who truly loved the cold, bleak beauty of our winters.

With Fargo padding alertly at my side, we were virtually assured of a roomy right-of-way on the sidewalk . . . of which we took full advantage. On the one hand, I was glad to see the tourists every year, for some of their activities contributed heavily to my income. And my Aunt Mae's. And Cassie's. Tourists were the main reason Ptown had a sizeable police force for Sonny to help oversee.

They put food on the tables of most of my friends. Yes, I was glad to see them. On the other hand, I didn't do overly well in crowds.

We reached John's office and were both happy to be off the bustling sidewalks and away from the heavy, exhaust-spewing traffic. John's secretary said he was expecting me. She gave Fargo a dubious smile, and said to go on in. I opened the door to his office, and we walked in to find him in conversation with Trish Woodworth, Sonny's girlfriend. She and Sonny make a handsome pair. Sonny with the wavy dark hair and always-tan skin of our Portuguese father, and Trish with light skin and baby-fine, whitish blonde hair, worn in a sort of Dutch cut. I imagine any other style would last about an hour.

We all said our good mornings. John, as usual, called Fargo *Denver* and had to be corrected. We chatted a moment about the bank's fete of yesterday. Then John sighed and pulled a yellow pad in front of him.

"Well, let's get moving on this. It's an unhappy, unpleasant affair here. We seem to have on our hands a case of date rape."

I looked up, startled. "*Mary was raped?* That's awful! But why come to you, John? Why hasn't she called the police?" I had a second thought. "My God, I just saw her yesterday at the bank. She seemed fine. When did this happen?"

John looked up and shook his head. What had been a round face in his youth was now somewhat elongated by a receding hairline. It gave him an overly solemn look like that famous portrait of Shakespeare, and belied his rather jovial nature. "Sorry," he said. "I misled you. It wasn't Mary who was raped. It was her young . . . er, friend. Maureen Delaney. And it was Sunday night."

I still didn't understand. "Maureen was with Mary yesterday. She seemed fine, too. If that happened to me, I don't think I'd be at a big affair anytime soon. I'd be sure everyone there, even if they didn't know me, would know what had happened and be secretly nudging each other."

Trish added a comment. "She's young, Alex. Kids recover fast. She's barely twenty-one. And maybe Mary thought it would do her good to get out. Just what is her relationship with Mary, anyway?"

"Don't ask me. I thought she was a niece or something."

"I think it's or something," John twinkled. "Mary referred to Maureen as friend and housemate. They work together. Or at least they both work for the phone company."

I lit a cigarette. John looked pleased and pulled a pack of his own from his desk. Trish wrinkled her nose at both of us.

"Housemate?" I repeated. Another thing not understood. "I never thought Mary had much luck with housemates. And Maureen her lover? There must be fifteen, sixteen years age difference there."

"That's not necessarily a barrier," John pointed out. "Sometimes those arrangements work out well. Anyway, let's continue. The night of Sunday, June fourth, Maureen met some female friends at the Bitter End. After a glass or two of wine, her friends left. They all had to work the next day. Maureen had Monday off. It was approximately nine thirty. Maureen vaguely remembers that she stayed a few minutes to finish her drink, and that she moved to the bar, rather than finish it alone at their table. That's about all she remembers." John paused and sipped from a glass of water on his desk.

"Did she know the man? Does she recall anything about him?" I asked.

"She doesn't recall much," Trish supplied.

"All she remembers," John continued, "is that he was Caucasian and may have had dark hair. She remembers a breeze, as if riding in a car, a large building, possibly light gray or white, and steps. The next thing she remembers, she was standing in Mary's kitchen with Mary shaking her and asking what was wrong. Mary recalls noticing a car just backing out the end of her driveway, though she didn't notice what kind or color. That was sometime after one a.m."

"I thought the building might be the old icehouse condos," Trish said.

"Good possibility," I agreed. I leaned over and put my cigarette out. "And what about the cops? What are they saying? I really don't understand why the three of us are sitting here."

John sighed and shuffled some papers. "They did not report it to the police. First, Mary didn't feel that Maureen was up to it. She seemed to feel that the police would not be sensitive to the girl's feelings and need of privacy, also that if the police knew, the press would know. And sometimes, unfortunately, that's quite correct." I shifted in my chair and wanted to disagree. I thought they would be as sensitive as anyone could be. They would perforce ask intimate and embarrassing questions, but they would try to be delicate. Leaks to the press, however, were an ongoing problem in any police department, Ptown being no exception.

"So," John finalized, "Let's try to find the man and find exactly what happened. If there was a crime we will, by law, report it. I've advised them of this. Then the question is, will Maureen be willing to go to an open trial and testify against this man? A quiet damages settlement may be more what she has in mind."

I raised my eyebrows at that, but John added nothing and stood up. We were finished. As we walked out of John's office, Trish turned to me. "Wait just a second. I have your authorizations to ask questions on Maureen's behalf and to check the medical records. I'll go get them."

"Then I take it she did at least see a doctor?" I asked.

John nodded. "Yes, Mary took her to the clinic, and," he added dryly, "somehow convinced them not to report it. Excuse me, Alex, got to run. I'm due in court."

I sat back down to wait for Trish. Fargo yawned, so of course I did, too. But I was far from bored. Of all crimes, next to murder and I guess child abuse, I hated rape the worst. Even if the woman was not physically injured, the damage to her psyche was enormous and often irreversible. Thus far, finding the perpetrator seemed unlikely. But by God, I'd give it my best shot. He was probably walking around feeling smug, and I would greatly enjoy slapping the smile off his face.

Chapter 4

It was almost noon when Fargo and I joined the slow, lock-step procession up Commercial Street. More tourists had surfaced as the morning passed, and though our progress was slow, it was pointless to try to move otherwise. The sun was warm, and a montage of good smells from numerous restaurants, exotic food shops and candy stores wafted past our noses. By the time we got to my "other office," the Wharf Rat Bar, Fargo was whuffling from trying to process all the odors at once, and I felt in need of sustenance.

Turning down the alley to the Rat, I tied Fargo to the big anchor outside its front door and went in. I took a plastic cup of water out to him and went back to pick up the beer Joe had placed on the end of the bar. I found my way to an empty table, still not used to finding the Rat so filled at the noon hour.

There were some locals at the bar, but most of the tables were taken by tourists, with one daily exception. The big table at the front of the room was always filled, in relays, by what Joe the bartender and I called the Ptown Blues Boys. They were a group of full- and part-time fishermen who came and went to have a few beers and sing the blues over low prices for fish, high prices for fuel, scarcities and quotas.

Their lead singer was Harmon, a disheveled character who sometimes fished and sometimes did odd jobs or beachcombed and frequently imbibed large quantities of beer. He had a heart of gold and the sure conviction that he was placed on this earth to thwart the drug dealers he saw on every corner. My brother Sonny said that Harmon had reported forty-two of the last five drug trades in Provincetown. The choir was in concert, and Harmon was warbling his solo.

"There's a little yellow seaplane docked right downtown this very minute. Now don't that just prove how brassy these dealers is gettin'?" His cronies looked blank. I imagine I did, too. Harmon explained. "Well, you know they just fly in here to gas up and maybe eat. And tonight they'll be flying out to meet the mother ship and pick up the drugs."

"Aa-a-haaah!" The round table replied solemnly. Now they got it. I didn't. I wondered if it would really pay to carry drugs in a small two-seater. I wondered if the little craft could land in Atlantic-class waves. I wondered why they would paint it bright yellow and gas up at the Cape's busiest town. I wondered several other things, including what I might have for lunch. I waved Joe over and decided on a pastrami sandwich with french fries and a half sour pickle and sat back to enjoy my beer.

I looked around at the tourists among us. They all seemed favorably impressed by the Wharf Rat's determinedly nautical décor. Fishnets hung everywhere, studded with starfish, clam shells and scallop shells. Long oars and boathooks were crisscrossed like medieval weapons on the walls, which also held old lobster pot markers, cork buoys and an ancient diving helmet. Kedge anchors hid in dim, dusty corners, ready to trip the unwary. A ship's telegraph, rescued from a long-scrapped ferry, with the indicator frozen on *All Astern Slow*, provided as good a motto as any for the Rat.

My lunch came and I looked it over with pleasure, debating

which food should merit the first bite. Then, remembering I was trying to eat more sensibly, I made a healthy decision. I would not add ketchup to the fries, and I would save a large bite of the sandwich for Fargo. Feeling terribly pure, I dug in.

While I ate, I mused about how much of the morning's information I could ethically tell Sonny. No names, that was a given. And he'd be pissed that they hadn't called in the police the night it happened. I knew the hospital would have urged Maureen to report it. She must have tossed a fit and said she'd swear it was consensual. I could feel that somehow John wasn't happy, either. I wasn't sure why, but I had wondered about his comment regarding damages. A little early to be on that track, wasn't it?

Well, I'd tell Sonny the bare bones. I wanted to ask him if there had been any similar occurrences of late or even any rumors. If he had *not* heard anything, I wanted to put him on the alert. We didn't need a rapist in town anytime, but especially not with the height of the season upon us. That was a frightening thought. I'd call Sonny when I got home.

"Frowns cause wrinkles, which make you look old and grumpy," announced a male voice. I wouldn't have to call my brother, it seemed, as he was now pulling up a chair to join me.

"I've a way to go to catch up with you," I replied. "But you'll be looking ninety in about a minute. I've got some interesting news."

"Well, let me at least get some lunch." He turned to Joe, who had followed him to the table. "Hi, Joe. Never mind the menu, I'll just ditto Alex, okay? Only make mine iced tea. I'm on duty."

He looked back at me and grinned. "All right. Make me frown."

"We've got a rapist in town."

"First I've heard of it." He shrugged. "What makes you think so?"

"I just left John Frost's office. He wants me to look around in a case of his. A young female client was apparently at a local bar, got something dumped in her drink, had a lengthy blackout and came to at her own back door, having been raped by an unknown male."

"Why didn't she call us?" *Now* he was frowning.

I picked up a french fry and formed my words carefully. Sonny was not going to like my answer, no matter how I phrased it. "She's only twenty-one, for one thing, and a foreigner to boot. I guess she feels humiliated and frightened as it is, and the thought of being questioned by authority figures is more than she can face. At least for now."

He was more than frowning, he was scowling. "So she can talk to Frost and to you, but she can't talk to me and Jeanine. We wouldn't exactly approach in full uniform with billyclubs and riot guns and drag her off to the station to an interrogation room, you know. We do have some feeling for a woman who's gone through that horror." He paused. "I assume she's hoping the guy has some money." Sonny was not stupid.

"Maybe so," I admitted. "But I take it you've had no other such reports?"

"None. Thanks, Joe." He looked at the food in front of him and doused his french fries in ketchup. I tried not to look wistful. "Actually," he said through his first bite, "Provincetown doesn't particularly lend itself to date rape. It's not a haven for straight kids like Lauderdale or the Hamptons. Which suits me fine. But, Alex, if you find the guy, you have to report it. Then we'll see if the victim can't be convinced to testify."

I nodded in agreement, and we both ate silently for a few minutes. Sonny took a swallow of tea and continued his thought. "The last date rape we had reported was two summers ago, and we never got the guy. We never even had a suspect. The young woman remembered virtually nothing, and there were no witnesses. She thought it happened somewhere in a car, and people who had been with her at a party said she left alone on foot. I don't envy you. It won't be easy."

"I haven't talked to the young woman yet. Hopefully she can help." I looked up, startled. Sonny had just laughed aloud. "Something funny?"

"Yes and no. Remember that guy Deloit? The guy who wore the raincoat and nothing under it. He raped several older women here in town, nothing funny about that. He had some fun beating up on a couple of them. And he knocked Ms. Weatherman down a flight of stairs. She's never walked right since. But remember how we finally caught him?"

"Kind of. I think I was still in college. Didn't Ann McCurdy have something to do with it?" Joe went by and I gave him a meaningful look, which I hoped would result in another beer.

"Yep, she and that dog of hers, Chaucer. She never could control him. He was part Afghan and part rottweiler, which made them the perfect pair: funny looking, assertive and about half a brain between them. That night Ann had closed some bar, came home with a snoot full, and decided to take the dog out without a leash. Chaucer runs right across the street and pins a guy up against a wall. The man is terrified, waving his arms and yelling for her to call off her dog. She's yelling for the dog to come back. The dog is getting more hysterical by the minute, barking and snapping. I think ten neighbors must have called the cops. I was brand new on the force then, working lots of nights, and I was in the car that answered."

I was laughing, too, now. "That's right! Didn't the dog rip the raincoat, and there stood your rapist in all his glory?"

"You got it." Sonny popped the last of the sandwich in his mouth. "But that was only half of it. We got the guy into the car. Ann says she'll be down in the morning to give a statement, and we leave. She takes Chaucer on down to the beach. A little earlier the Coast Guard down at Truro had launched a weather balloon. But something went wrong with the inflation process and here's this funny jellyfish-looking thing drifting along only about two hundred feet up, headed out over the bay on a night that had turned foggy with a full moon trying to shine through."

Sonny reached for my cigarettes, as usual. But this time he got punished. Joe picked that moment to deliver my beer. Sonny glared and continued.

"Now, unknown to any of us, Ann had been scared she might encounter the rapist when she had first left her house, so tucked in

26

her pocket was an old pistol her father had lifted off some German guy in WWII. She decides the balloon is a UFO, pulls out the pistol and starts blasting away. The dog is running in circles barking, and by now, a couple of other mutts have joined him. And our phone is ringing again."

I retrieved my cigarettes and lit what I believe was number four. "Sonny." I shook my head. "This can't be real."

"It's gospel. By the time we got there she had emptied a nine-round clip into the balloon, and it was slowly coming down into the water, thereby becoming a navigation hazard, as opposed to an aviation hazard, and Annie was yelling at it, 'That'll teach you little green bastards to stay home!'"

I wiped my eyes with my napkin and gasped, "Then what?"

He lifted his hands palm up. "Then nothing. We took the gun, caught the dog, drove everybody home and went and called the Coasties to come get their balloon. What should we have done? Arrest her? We had about twenty different counts to choose from. But arrest the person whose dog had just made Ptown safe for women again? Later, the Board of Selectmen gave her and the dog a plaque, while we all stood behind her, smiling, as the media did their thing. It was a heart-warming moment . . . well, you know, I guess in a way, it really was." He smiled and stood up. "Thanks for lunch."

He was gone before I realized what he had done, but I fixed him. He had left several fries, covered in ketchup, and I ate them.

Chapter 5

Not wanting to take Fargo with me to Mary's, and with a little time to kill, I aimed us toward home. I was strongly tempted by a nap in the sun, but was afraid I'd oversleep, so I opted to water my garden instead. But first, as usual, came a little game or two with Himself.

I would twirl the nozzle in a circle, thereby making the stream of water act sort of like a jump rope. Fargo would leap over, try to crawl under and finally stand in the middle of the spray. Then I would aim it at random around the yard, and he would attack it, barking ferociously. Hey, he made the rules. I just handled the hose. Finally, I'd get to my tomatoes, which were doing well. And I'd branched out this year. Already I had a few small radishes showing, and the lettuce seemed healthy once I'd learned to share my beer with the slugs. They would crawl into a shallow bowl to drink it, and drown. Well, I can think of worse ways. I had even added a few flowers, though I sometimes mixed up their names.

Gardening had taken on a new importance to me. Previously,

I'd had a lover who always made sure I knew that puppy-Fargo was lying in the zinnias, another who wondered vocally why I made no attempt to plant in ruler-straight rows, another who felt she had to be within touching distance anytime I worked in the yard (or did anything else) and, finally, one who stripped off the best tomatoes and stood in the garden eating them because she knew it looked sexy. I had begun to pretend I was too busy to garden.

Cindy had taken a different tack. What and how I planted was my business. She would enjoy anything I grew—floral or vegetable. She had a small plot at my aunt's where she had put in squash, peppers and something else, which she would happily share when they got ripe. Meantime, they were her sole concern. I found I took great pleasure in hearing her observe casually that my petunias were growing fast, or she couldn't wait for the first radish. But mostly I took great pleasure in fiddling around in *my* garden.

Time to go to Mary's. I changed my shirt, checked Fargo's water and dry food and broke the news that he wasn't going. He collapsed pitifully in his bed, nose between paws, eyes rolled back. I knew he'd be asleep by the time I had gone a block and told myself I didn't feel guilty.

Mary's shining vehicle was in her driveway, I looked at my car and I wished I had parked on the street. Anytime I went to Mary's, I was mentally handed a list of things I should wash, clean out, scrub or vacuum. She met me at the back door and stood while I wiped my shoes on the mat. Only then did I notice some small pieces of cut grass on the sides of my damp shoes. Oh, God.

"Come on in, Alex. Maureen is in the living room."

I followed her, and as we entered the room, I felt some change from the usual. Looking around like the professional observer I am, I noted a vase of daffodils by the window and a chorus line of bright paperbacks stretched across two bookshelves which had always been empty except for a few of Mary's thick, gray manuals and how-to books. On the coffee table rested a plate of pastel-iced petit fours and a tray holding a pitcher of tea and three glasses. The room seemed warm, almost gracious.

Maureen sat on the couch in a T-shirt and cut-offs, looking

29

very young and very pretty in a wholesome, scrubbed way that belied even the few years she could claim. Mary pointed me toward a chair and sank onto the couch beside Maureen. They weren't quite touching, but the separation was far from six degrees. Obviously, Maureen and I were not going to talk alone.

"Well," I began, "I can at least save you explaining why I'm here. I happened to see John Frost this morning and he told me what happened." I turned to Maureen. "I'm terribly sorry, and I promise you I'll try very hard to get the bastard."

"It's so nice of you to come, Alex. Mary tells me you're so smart, I know you can help me." She bestowed a brilliant smile.

"I'm flattered, and I'll certainly make every effort." She had flustered me a little, and to have something to do, I reached for a petit four, fully expecting Mary either to slap my wrist and tell me they were for later or to move them out of reach now that I had one. Instead, she smiled and nodded. "That one's strawberry. When you finish it, try a yellow one. I think they're best. They're lemon."

Between them, they got the tea poured and sugared and lemoned. Mary peered at me nervously, and Maureen's hands were tightly clasped in her lap. Looking for a conversational gambit to relax us all for a few moments, I again noticed the books in the case and commented, "You've added a bit to your library, Mary. They look very nice there."

Mary laughed. "I saw in the paper the library was selling off some old books. Maureen's a mystery buff, so I stopped by for a look. They seemed a bargain, so I bought this bunch."

I looked more closely and noted that she had bought what must be the entire output of Dorothy Sayers, Ngaio Marsh and P.D. James. "Well, you did great, even by accident. Sayers and James are timeless and matchless. And Marsh may be dated, but she's fun. Have you started any, Maureen?"

"Just this one so far. And it's a right laugh, isn't it? Sure, the old bloke got his comeuppance, I'd say." She indicated a book on the end table.

It was entitled *Death of a Peer*, but Marsh had done in several peers in her day, and I couldn't remember any details about this one. So I made a non-committal "uhhhmm" and got out pen and notebook, and we got underway.

I spoke softly, and, I hoped, nonthreateningly. "Maureen. The worst is behind you now, and the sooner we get this man into custody, the sooner you can really sleep easily and move past it. So I need to know everything . . . *everything* you can remember, no matter how small or irrelevant it seems. For example, over the past few weeks can you remember a man following you or paying unusual attention to you or acting differently around you? Anyone at work or in a store or elsewhere?"

She took a long drink of tea, as if her throat were dry. "No," she finally answered. "I can't recall anything at all unusual. I don't know about someone following me. I probably wouldn't have noticed, I never thought of it."

"Okay, something may come to you later. Let's move on to Sunday night. I understand you had worked Sunday. What happened from the time you got off?"

Mary leaned a little forward and spoke. "We both got off about three. We came home, did a few chores and made dinner. We watched the news while we ate and then straightened up. Maureen had promised to meet the three girls she used to share an apartment with for a drink at the Bitter End at eight o'clock."

This was what I'd been worried about. Mary was bound to be in control. And I couldn't let her be. And she wasn't going to like what I had to say. "Thanks, Mary. That pretty well covers the at-home portion of the evening. Now, I think, the rest of the evening, I'd better hear from Maureen. If she should forget anything, maybe you could add that later."

Damned if she didn't fool me again! "Of course, Alex, sorry. I just want to catch this guy so badly, I'm churning my wheels. I'll shut up." Our Mary had undergone quite some change! I'd expected my eyebrows to be smoking. Instead, I'd encountered Lady Affable. She patted Maureen's knee and left her hand casually

31

there. There were three women with whom I might feel comfortable making that gesture: Cindy, my mother and my Aunt Mae. Mary and Maureen were not relatives.

Maureen covered the hand with her own and continued. "My ex-roommates and I don't get together very often, what with us workin' different places and all." The Irish surfaced now and then. "So Sunday night we were to meet at eight. I walked over to the Bitter End and they already had a table in back and were drinking their wine. I sat down and ordered a glass for myself." She lifted her glass of tea and looked at it as if she wished it were wine.

Maureen's account of her evening with *les girls* was deadly dull and sounded rehearsed. Well, she'd had almost a week to go over it again and again in her mind, so no wonder. But it was unhelpful. Finally, her friends had remarked that they all had to be at work early in the morning and had left around 9:30. Maureen had an almost-full glass of wine and had elected to finish it at the bar rather than alone at the table. She thought she might have spoken briefly to a young man in passing, but wasn't sure.

There her memory stopped. She basically remembered nothing until standing in the back doorway of Mary's house at approximately, according to Mary, 1:15.

Maureen did not remember spending time with anyone at the bar or recall leaving the building at all. She vaguely remembered a car, possibly dark in color. "I think it had gotten foggy," she added. "I'm not sure. And there was a man driving, a white man, but he seemed dark to me . . . tanned, I guess." She put her hands up to her face. "I remember wind. It was windy in the car."

"You mean your window was rolled down? Or maybe it was a convertible?" I asked.

"Convertible, yes! Oh, yes, sure and it was a convertible! I felt cold." She grabbed Mary's hand. "Is it coming back to me, darlin'? Am I going to remember? Must I remember it? Oh, God."

Mary held both her hands. "Shush. It's all right. The more you remember, the better. We'll get through this, don't you worry.

Now, keep thinking. Is there more you can dredge up? Try, dear, try! Alex is going to help you."

I felt like some sort of brutal voyeur. This was terrible for both of them. Obviously Mary was deeply involved here, and I was making both of them recall a night of hell. "Maureen, about the car, can you remember anything more? What color was the upholstery? What color was the top? Did it have a hood ornament?" I lit a cigarette, and Maureen leaned over and took it from me with a shaky hand. I lit another and noticed I wasn't so steady myself. Perhaps when rape happens to one woman, it happens to us all.

She blew out a cloud of smoke. "The . . . top, the top was . . . down. I don't know the color. The upholstery was light . . . white or gray. Or light blue. I don't know about hoods, what kind of ornament? Where?"

Mary answered and I didn't stop her. "On the very front of the hood—the bonnet—some cars have a little decoration. Cadillacs have a sort of shield. Lincolns have a kind of silver rectangle with a line across it."

I sipped my tea as Maureen thought. Finally she answered. "It was silver, yes. A circle with a sort of upside down Y in it, I think."

"Mercedes!" Mary triumphed. "A Mercedes convertible! Alex, surely that's a big help!"

I nodded with more enthusiasm than I felt. It would have been more help last Sunday night. By now the car could be back home in Indiana or halfway to Phoenix.

"Yes, it's a great help." I smiled at Maureen. "Does the car lead you to visualize the man a little clearer?"

She shrugged. "Tanned." She shook her head. Suddenly she buried her face in her hands and began to cry. It was difficult to hear her, and I finally moved and knelt beside her. "He was young," she whispered. "Young and gorgeous . . . with a face like a b-b-beautiful pirate. Curly black hair all blowing in the wind. But I was so afraid, I knew I must make him stop the car. I must get out! But I couldn't say it. I tried and tried. B-b-but I couldn't. I couldn't—*speak!*" She cried as if her heart were broken. Mary looked as if she'd like to kill.

I patted Maureen's shoulder as I rose. "All right, that's all a help, too. I'm sorry to drag you through this. I really am. Let's give it a rest for today. If you remember anything else, though, please write it down and tell Mary. I'll give you a call tomorrow."

Mary disengaged herself from the couch and walked me to the back door. She looked drained. "Is any of it really a help, Alex?"

"Some. There can't be too many Mercedes convertibles in town. The question is, is it *still* in town? The description of the man can be helpful later, hopefully."

Mary nodded tiredly and I turned to leave. "Oh," I recalled. "Mary, I need a favor. Trish Woodward bought a little boat down in Eastham or somewhere. Sonny wants to help her move it up here this Saturday morning, but has no trailer. Would it be possible for them to use yours?"

"I guess so. I may not be here, but I'll unlock the garage." She didn't sound thrilled. "Tell them that when they bring it back, they should be sure to hose it down and dry it off. I'll leave my hose out . . . and some drying rags. And when they put it back in the garage, make certain they close the door and turn the handle to lock it. I guess that will be okay." She sounded far from sure. I thanked her and walked toward my car before she could recant.

As I backed out of the driveway, I remembered something else. The only time in my life I'd been offered refreshments in Mary's home . . . and I forgot the lemon petit fours!

Chapter 6

Turning out of Mary's street, I realized I had to go right past the place where Maureen's three ex-roommates lived, and decided to chance it that one or more of them might be home. I parked and climbed the stairs to the garage apartment and felt the sun beat warmly on my back. Were we headed for a hot summer? The main door was open, so I rapped on the screen doorframe and called out, "Hello, anybody home?"

A young woman in a short robe, toweling her hair, arrived. I introduced myself and asked, "Are you Ruth or Nadine or Clare?"

She smiled. "I'm Nadine." I explained my errand, and she held the door open.

"That's terrible! God, I hate to hear of rape! Come on in."

I walked in and immediately felt stifled. The ceilings were low and probably uninsulated. The windows were few, small and faced the wrong direction to catch the prevailing breeze. The apartment smelled of steam from a recent hot shower, shampoo, deodorant and an elusive scent of cucumbers.

Two kitty-cornered single beds doubled as couches in the living room, and pretty well filled it except for a small coffee table and a bureau, its top crowded with a TV, a small CD player and a lamp. A tiny kitchenette huddled in a corner, jammed with a cube refrigerator, micro, toaster and coffeemaker. I could see into the bedroom, which held two single beds separated by a small table with lamp. I assumed another bureau might be beyond my sight. A tiny bathroom showed a stall shower, steam-coated mirror and a sink about the size of a cereal bowl. The edge of the toilet peeked coyly around the half-open door.

Nadine kicked the bathroom door closed and pointed toward a figure reclined on one of the couches. The figure wore shorts, a halter and what looked to be a plaster mask, covering her entire face except for a round mouth-circle and two green circles where I hoped her eyes were. "This is Clare."

"Hi, Clare. I'm Alex."

"Hi," Clare responded. She tried to smile, but the plaster cracked alarmingly and sent a shower of small fragments onto the pillow. She removed two thick slices of cucumber from her eyes, thereby solving that little mystery, and sat up. "Did somebody really get raped?"

I said yes, but did not identify Maureen as the victim. I merely said I was interviewing people who had been at the Bitter End and might have seen something helpful. Clare and Nadine tried to be obliging, but had little to offer. No one had tried to join their table. No one showed special interest in any of them. No one had acted strangely. "At least, no stranger than always," Nadine had laughed.

They more or less confirmed the timeline Maureen had given me, and that was that. By that point, I felt pretty steamy myself and was glad to leave them.

In the car I put down all the windows and took deep breaths. The thought of three people living in that warren was claustrophobic. If you factored in Maureen, it took on the characteristics of a string quartet performing in an upper berth.

Now running late, I picked up Fargo and headed for the cottage. Once there, we went about our chores. He checked out every square inch, looking for Cindy and/or Wells, her young cat, a little black beauty with three white socks and one white spot that looked as if she'd dipped her chin in the milk. According to orders, I took the package of chicken breasts out of the freezer. In a burst of domesticity, I removed the packaging, put the meat in a shallow bowl and splashed some marinade on it.

I called Sonny and delivered Mary's message regarding the boat trailer. He said "Yeah, yeah, yeah" at the end of it, which irritated me somewhat.

"Look, Sonny, you begged me to do your dirty work and I did it. Now please at least do what she asks. If you don't, I'm the one who'll pay for it. Wash and dry that damn trailer or don't use it at all!"

"Oh, hell, Alex, you know I'd wash off the salt water and either dry it or park it in the sun, anyway. I don't need to be lectured like a twelve-year-old. Does she want rental for it, too?"

"Of course she doesn't, but if you're smart, you'll take her a lovely pot of spring flowers."

"Oh. Yeah. Okay. Thanks for calling." He rang off and I smiled a very sisterly smile. Sonny prided himself on good manners. It was a real blow when he had to be reminded of something. Fargo and I moved to the backyard, where I dumped some briquettes in the grill and lit it, and Fargo surveyed the scene and then looked at me questioningly. I answered his question. "Cindy will be here soon, and I imagine Wells is up at Aunt Mae's being spoiled." At the mention of Aunt Mae, Fargo looked thoughtfully up the slope toward her house, apparently decided the walk was not worth it and lay down on the grass.

I sat down in one of the lawn chairs, propped my feet on another and had that first bitingly cold bitter swallow of freshly opened beer, lit cigarette number four and decided life was good.

It got better shortly. Cindy arrived in a smiling TGIF mood. We made dinner and ate it in the kitchen. A breeze had come up, and it held a leftover spring chill somewhere around the edges. We lingered over coffee and swapped accounts of our day. Cindy was, of course, horrified at the tale of Maureen's rape. I cautioned her to silence and she nodded.

"I understand. She still needs privacy around this. Although she'd better be prepared for lots of publicity when you catch him."

I was touched by her faith. "That may not be tonight," I said lightly. "She really hasn't yet come up with much to go on." I sipped my coffee thoughtfully. "Cindy, let me ask you. If you knew you had in some way been drugged and were in the car with a woman who frightened you, and who you were sure had thoughts of raping you or harming you in some manner, would you say later, that with the wind blowing through her hair, she looked like a beautiful pirate?"

"No." Her answer was quick and firm. "I would not. In an effort to describe her, I would mention the hair color. And I would maybe say she had an attractive face. Or maybe—yes, I'd more likely say she looked like a movie actress, something like that. The beautiful pirate bit sounds too romantic, like she found him thrilling . . . maybe a little scary, but thrilling."

She stood up and took a small melon from the refrigerator. She cut two slices and turned back to the table. "And there's something else. Who'd be driving this fancy, expensive car with the top down, on a windy and cold, wet night?"

I stared at her, fork in hand. It made no sense. And Super Sleuth here hadn't thought of it. Then she gave me further reason to wonder which of us was the detective.

"The two things," she explained, "almost sound as if Maureen is remembering a previous time with him, when she wasn't afraid. When it was a lovely night with the wind in his hair, and his pirate profile didn't frighten her. Maybe the drugs and the trauma have got her mixed up."

I blew out a deep breath. It made sense. Maybe Maureen really knew the guy and couldn't bring herself to realize it. I'd have to figure out a way to get around that with her.

Cindy scraped an errant seed off the side of her melon. "Have you any idea where he took her?"

"Not really. Maureen remembered some steps and a light colored building. Trish thought it might be the old icehouse condos. And it has to be someplace near Ptown or just possibly North Truro. He wouldn't want to be carting her around passed out or have the drug wearing off. There's a big motel over near Pilgrim Heights. And there are plenty of big white houses in town. But motels or B&B's have people around. It sounds as if she could barely walk . . . if that."

I finished my melon and Cindy picked up the plates. "Most people would probably assume Maureen and her boyfriend were just drunk, if they paid any attention at all. But, Alex, I keep going back to John Frost. Why did they go to him instead of the police? No offense to Sonny, but is there any reason to think the cops would mishandle it?"

"I can't think of any. They've all had various types of sensitivity training. If there was reason to think Maureen was especially vulnerable, I'm sure Sonny would have had Jeanine handle at least the opening phase of it. She's a good cop and a very warm, caring woman. No, they wouldn't screw up." I got up, too, and poured us some coffee. We both went back to the table and I lit cigarette number . . . could it be six? For shame! Naughty!

"Uh-huh." Cindy still wasn't happy. "So they probably went to Frost, thinking of suing for some kind of damages?"

"I assume so."

"But, Alex, how do they know the rapist has any money to give them?"

I had no answer for that one. "Just hoping, I guess." It sounded weak.

Cindy smiled. Then she changed course. "What's your schedule for tomorrow?"

"Busy, I'm afraid. I need to talk to the bartender at the Bitter End and the doctor who treated her, if he's available."

She nodded, amicably enough. "I figured something like that.

39

Just remember, Lainey and Cassie and Trish and Sonny plus Peter and the Wolf are coming to dinner."

I silently blessed her for not going into some diatribe about my working on a weekend. "I'm sorry. I'll get finished as fast as I can. What do you need me to do?"

"Just make sure we have whatever forms of alcohol we may need, plus mixers and ice. I can handle the rest of it. Oh, check the charcoal. Sonny's bringing steaks to go with the lobster."

"Going first-class, huh? Oh . . ." I had a sudden thought. "Uh, where are we eating?"

She laughed. "The house." I liked this woman. It was never *your* house or *my* cottage. It was just *the* house or *the* cottage, a quiet statement that we were both at home in both dwellings. "They're due at seven, so please be home in time to sit down and have a quiet drink with me before they get there." She gave me a kiss that promised nice things later.

And Cindy did not break promises.

Chapter 7

By 9:30 Saturday morning, I was underway. I left Cindy, Wells and Fargo comfortably propped up in bed, one of them with a mug of coffee and a rare cigarette. I paused at the bedroom door. "What a lovely, heart-warming scene," I said enviously. "If you'll all stay there while I get my camera, we can make it our Christmas card."

"It's not our fault you don't know a weekend when you see one," Cindy gushed sweetly. "Go make the town safe for American womanhood." She put her arms around the animals in a Madonna-like pose that totally distracted me from my planned duties. Seeing my expression, Cindy laughed. "Get out. I have to get moving, too, in a minute."

I got. But I fixed them. On the way to the house, I stopped at the bakery and picked up a walnut and cranberry croissant and a French cruller. Working PI's need sustenance.

Pulling in the driveway at the house, I was totally surprised to see Maureen sitting on the back steps, sipping coffee from a paper cup.

"Well, hello there. Everything all right?"

"Oh, yes. You see, Mary decided to go along with Trish and Sonny. You know, just to be an extra hand."

I burst out laughing. Mary's reformation only went so far! Obviously she couldn't bear the thought of someone using her trailer without her presence. She'd be telling Trish and Sonny every move to make all morning long. They must be thrilled along about now, and it would only get better.

Maureen gave me a knowing grin but remained neutral. "Your brother seems very nice," she said. "And so is Trish. They brought Mary a lovely pot of dahlias. Anyway, I wanted to talk to you, so I took a chance and came over."

"You walked all the way over here?" I was surprised. They lived way down in the East End. It would have been quite a hike for her.

Maureen stood and stretched. She had quite a body. "No." She grinned again, and again I noticed what a pretty young woman she was. "I stole Mary's lorry." She nodded toward the street and I saw the shiny SUV parked under my neighbor's shade tree.

"I don't imagine she'll mind." I smiled back. Maureen seemed to warrant smiles. "But that reminds me of something I need to ask you. You see, the man who attacked you may have just been an opportunist. What I mean is, let's say he had the drug, and he hung around bars looking for possibilities. There you were . . . alone. He dropped it in your drink, and that was it." I propped my foot on the step and leaned my arm across my thigh.

"On the other hand, he may have known you at least slightly . . . had sometime previously chatted with you, maybe had danced with you or bought you a drink. He had thought he was making progress. Then he finds out you and Mary are lovers, and he's pissed. He raped you sort of in revenge." I tilted my headed to look at her more closely. "You *are* lovers aren't you? I know that's technically none of my business, but when a crime is committed, privacy doesn't count for much."

She dropped her eyes away from mine. "Oh, I don't mind your asking." She looked back up with a tremulous smile. "I can't tell you when I've been so happy. Until this dreadful thing! Mary is awfully good to me, and . . . and she needs a bit of looking after, too, you know." Unsurprisingly, she was blushing. Well, I'd heard of worse reasons for relationships.

"Come on inside and I'll make some fresh coffee." I even offered her a pastry. She seemed to turn slightly pale and refused. I supposed her nerves still weren't what they should be. But mine were fine and the cruller disappeared before I even poured the coffee. When we were settled at the kitchen table I asked, "Well, what can I do for you?"

"I think I remember a couple of things. But they sound sort of crazy. I think I must have dreamed them, but Mary said I must . . . tell you." She trailed off apologetically.

"Mary's right. What do you remember?"

"Well, the stairs. I'm sure now they were indoors, and they had green carpeting and were very narrow. And dimly lit."

"Dimly lit? Stairs in a hotel or any public place are usually brightly lit."

"These weren't. They had little fixtures spaced along the wall, with dim little bulbs. And then upstairs, I . . . I was on the bed and he was . . . doing it. I was staring across his shoulder. He was hurting me, but I couldn't tell him to stop, couldn't scream. The doctor told me later some drugs affect you like that. Anyway, I think I saw some cups on a shelf . . . not like this." She picked up her coffee cup. "Cups like when you win a game, you know, with two handles."

"Okay." I nodded. "I'm with you. It's beginning to sound as if you were in a home, not a motel or B&B or some kind of warehouse."

"That's what Mary said. Whatever it was, it was big. I just feel like it was big."

"All right, we'll assume it was big." I smiled and finished the last of the croissant. Working gave me an appetite. "Anything else?"

She gave an embarrassed little laugh. "I hate to even say this, it sounds so silly. But when we came out of the building, we walked across some grass to the car. My legs were beginning to function a little, with him helping. Off on the edge of the grass, way over, I saw a telescope."

"A telescope?" I began to try to think of something a half-drugged, scared girl might mistake for a telescope. Everything I thought of made even less sense. A car muffler? A log? A length of pipe? A machine gun . . . oh, hell, she had to have dreamed it.

"Yeah, well, we'll have to think about that one. But, tell me, Maureen, are you absolutely certain you didn't know this guy? Even slightly?"

"Oh, no! Oh, I couldn't have, Alex! Now, sure I would remember him, wouldn't I?" She looked like tears were moving in.

"Yeah, I guess so. Probably. Forget I asked." I stood and brought the coffee carafe back to the table.

Under control now, Maureen stood, too, and put her hand on my arm. "No, no more coffee, thank you, Alex. I'm taking up your morning and I'm sure you're busy. Thank you for listening to my natter." Her face seemed suddenly close to mine.

"It's my pleasure and my job," I replied gallantly, but she was right. I was anxious to get moving. I did have a lot to do, and I was strangely jumpy. "We'll get this guy, don't you worry, so you can relax and stop looking over your shoulder."

"That would be wonderful," she sighed. She managed a half-smile and left.

I put her cup and saucer in the sink and refilled my cup, picking up the phone with the other hand. I called Nacho at the police station. Nacho was Mary O'Malley, who had been dubbed Nacho when we were in high school, because she was always eating nuts, chips, popcorn, nachos, candy bars. She still weighed about 110, had beautiful teeth and smooth skin. But she was also pleasant and was hard to hate. She had a love affair going with computers, and they came up with anything she asked, unlike the little smoking bombs they so frequently threw into the center of my screen.

I asked her to find me a dark Mercedes convertible with Ptown connections, and she agreed.

"And I can tell you off the cuff, Alex, there are two in town.

One is dark gray and belongs to the couple who own the Chambered Nautilus B&B. The other is actually an ancient four-door black model that I think must have originally belonged to Hitler. Old Don Clarke owns it and occasionally uses it to troll for young men."

We both laughed. Skinny, red-necked Clarke with his slicked-back, thinning hair had been trolling since we were kids. Rumor had it he baited the hook with cash. "I know about Dapper Don. Anything interesting about the B&B guy?"

"Not much. His wife goes to my hairdresser. She's gorgeous. Your heart would go pitty-pat."

"Alas, my heart is not free to go pitty-pat. I'll drop in later and see what *your* trolling brings in."

I put my finger on the disconnect button for a minute, while I ran my eye down a list of numbers taped to the wall above the phone. I found the number for the clinic and dialed. I asked which doctor had been on emergency room duty the night of Sunday, June fourth. After several minutes of jolly music, I was told it was Dr. Gloetzner. No, I could not speak with him. He would not be in until Monday morning. Could someone else help me? I said no thanks and hung up.

Well, I wasn't making much progress with interviews. Maybe I'd do better with the bartender at the Bitter End. I changed into some decent slacks and shoes, and a fresh shirt and then had to make the big decision. Walk, and face the sidewalk traffic. Drive, and face the street traffic. I made a fast check of the liquor cabinet and decided on the car.

Fortunately, the bartender on duty at the Bitter End had been on duty Sunday night. Unfortunately, he simply refused to believe spiking a drink could have happened there. "No way. Couldn't be. We don't run that kind of place. We don't have that kind of crowd. Nobody did that while *I* was behind this bar!"

"Look," I said, "Nobody is trying to blame you or say the place is sleazy. Who ever knows when some psycho walks in? They don't always have little horns and cloven hooves."

His jaw set in a stubborn line and his lower lip jutted out. "Nope. We don't cater to psychos."

I wondered who did. "Well, barkeep, it did happen. You know Maureen Delaney?" I felt I had no choice but to identify her.

"It was her? Now, see, that just proves my point. She's that pretty, redheaded Irish girl, right? She's a *nice* girl. I mean, she's friendly enough, but she don't come on strong to the guys. She's not loud, doesn't show off. Anybody come on too strong to her, she'd tell him off in a hurry."

I had a distinct feeling he spoke from experience, but all I said was, "He wouldn't necessarily get fresh. He might just drop some powder or liquid in her drink."

"She wasn't even with a guy that night. Hasn't been for a month or so."

"She used to come in with a man?" I looked up sharply.

"Yeah, once or twice. Nice-looking guy, dark curly hair. Wore expensive clothes, kinda highbrow for in here, you know? Haven't seen him for quite awhile, though."

"Did he look like a pirate?"

The bartender stared at me and then laughed. "You crazy? There aren't pirates nowadays. Although . . ." he added thoughtfully, "He mighta been a movie pirate. Like Johnny Depp or something."

"Have you any idea who he is?"

"Nah. Rich college kid would be my bet."

We chatted awhile longer, but I learned nothing else. Finally, I gave him my card. "If you think of anything, or if you see anything unusual, call me or the cops. They know about this. Keep a close eye on your bar. And you might warn the other bartenders. Oh," I added on my way out, "We're trying to keep quiet about who it was, save her some embarrassment if we can."

"Sure. I'll tell the other guys. But I won't use her name around no one."

I hoped he meant it. Looking at my watch, I realized I still had plenty of time before I needed to get home and give Cindy a hand for the evening's festivities. I decided to walk over and see if Nacho had brought in a worthwhile catch.

When I walked in, she saw me and waved me into her office. Foregoing the amenities, she got right to business. "Ptown's getting more affluent," she informed me. "We have another Mercedes registered in town. Black with a white top, belonging to one Barbara Thomasen. Age fifty-seven. The address is a condo up near you. No second driver listed on her insurance." Nacho had gone full out to get thorough information.

I nodded. "I know her . . . slightly. Her lover died last year in some weird accident. She's bursar for a small college down in Connecticut. I doubt she's taken to dressing in drag and raping young women."

"She could have a son . . . or a nephew who uses the car." She reached in her desk drawer and pulled out a tin of peanuts and pointed it toward me. I shook my head no.

"I'll keep her in mind. Anything else?" I waited while she washed some nuts down with a soda.

"Yeah. I took a chance and ran the car we want as being from within the Boston city limits, before I went statewide and then maybe into Rhode Island and probably Kansas and Minnesota." She grinned and took another swig of soda.

"You're gonna love this one, Alex. Dark blue with white top. Registered to that Beacon Hill scion of the aristocracy . . . one John Lanham Sanhope."

I had to stop and think a minute. The Sanhopes. Of course! They had an old sprawling house, complete with guest cottage and garages that used to be a stable . . . up on the crest of the hill near the end of Bradford Street overlooking the marsh and half of the Atlantic Ocean. They also had some sort of mansion in Boston and split their time between here and there. They had money. Big money, *really* big money. I tapped my finger on Nacho's desk.

"Didn't their name used to be Santos?" I asked.

"Um hmmm." Her mouth was full again. "Years back, when papa Santos still worked on a fishing boat. Before they got rich and decided not to be Portuguese anymore."

"Right. I remember now. They're in banking or something now. But isn't *our* Pete Santos kin to them?" I stood and looked into the main room, hoping to spot Officer Peter Santos.

"He is, but he's not here. He left a few minutes ago to go up to the Wharf Rat Bar and get some lunch. Then he's going to his mother's to mow the lawn." She stood too, now, and clicked off her computer.

The Rat. I had to get up there, to my "other office," to catch Pete and maybe get myself some lunch. "Thanks, Nacho, thanks a million!" I was headed for the door.

"You owe me a bag of potato chips."

"You'll get 'em, Nacho, you'll get 'em!" I was gone.

Chapter 8

I made no friends on the way to the Rat. I must have said *excuse me* a dozen times as I squeezed, shouldered, dodged and detoured my way up Commercial Street. And it was no better when I got there. People were out in the alley waiting for tables and my, "Sorry, pardon me, meeting a friend inside," as I pushed past them earned me only dirty looks and grunts.

Inside, I finally spotted Pete Santos, back near the kitchen door, nursing a beer and turning hopefully toward the kitchen every few seconds. I was about to take his mind off food.

"Hiya, Pete, may I join you?"

"Sure, Alex. Sit down before somebody knocks you down. It's crazy in here."

I sat. God help the native during tourist season. I snagged a waiter by the simple expedient of sticking out my arm and blocking his entrance to the kitchen. Glancing at Pete's beer, I ordered, "One Bass, one Bud. A Caesar salad with seared scallops and some of Billy's little corn muffins. Put it on his check," I pointed to Pete, "And give the check to me later. Thanks for fitting us in." Both Pete and the waiter looked a bit startled, but I smiled sweetly and let my arm fall back into my lap, and the waiter continued his way to the kitchen, scribbling on a pad.

Pete took a swig of his beer. "Thanks for the treat. You win the lottery or something?"

"I'll be billing a client," I said grandly.

"Ah, then I'll have dessert."

"Have two." I leaned across the table, so I could speak without shouting. "I'm here to pick your brain. You're kin to the Sanhopes, aren't you?"

"All the way back to when they were not Sanhopes. Old Peter Sanhope, *né* Santos, was my grandfather Augie's brother. They both worked on *their* father's fishing boat."

"Tell me the story, then to now. How did he get to be a Sanhope?" Our beer arrived and I took a grateful sip.

"A tale of tragedy and treachery, love, greed, power . . . and piles of money."

"My God, Pete, it sounds like a real swashbuckler! Give."

"It was right after WWII. Old Pete and Augie and the rest of the crew were at sea on the boat when she developed some engine problems. They got a tow into Boston to a shipyard, but parts were still hard to get, so everyone but Augie and Pete went home. The two young guys stayed with the boat as sort of caretaker watchmen, and would bring her home when she got fixed."

He looked at me to make sure I was still with him. I nodded. He continued. "Well, one afternoon Peter was sitting taking the sun in some park, and here along came Miss Grace Lanham, out walking her little Boston terrier. I guess Grace was a real beauty. You can still see it in her now, and she's damn near eighty! And she was rich. Her father owned some stock brokerage firm in Boston. Grace and Peter looked at each other and that was all it took." He laughed. "If you believe old Pete, he had her then and there under a bush by the park bench."

I raised my eyebrows. "How did the terrier feel about it?"

Pete answered just as solemnly. "According to Uncle Peter, the dog kept score. Anyway, it was hot and heavy till the boat got fixed. I don't know if that would have been an end to it, but about the time Peter got back to Ptown, Grace discovered she was, as they said, in the family way."

"Uh-oh."

"Yeah, two families, miles apart in every way. And spoiled little Grace yelling, no abortion, no adoption . . . marriage! She wanted that man."

We held our conversation in abeyance while the waiter graciously slammed Pete's fish and chips platter, and my corn muffins and salad plates onto the table and hurried back to the kitchen.

I took a fast bite and got back to the subject. "So they married?" I asked through a full mouth.

"Yep. They took Portuguese Peter and cleaned him up and changed his name to Sanhope, which sounded much more like somebody Amazing Grace would marry, and got them to church. Then somehow they got him into the university for four years."

"Amazing Grace?" I smiled.

"Everybody calls her that—with good reason, but don't let her hear you. Anyway, all was well. They were happy, and Peter actually liked college and was doing very well. The baby came along— a little girl—and then the troubles started. She only lived a month or so. I think they called it crib death, right?"

"Yes. Sudden infant death syndrome or SIDS, I think they say now. How sad."

"Well, they got through it. And Grace got pregnant again, with Robert, and then with William. *They* were both healthy kids, thank goodness. Peter graduated and they put him in some gofer job at the brokerage. But come to find out he loved the business and was a genius at it. Before you know it, he's got them with branches in a lot of big cities all over the country, and into investment banking as well. Next thing you know, it's Lanham and Sanhope, Inc., and when old man Lanham died, Peter became CEO and Amazin'

Grace got herself elected Chairman of the Board. The all-American success story." He leaned back and drank some beer thirstily, as I finished the last bite of Billy's fluffy, wonderful corn-bread.

"So that's it?" I asked. "They lived happily every after?" I lit a cigarette, and Pete looked wistful. I was sorry, but not sorry enough to put it out. I did, however, order us two more beers.

"Not so happily, no," Pete said rather sadly. "There was talk that old Peter couldn't always keep his pants zipped. And then there was the big house he bought and added onto down here, the one Grace has now. Peter may have become a lah-di-dah Sanhope, but he was still part Santos. He loved Ptown and never forgot his roots. That didn't especially suit Grace. It was a thorn in her high society side. I think she was torn. She loved the water and scenery. She hated calling fishing folk her in-laws. She's never been com-fortable around us . . . although all us kids get along okay whenever we do get together."

The beers came, and I poured some into my glass as I asked, "That's not often?"

"No, not often." He sounded regretful. "You see, there was always a bunch of Santos kids running around here in Ptown. But the Sanhopes only had William and Robert, and they went to the fancy schools. So that meant mostly just summers and holidays down here. Then Robert grew up just in time for Vietnam, and that was two Sanhopes down."

"He was killed in action?" I was appalled. All the money in the world couldn't make up for the death of two children! I leaned back and blew smoke toward the already smoke-yellowed ceiling.

Pete shrugged. "That's the general story. Actually he was doing something for the CIA in Laos. He disappeared. Months later his body arrived at the U.S. Embassy in Saigon, neatly chopped up, packed in a barrel of salt."

"Jesus Christ!" I exploded, feeling my lunch churn in my stom-ach. "Did Grace know that? I'm surprised she didn't go out of her mind!"

"Amazing Grace earned her nickname. She stayed as tall and proud as ever. It was Old Peter who kind of fell apart. You know, lots of booze, more women, less time at home. But fortunately their other son, William, was all you could have asked for. He took over the business and did well at it. He managed to stay alive a reasonable amount of time and had three children who are all still healthy. Then Uncle Willie had a heart attack about twelve years ago."

This all sounded like it ought to be a TV miniseries to me. "So Grace has outlived all three of her children?"

Pete nodded. "And her husband. Old Peter was flying his twin-engine plane up to Sydney, Nova Scotia, back in 1982. He had two pals with him for a so-called fishing trip . . . but there were also three young women on board. It was foggy, and he put them into the side of a mountain. That was really tough on Grace."

"Tough?" I snorted. "Understatement of the year! Poor woman. She's lost all her kids, and her husband augers in a plane full of the party set. So who's left for her to talk to? The upstairs maid?"

Pete pushed his empty plate aside and snagged one of my cigarettes. Did I supply the entire Provincetown Police Department? "A little better than that. There's three grandchildren . . . William's kids. Francesca is the oldest, married with two daughters, down in Washington, D.C. There's Richard, he and Lillian have no kids so far. He runs the business now . . . doing great, I hear. And there's the *oops* kid . . . about twelve or fourteen years younger than the other two, Jack, graduating Harvard tomorrow, in fact."

"Ah, *Jack*." At last! I leaned forward. "Does Jack by chance drive a Mercedes?"

"Yeah. Navy with a ragtop, really sharp. Why?"

"This is not easy to say, Pete. But a young lady, a client of John Frost's, was date raped Monday night, and some of her information is pointing toward Jack."

I was totally surprised at Pete's reaction. He leaned back in his chair and roared with laughter. "Jack? John Lanham Sanhope?

Rape . . . date or otherwise?" He wiped his eyes with his napkin. "Oh, Alex, you've got to be kidding."

"I'm afraid not," I answered a little stiffly. "Several things point toward him."

"Oh, sure." Pete got his laughter under control. "Like a curly-haired, good-looking guy with a Mercedes and lots of the ready having to rape a girl? Alex, he travels with a broom to beat 'em off! My brother Augie and I could be happy till death with his rejects! You're way off on this one."

"Oh? His looks and the car fit. How about the house? Maybe some back stairs, dimly lit? With a green carpet? Maybe a bedroom with some trophies—you know, cups—from athletic events? And, I admit this is probably silly, but does he have a telescope?" I watched Pete's laughter die and his eyes turn from merriment to concern.

"Jesus, Alex. Jesus. What are you saying? The girl told you she remembered all those things?"

"Yes."

"I still don't believe it. All kidding aside, Jack isn't the rapist type. He's never taken girls that seriously. He really is like the old adage about the trolley . . . if you don't catch this one, there'll be another in ten minutes. And believe it or not, he's a good student, and he's still got law school to get through. Girls are . . . *handy*, I guess . . . and fun, but they're not his life. And God knows he's got nothing to prove. I don't understand what the telescope has to do with it. It's been out in the yard—out on the point—ever since I can remember."

I shrugged. "A lot of people aren't what they seem, Pete. We've all got a dark side. About the telescope, the girl thought she saw one through the fog that night, and how many mounted telescopes are there in town?"

"Alex, I ask you, please not to ruin his life with this! Trust me, Jack is one of the good guys." Pete grasped my hand across the table. "Let me talk to him first, before you do anything. I'm sure there's a simple explanation. Please!"

I tried to think of the best way to handle this. Maureen had been very convincing, but so was Pete. And for some reason I would have been hard-put to explain, the fact there was a telescope in the yard made me more inclined to believe Jack was innocent.

"No, Pete, you don't talk to him. I do. You can set up an appointment. Tell him to be at my house Monday at two o'clock."

"He won't be here until Monday night. Augie Jr. and I are going over Monday with my pickup to help him clean out his room and cart stuff up here. Would Tuesday be okay?"

"I guess so, God forbid we should interrupt a Harvard graduation. But you don't tell him why I want to see him. Tell him . . . tell him a car like his may be involved in a crime. Don't tell him the real reason, Pete. If I think you've warned him, I'll go straight to Sonny and Jack will be arrested in five minutes. I mean it."

Pete stood up and looked at me with a kind of disappointed dignity. "You forget, Alex, Jack may be my cousin, but I am a cop. I will not tell him." He laid fifteen dollars on the table. "This should cover my lunch." He turned and left.

And I felt as if the Rat were a very good place for me to be at that moment.

Chapter 9

I decided to finish my beer and have another cigarette. Something told me just to quit counting before I added more guilt to my day. As I sat at the table, idly watching the lunch crowd thin, I kept going back to that damned telescope.

According to Pete, it was "way out on the point" of the land. That would put it considerable distance from the house, which sat back in the center of the property. I didn't know the place well, but as I recalled it from going to some charity party with my mother several years back, you didn't go near the point to reach the *mews*, as they called the converted stables/garages. It seemed very chancy to me that Maureen, still drugged, staggering, recently raped, scared, and probably in pain, would notice a telescope set many feet away and blanketed in fog. And probably draped with some protective cover, anyway.

She almost *had* to have been there before and noticed it. Suppose she and her roomies had been at some party Jack had given. Maybe he'd wanted to have sex with her, and she'd maybe led him on and then said *no*. He apparently wasn't used to being turned down and maybe it made him all the more intrigued. So Sunday night, he added a little something to her drink. She remembered the telescope, but either she really didn't remember being there before . . . drunk? . . . maybe drugged then, also? Or she didn't want to admit it. Maybe afraid it would make her look bad or upset Mary. It worked for me.

I looked at my watch and waved for the check. Cindy would be in need of my expertise. Well, she'd at least appreciate another warm body trying to be of some help.

I headed for the liquor store and then for home. On the way, I stopped at the flower shop and picked up what the florist called "a romantic little French nosegay." I knew Cindy would have taken care of flowers for the living room and for the dining room table, but the nosegay was just for her. She loved it. And that made me happy.

With Fargo's help, I got out some extra lawn chairs and little tables and filled the grill with briquettes and got out the utensils I figured Sonny would need. I knew he would insist on doing the outdoor cooking. I set up the bar on the lowboy in the living room. Cindy and I agreed that it seemed to be turning cloudy and might become too cool to eat outside, so I set the dining room table. Finally, I fed Fargo, in the vain hope it might make him less interested in our dinner.

Cindy and I looked around, looked at each other and declared all in order. Time to shower and change and have that one relaxing drink before becoming hostesses.

Half an hour before party time, I mixed us both a bourbon old fashioned and carried them outside where she sat. She had her feet propped up on another chair, and I assumed she been on them most of the day, though she looked fresh and vibrant.

She asked about my day, and I told her about my lunch with

Pete Santos. I could tell she felt bad for Pete, but she said she didn't see I'd had much choice in the way I handled it. Perhaps when all was settled we could have him and his girlfriend for dinner or something. I grunted, got up and lit the grill. One dinner party at a time, please.

I started to tell her about Maureen's visit and Nacho's car-tracking success, but was cut off by the arrival of our first guest. Lainey walked up the drive, bearing one of her pecan pies. With Lainey's pies, you didn't think of calories or carbs or cholesterol, you just thought of how it *tastes!*

"Where's Cassie?" I asked, as I gently relieved her of the pie. "Don't tell me she had to make a flight?"

"Oh, no. No, we're actually going to make our dining room a real dining room after only seven years of a card table and some rickety chairs and shelves. Peter and the Wolf have a small break-front they want to sell, and Cassie went to take a look. She'll be along shortly."

Peter and the Wolf were two older gay men who ran a B&B patronized mainly by mature gay men, who were said to appreciate the good-looking young houseboys employed there. Their names were actually Peter Mellon and Frank Wolfman, but years ago, someone had used the sobriquet *Peter and the Wolf.* It had stuck, and thus were they usually called. They sort of fit the names. Peter was not tall and becoming quite rounded, complete with a shiny bald top. If anyone had needed Friar Tuck for a movie, Central Casting would have sent him along. Wolf, on the other hand, was tall and lank, with sharp gray eyes and a sarcastic grin that framed very business-like molars.

Lainey was in fact followed by Trish and Sonny, who pulled into the drive and began unloading steaks, which Sonny took out to the grill, while I got the lobsters from the kitchen. I brought him out a drink while he checked the state of the fire and doused the meat with various sauces he had concocted. I noticed he was limping, but had no opportunity to ask about it, as Cassie picked that moment to arrive and handed me a DVD with the explanation, "I brought this along to watch after dinner. It's a docudrama about Amelia Earhart. Supposed to be good, with really fabulous aerial shots."

"Oh, that's a splendid idea!" At least I hoped it was. I knew Sonny and I would be interested. I wasn't so sure of the other five. Well, we'd see. "I'll just go put it safely in the house." I arrived at the back door the same time as Peter and the Wolf, who was carrying one of Peter's applesauce walnut cakes with some sort of butter crème icing. I knew it would be moist and delectable, and was already thinking with pleasure of tomorrow's leftovers.

We all gathered in the yard to keep Sonny company in his cooking. He's one of the few people I know who can broil a lobster on a grill, get it evenly cooked and serve it up unburned. And he broiled a good steak as well. We had our drinks and munched on crudités with a dip of yogurt, dill and just enough bleu cheese to give it some pizzazz.

The clouds were definitely moving in and a cool breeze was trying itself out in tentative little puffs, growing more self-confident as time passed. Eating inside would prove a wise choice.

The table looked lovely. A white damask cloth held light blue dinner plates with silver filigreed edges, and creamy white salad plates with a thin blue rim, and was set with graceful Royal Danish flatware . . . all from my grandmother. The wine and water glasses were plain and clear with simple rope stems, all set off by Cindy's centerpiece—a lovely grouping of narcissi, blue hyacinths and pale pink tulips in a bowl of streaked cobalt.

It was simple and elegant and I was very proud of us.

"Just look, Cassie," Lainey expounded. "See what you can do when you graduate from card tables."

Everyone laughed and Peter answered, "And now you've got a great little breakfront as soon as we can figure out how to get it over to your place."

"Well, whatever you do, don't borrow Mary Sloan's boat trailer and tie it onto that to move it," Sonny said with a sigh.

Trish looked startled when the table erupted into laughter.

Wolf was the first to speak. "So she finally got you, too? That makes about half the town now. What happened?"

Sonny looked embarrassed and Trish answered. "We borrowed Mary's trailer to move a little boat I just bought. Unfortunately Mary came with it . . . the trailer, I mean. We got the boat into the water okay, then Mary said she'd pull the trailer out. She accidentally put Sonny's Explorer in reverse and damn near ran him over. Sonny was barefoot, and when he jumped aside, he came down on a big rock. We think he broke his middle toe."

"You have just joined a large and unexclusive club." Wolf smirked. "Mary's hell when it comes to getting boats in or out. She left me standing in a hole with a sprained ankle, and she let Alex walk home in the rain with a badly scraped shin."

"Don't forget me," Lainey chimed in. "She roared her truck out while I was still in the water. I got so much sand in the face, I went around for a week explaining I really didn't have pink eye. But, Sonny, did you take care of that toe?" Lainey was a nurse at the clinic, and never really went off duty.

"Taped it to the next one. What else is there to do?"

"Not much," Lainey admitted. "Try to stay off it. Ooo-oh, look at all this!"

Cindy and Peter and I had brought in the food. Platters of steak and lobster, a large bowl of lightly curried rice with raisins and small chunks of mango and toasted almond slivers, a bowl of mixed salad greens with a dressing of boiling hot olive oil and vinegar, and fresh basil. And, finally, white corn muffins with kernels of shoe peg corn and chips of crisp bacon in the centers.

Wolf poured the wine, to save Sonny's foot, and we settled in to a truly scrumptious meal. Conversation understandably faded to various murmured comments while we all took the edge off our hunger.

Then Cassie looked toward Sonny. "Speaking of Mary Sloan, her girlfriend had a terrible thing happen, didn't she? Any luck finding who raped her?"

The table went dead silent and silverware stopped wherever it was.

Finally, Sonny answered. "There . . . uh, there is a possibility such an event occurred. But I'd love to know where you garnered that information." He always gets pompous when he doesn't know what to say.

Cassie shrugged and pointed. "Peter told me. He said Freddie, the cook at the Bitter End, called to reserve a room for two friends next weekend and told him what happened. Why? What difference does it make?"

"Well," Trish explained, "It's just a matter of protecting the victim from any embarrassment . . . you know, town gossip." She looked embarrassed herself. Certainly she hadn't phrased it very tactfully.

And now Wolf made it worse. "Dammit, Peter, Freddie *asked* you not to blab it all over!"

Understandably, Cassie started working up a head of steam. "So I constitute 'blabbing it all over?' So what am I? Chopped liver?" She looked around at seven guilty faces. "But *you* all knew, didn't you?"

At that point we all needed something to do. Lainey dropped her napkin and started a floor search. Cindy decided the centerpiece needed some adjustment and was making a royal mess. Trish grabbed the breadbasket and ran for the kitchen. Peter picked that moment to stand up and start serving salads.

And Cassie continued her accusatory screed. "I guess Sonny told Trish and Alex, and Alex told Cindy." She was wrong, but I felt this was not the moment to correct her. "Freddie told Peter and the Wolf. And," she addressed Lainey's back in a voice that carried throughout the house. "And *you* . . . *you* knew. You've been working the ER for a couple of weeks. You—my lover, my friend, my *mate*—you knew! But you didn't tell me! Why am I the only person in town who *didn't* know?"

Lainey straightened up and snapped. "Yes, I knew. I also work under certain rules of patient confidentiality. Now you know. So do the neighbors. Feel better?" She polished off her wine and set the glass down with a thump that made me grateful for a thick table pad.

61

Now it was my turn. "Wine, we need some wine here!" I went to the sideboard for a bottle that was "breathing." "Isn't this a lovely little wine? Sturdy enough for steak, light enough for lobster, a cosmopolitan little—" Seven voices put aside other concerns long enough to chorus, "Shut up, Alex!"

I went around the table, pouring wine. As I got to Sonny, he was wrestling with a lobster claw. It broke off unexpectedly and skipped merrily across the table, landing in Cindy's ramekin of drawn butter, making a fine spatter on the tablecloth and then rolling onto the floor, where the ever-alert Fargo darted from under the table and began slurping at the butter. I had been watching the claw's progress and consequently filled Sonny's wineglass to overflowing.

"Alex! What the hell—"

Trish was already up and wiping his shirtsleeve with her napkin. "It's all right, Sonny, just a little mishap. Don't get snarly just because you're miffed I knew about Maureen first." That earned her a glare and a wordless gargle from Sonny and inquisitive looks from everyone else.

I was no longer concerned with the success of our dinner party. It was obviously unforgettable. My worry now was that the crystal and china would survive it.

Chapter 10

We got through what was left of dinner with the age-old crutch of an in-depth exploration of the weekend weather forecast, augmented by a detailed exchange of various recipes no one would ever remember.

Trish, Cindy and Peter, the truly civilized among us, eased us into the living room for coffee and dessert and plugged in the movie of Amelia Earhart's last hours. I love the description of a movie as a *docudrama*. It gives you total, individual choice of what you can consider to be absolutely true, possibly true or no-way true. These choices can lead to a lively discussion among the viewers, and I didn't think any one of us was up to that. I hoped no one would lead us into it.

What I knew to be true was that Amelia was on a west-to-east global flight in a beautiful little twin-engine Lockheed, accompanied by her navigator, an ex-naval officer named Noonan who had resigned because of alcohol problems. They were about to fly their longest leg of the journey, from Lae, New Guinea, to Howland Island, an infinitesimal blip in the middle of that trackless watery desert of the Pacific Ocean.

Personally, I wouldn't want to make that flight with a cockpit full of radar, loran and global positioning gear—much less with the limited navigational aids of 1937. And a navigator who may or may not have been drunk the night before. But away they went, so heavily laden with fuel they barely made it off the end of the Lae runway. Flying dead reckoning with no firm idea of wind speed or direction.

Theoretically they had a little help from the U.S. Navy, who had stationed some ships en route as they neared Howland, to fix her position via radio directional beams and tell Amelia where she was. But it didn't work out. The ships presumably heard her brief calls, but she couldn't receive their requests to broadcast longer so they could get a fix, because—unbelievably to me—she had scrapped a trailing antenna at Lae in order to carry about two more gallons of fuel. And lost she was. Eventually out of fuel, she and Noonan crashed somewhere at sea and perished.

But, there was a possible alternative scenario. United States intelligence sources believed that Japan was building an airstrip and fortifications on the island of Saipan, preparing for war and violating some treaty or other. Earhart would pretend to be lost, per her radio calls, but actually bypass Howland and fly to the much larger Saipan, where she would get a great aerial view of whatever military preparations were going on. Then she would make a genuine low-fuel emergency landing on Saipan. The Japanese would doubtless radio the U.S. Navy that the famous aviatrix was safely down and to come and get her. Everyone would have a cup of tea and it would all be terribly civilized.

The problem was an inexperienced young Japanese officer who was the first to reach them after they made a landing in shallow waters nearby. He was not so green he didn't recognize a couple of nosy bastards when he saw them, so he simply shot them. Then he radioed Tokyo and sat back to await his promotion. Tokyo panicked. In 1937 you did not yet go around shooting Amelia Earhart or ex-U.S. navy officers. They yanked the lieutenant and his squad off the island and put the fear of God into the natives. It simply never happened. The Japanese were most helpful in the unsuccessful search of the vast sea for Amelia. The Americans were suspicious but helpless.

The truth has remained unproved. As we discussed it after the movie, Cassie and Sonny opted for the ran-out-of-gas version. Wolf and I went for the Saipan caper. Everyone else appeared somehow to have drifted into the kitchen, where they seemed to be having great fun helping Cindy clear up and put the food away.

The four of us left in the living room were discussing the movie with growing determination that our individual opinions were correct. Our conversation was declarative and perhaps, suitable for the hard of hearing. I wouldn't really have called it an argument. Not actually. Suddenly Cindy appeared in the doorway wearing the sweetest smile I have ever seen. "Alex, darling, could I borrow you for just one tiny second?"

"Sure." I walked into the kitchen and she yanked my arm, pulling me into the pantry and closing the door. For one delirious instant, I thought she simply could not bear to be without my body for another moment. I soon learned that any designs upon my person were not friendly. She poked a schoolteacher finger hard into my chest. "We will not have any more disagreements in this house this night! I don't care if they marched that airplane woman naked through the streets and the emperor cut off her head with an antique letter opener! Let . . . it . . . go! Now get back in there and be charming. Oh, don't let Wolf drink any more, he's not making sense. Now, go."

I went. I was charming. Peter got Wolf onto his feet, explaining, "It's getting late and much as I hate to leave you lovely people, we have to get up and make brekkers for a bunch of silly queens in the morning. Cindy, Alex, I can't *tell* you what an unforgettable time we've had!"

I just bet he couldn't, although I was sure he'd manage to tell everybody else in town. But I smiled and murmured little nothings as I escorted them to the front door, with Wolf swaying and muttering about that brave young woman dying for her country, that we should all go and throw flowers in the ocean for her.

That started the exodus. Sonny and Trish went out the back door, with Sonny insisting he could drive perfectly well, broken toe or not. Trish said it wasn't his toe she was afraid of. I have no idea how that played out. I closed the door and returned to the living room, where Cindy, Lainey and Cassie were in a three-way embrace. Cassie was apologizing for her outburst and obviously not meaning a word of it, and throwing in little snipes like, "If only I had known I was just supposed to be a leper I would never have said a word."

I broke up the hugfest and sort of danced Cassie to the door, assuring her it was nothing at all, which earned me a sour grin and a rather snappy pat on the cheek from Lainey, and they were gone.

I leaned against the door. Cindy stood in the middle of the room looking dazed. "Is everybody gone?"

"Yes."

"Lock the damn door."

"I already did."

"Then come and make me a drink. And tell me none of this happened." She tottered into the kitchen.

I made the drinks and we sat at the table staring at each other. Then we both burst into laughter. "My God, what a disaster," I managed to say.

"I'll never forget that lobster claw making a true three-pointer into my butter cup, and then your pouring wine all over Sonny's sleeve." Cindy giggled.

"Yeah, well, you did a fine job on the centerpiece, my dear!"

"I know. And I don't even know why." She giggled again and then sobered. "Alex, was it a bad thing that you told me about Maureen being raped? Should you have kept it secret?"

"No, I don't think so. I thought about it before I told you, but I decided it was okay. I think, actually, Cassie stated it pretty well . . .

66

you are my lover, my best friend and my mate. If I can't trust you, we've got bigger troubles than some unfortunate gossip getting spread."

I lit cigarette number something, and decided not to even wonder. "You see, things like Maureen's attack are part of my job. Sometimes my job gets me down, or confused or excited or whatever, and I need someone to talk to. You are that person. I trust you."

She reached for my hand and squeezed it. "I'm glad. I wonder why Lainey didn't tell Cassie."

"Knee-jerk reaction. Medical people hate to share information with any layperson. I think it's one way they preserve that holy mystique. Sometimes I wonder that they even share anything with the patient."

"You're bad. But you don't share *everything* about your cases with me, do you?" She looked at me coquettishly over her drink.

I shrugged. "Mostly. Maybe I skip a detail here and there."

"Aha! Like you might just have skipped the unnamed person who had coffee with you this morning?"

I frowned for a minute, trying to think what she meant. It had been a long day. At last I got it. "Oh, you mean Maureen? She was sitting on the back steps when I got here this morning. How did . . . ?" Then the penny dropped. "Ah, the cup in the sink, her lipstick on it probably."

"As long as it wasn't on you." Cindy smiled, and I had an insane, momentary feeling she looked just like Wells. "What did she want? Why come all the way over here and hang around? She could have just phoned."

"She had thought of a couple more things." I filled her in on my general conversation with Maureen, and then addressed the specifics.

"Added to Nacho IDing the car and what Pete Santos told me, it really pretty well narrows it down to Jack Sanhope, I think."

"What did she come up with?" Cindy did not sound particularly friendly.

"Nothing big, for example, she remembered the stairs she went up were narrow, dim and green-carpeted. She recalls seeing some athletic trophies on a shelf while she was . . . er, in bed. And for some reason, she spotted a telescope out in the yard. I'm almost sure she'd been there before, even though she may now have blocked it." I sipped my drink.

"She really led you right to the Sanhope kid, didn't she? Everything she remembered had his name all over it. You just followed the breadcrumbs. Have you ever considered, Alex, that most people in stressful situations remember trivia? They don't remember the hold-up guy had on a red jacket, they remember he had garlic on his breath. They don't remember his accomplice was tall and skinny, they remember she was wearing blue eye shadow. And I don't think Maureen blocked a damn thing," Cindy went on acerbically. "I think she remembered them all along. I think for some reason she's leading everybody on at her own pace. She wants something from you, Alex, though I'm not sure what. It may simply be your sweet bod . . . *if* she's gay."

"You don't think she is?" She was confusing me now.

"Well, think back. According to what you told me she said this morning, she never really admitted to sleeping with Mary. I think she is whatever is handiest, richest or most likely to advance her cause . . . whatever that may be at the moment. Never mind the grammar, you know what I mean."

I sat back in my chair, surprised at the dislike in her voice. "Wow, ma'am! You don't care for our little Irish colleen?"

"I think she is a conniving opportunist. And if she ever really comes on to you, I'll bop her one in the head with a baseball bat!"

I laughed very heartily, and then said with just the right amount of casualness, "Oh, I don't think we have to worry."

Cindy smiled. "That would be about ten seconds after I bopped *you* in the head." She stood and headed for the bedroom.

"I'll be right there," I called after her. "I'm just going out with Fargo for a sec." And, please, God, don't let Maureen be walking up the driveway.

68

While Fargo went on patrol around the yard, looking for just the right spot on just the right bush, I thought of Cindy's intensity about Maureen. It made sense when you factored in a tiring work week, a long day, a catastrophic evening, a late hour and more to drink than usual for my beloved. She'd probably either be embarrassed or forget all about it by morning. On the other hand, Maureen *had kind* of dodged the Mary issue.

By the time Fargo had peed and declared the yard free of intruders, we had been outside for several minutes. Inside, I closed up the house and turned off lights and went into the bedroom. Cindy was already asleep.

At least, I guessed she was.

Chapter 11

When a dog decides it is time to begin his day, he does not factor in what he had to drink the night before, at what hour the lights were turned off, what day of the week it is or what plans may be had for that day. He simply knows that he is awake and ready to embark on whatever today's journey may be . . . and so, consequently, are you. You can either get up or you can shoot the dog.

I knew of one small restaurant that opened at the crack of dawn, and stopped there on the way to Race Point to pick up a container of coffee and a slab of hot Portuguese fried bread, liberally smeared with butter and beach plum jelly. I consumed it in about four bites plus one for Fargo as we drove. I got down a shudderingly hot belt of coffee, and felt much better about the world in general.

I parked the car and Fargo took off down the hill to the water's edge where he ran all-out, zigzagging for no apparent reason except the pure joy of feeling the sand skid beneath him. The air was cool, but the still-red rising sun held out the carrot of warmer rays to come, and the ocean lapped ashore with feisty little wavelets not quite daring to reach my shoes. But I had the feeling it was all a big bluff. The sun had just a touch of haze, barely enough to put it half a degree out of focus. Away from the shore, the swells were bulky, with an oily look, and breaking sullenly out where the beach began to shelve. What wind there was came from the east. My bet was rain before nightfall.

So Fargo and I enjoyed our solitude. One of us running, trotting, prancing saucily up to the waves, snapping at the foam, dashing ashore, exploring every smell of possible interest. The other, walking slowly, camera in hand, waiting for the photo op. It came, with two seagulls screaming and fighting over a small, very dead fish head. It went, as Fargo broke up the fight and peed on the fish, just to prove he'd won.

I turned back toward the car, sipping the cooling coffee, lighting the first cigarette. Fargo dashed by, chasing a flock of sandpipers that whirled and dipped enticingly, perhaps just to keep him interested. And we went home.

I stopped for pastry and papers. I could never figure out why we had to have two Sunday *New York Times*. Nor could I figure out how we could get along with just one. We needed two puzzles. And two TV schedules. We each liked to read various sections, like the Book Review, during the week. Whatever. I lugged two of them into the house.

Cindy was up and dressed, looking alert and cheerful, her difficult mood of the night before apparently evaporated. I plopped a paper in front of her, put the other one across the table for me and turned to feed the dog. "How was the beach?" Cindy asked. "I was half awake. I should have gone with you."

"We would love to have had you. It was splendid, but . . ." I pressed the back of my hand to my forehead as if receiving a vision. "I foresee rain in the near future. We should breakfast *al fresco.*"

"Invite him if you wish," she sighed. "Personally, I can go a long time without guests for a meal."

"Okay, scratch Al." I grabbed the bag of pastries and two mugs of coffee. "First one out gets first choice of the goodies." I ran for the back door.

She followed slowly, finally placing napkins, the two puzzles and pencils on the outdoor table. I reached for the goodies bag and she moved it away. "No game. You already had breakfast."

"Now why would you say a thing like that?" I asked indignantly.

"The jelly on your shirt."

"Oh." I handed her the paper bag. "Help yourself."

We ate and fiddled with the puzzle. I looked at the high-end real estate ads with photos, to see what I might "buy" this week. There was a rather nice estate in Greenwich, CT, but at 3.7 mil, it seemed a bit pricey, so I moved on to the food section. It featured three soups I'd never heard of, which might be at home in Greenwich, but would be foreign indeed on my table. It was just as well I'd saved my millions.

Cindy gathered up the debris and headed inside, murmuring something about the dishwasher. I strolled around the plantation, pulling a weed here and there. Then I put the circular metal cages around the tomato plants, though somehow the cages made them look even smaller and more vulnerable. I wished they would grow faster. I hoed my hydrangea plant and sprinkled some used tea leaves around the roots. A suggestion from Aunt Mae. From the garage I took a jar of flat beer, also an Aunt Mae idea, poured some into a shallow bowl and placed it near the baby peppers in case the slugs came a-wandering. And then I felt a large *splat* on the back of my hand and looked down, relieved to see it was a giant raindrop. Then I felt another on my back, on my head, my back again.

My prophecy was coming true a little early. So much for the beer. I poured it back in the jar, grabbed the hoe and trotted for the garage. By the time I got in the house, it was coming down hard.

Cindy had done the only sensible thing for a rainy Sunday afternoon, and gone back to bed. She was curled up under a light throw reading *The Week in Review* while Gershwin's *Concerto in F* played in the background. I took a fast shower and stretched out beside her. The CD had switched to my favorite of the selections,

Cuban Rhapsody, and I kept the tricky rhythms softly with my fingertips on the bed.

I pulled the throw to cover us both and felt her welcome body warmth. I moved my head down to her stomach and massaged her legs lightly. While she read she tried desultorily and unsuccessfully to subdue the shower-damp cowlick left in the crown of my hair. The rain against the windows beat a counter tempo to the music. It was a friendly timeless time.

There was no passion. Passion would come later. Then mouths would kiss and tongues would explore and insist. Hands would stroke and grasp and give and demand. Bodies would quiver and move unbidden, as if controlled by a master puppeteer. One of us would give a small, sharp cry. The other would take a deep, almost sobbing breath. But it was not that time . . . not yet.

It was an early, cloud-induced dusk and still raining when I awoke and heard Cindy doing something in the kitchen. I pulled on jeans and sweatshirt and went to investigate. As I walked into the room, she turned and smiled and raised her arms. "Caught me. I surrender."

I pulled her toward me and whispered into her hair. "Stealing lobsters is a dangerous pastime in this area." I gave her a kiss and she turned back to the counter.

"I wanted to do something with the food from last night while it's still good to eat. There's rice in the blue bowl and some salad greens in the yellow bowl. I left you and Fargo a lobster plus a steak. And there are muffins in the plastic bag. Just nuke everything but the salad."

Yawning, I asked. "Could it be you are leaving me?"

"Yep. I want to check on Wells. Aunt Mae may have had enough of her by now. And I need to get some clothes together for tomorrow."

"You didn't leave me all the food, did you?"

"Certainly not. Wells and I will also enjoy surf and turf together." She kissed me again. "Talk to you tomorrow?"

"Yes. And miss you tonight."

"That's good. A little, not too much, but a little." She stroked Fargo for a moment, picked up a plastic bag and went out, calling over her shoulder, "My God, there's a big boat out here with animals marching into it."

I popped a beer and nuked the rice and meat and muffins as ordered, and put some dressing on the salad. It was almost as good as it was last night, and I realized I was starved. Somewhere along the way, lunch had been misplaced. I turned on the TV and watched the news while we ate.

The food was so good and my mood so mellow, not even world and national events could get me down. I did miss Cindy . . . a little. And I was pretty sure she was missing me . . . a little.

Chapter 12

By Monday morning at 10:30 the rain had stopped, the sun was out, and Fargo and I had long-finished our early beach run, where, lying flat on my stomach and shooting directly into the sun, I had gotten a fabulous shot of driftwood, a small tree limb, half-buried in sand, arms reaching skyward in a plea for freedom. Afterward, I tried to yank it loose and take it to Aunt Mae to be made into a planter for herbs, but it was too big to handle. So we headed for the car.

And now, I was ready to visit Dr. Gloetzner and collect the information I was pretty sure would finish off one Jack Sanhope. Rapists were rarely so thoughtful as to use condoms, so Jack's DNA should be easily provided by semen samples, recovered from Maureen's visit to the emergency room early Monday morning.

Fargo begged to go along, and who was I to be disagreeable on such a promising day? En route we stopped at Evans' Grocery, mainly because they delivered. There I purchased three large bags of potato chips, tortilla chips and pretzels, plus three tins each of mixed nuts and bridge mix. That should hold Nacho for an afternoon! And, I thought happily, tucking the receipt into my wallet, they were a legitimate expense item.

I parked in the shade, lowered all the windows and presented myself at Dr. Gloetzner's door promptly at 11:00. He was a slight, balding man with a bit of a ski-slope nose and a rather prim mouth, and the first words out of his mouth were to ask for my credentials and Maureen's letter permitting release of medical records to me. He called through the open door to his secretary and asked her to make copies of both documents, and then seemed to relax.

"You want to know about Maureen's experience of June fourth," he reminded us both, as he opened the folder in front of him. "Well, there were some abrasions in and outside the vagina, as well as some mild interior bruising." He stopped.

"Indicative of rape," I concluded for him.

"Good word, indicative." He looked up at me with a surprising grin that made him almost handsome. "Could be indicative of rape. Could be indicative of a good old-fashioned enthusiastic romp in the hay."

To say I was shocked was an understatement. "Ah . . . well . . . ah, what about other signs of rape? An attack?"

"Sorry, Ms. Peres, there were none I could find. No bruises on her neck, arms, back or breasts. None on her knuckles or feet to indicate she tried to hit him. No torn fingernails saying she might have left some scratches on the brute. There were a couple of very mild bruises on the inner thighs."

"Aha!" I began to breathe again.

"Ah, no, I fear. Those usually occur when the woman is on top during intercourse."

"Damnation!" I was floundering. I leaned forward and tapped the folder. "Drugs. She said she was drugged. You tested for drugs?"

"We always do. There are a bunch of them around, choose your date rape drug *du jour*. We tested for GHB, for Ketamine hydrochloride and for Rohypnol . . . the most popular of the bunch at the moment. They aren't always easy to isolate, and they rarely remain in the bloodstream at all past twenty-four hours. Once in a while traces have been found at seventy-two hours, but that's very unusual. We found none." He leaned back in his chair.

"Doctor, I don't understand. If the rapist administered the drug at, say, ten o'clock Sunday night and Maureen got to you at—what?—three o'clock Monday morning, that's only five hours. Why wouldn't the drugs show up in her blood?" I was now on the edge of my chair.

"They might have," he agreed. "But she walked into the ER at . . ." He looked down at the folder. "At ten seventeen a.m. Wednesday, June seven, with her friend, a Ms. Sloan."

"*Wednesday morning*?" I felt as if I were hurtling down a rabbit hole.

"Yes. Ms. Sloan said Maureen had been too distraught to come in earlier." His face was deadpan.

"And semen residue?" I asked hopelessly.

He shook his head. "If there had been any, it was all douched cleanly away." He leaned back in his chair and looked at me kindly. "I really am sorry to be so unhelpful, but that's simply the way it went. She may indeed have been drugged and raped, but I have absolutely no conclusive proof or even strong indicators that she was. Whatever might have been there was gone. Often, women who have been raped are so upset they do foolish things. I'm just sorry her older friend didn't have better sense about preserving evidence and getting her here at once."

He tapped his fist lightly on his desk. "I don't like to think of a man getting away with rape because of foolish technicalities. But I can't change what I found. There is one other thing I can tell you, which may be of interest. Rape or romp, that night's athletic sexual encounter could have injured the fetus. Maureen is lucky there was apparently no damage."

"She's pregnant?" I wasn't sure we were both still in the same room. "You can tell so soon?"

"Oh, that was misleading." He waved a hand apologetically. "No, she did not get pregnant Sunday night. She got pregnant, I would say, approximately April tenth . . . give or take a week. Ms. Peres, you look pale. Are you all right?"

"I was fine when I got here," I muttered. "Yeah, I guess so. So she's about two months pregnant . . . and who the hell is the father? What did you do when you realized that?"

"Who indeed? I referred her to our Obstetrics Department. What else was there to do? And, now, Ms. Peres, much as I hate to rush you . . ."

"Yes, of course. Well, Dr. Gloetzner, thank you for your time. Forgive me if I seem a little scattered. This is turning into the case from hell." We smiled sadly at each other, shook hands and parted. His secretary pressed my license and Maureen's release gently into my damp hand on my way out.

I stood on the clinic steps, breathing deeply of the sun-warmed air, getting the hospital smell out of my nose and mouth. In Gloetzner's office, I had been deeply shaken. Now I was getting boiling mad. I walked to the car and let Fargo out to find a friendly bush. Meanwhile, I was going to track down Mary and/or Maureen and find out what the hell they had been up to, if I had to pull them off the top of a phone pole. Jesus, I hoped Maureen wasn't climbing phone poles. Well, at least I had answered one question. Now I knew why Maureen had turned green when I offered her a nice greasy French cruller.

I reach into the compartment for my cell phone and checked for Mary's number. Then I stopped. I'd better talk to John Frost before I waded deeper into this quagmire. I dialed his number and, miracle-time, was put right through. I asked if I could see him right away. He hesitated and said that he and Trish were just thinking of some lunch.

"Fine," I said. "Have it at the Wharf Rat. I'll be there in ten minutes." I hung up before he could answer, recovered Fargo and slammed the car into gear.

By the time I looped Fargo's leash around the big old anchor outside the Rat, I had calmed down a little. I brought him out water and a small bowl of Billie's beef stew, to avoid the collapse that had seemed imminent as he raised his head and whuffled at the aromas coming out the Wharf Rat door.

I went in again, spotted Trish and John and joined them as they both sipped Sprites while waiting for their lunches. I felt no such compunction and ordered a Bud plus my usual lunch of pastrami sandwich, french fries and half sour pickle. It was my favorite, and that way I could honestly tell Cindy I'd had a healthy meal of protein, grain, vegetable and a little something green.

John addressed his broiled scrod and sautéed summer squash, while Trish chewed manfully at what looked like a bowl of grass clippings. They both eyed my plate with envy. I was making little progress emptying it. I was too busy bringing them up-to-date.

I told them of my earlier visit to Mary and Maureen, the comments of her ex-roommates and the bartender. I recounted Maureen's Saturday morning visit and got a look from Trish that reminded me strongly of Cindy. Finally, I informed them of Nacho's luck with the car and my luncheon with Pete Santos.

John looked genuinely distressed. "I know it's natural that Pete would stand up for his cousin, but I find myself wondering if he's right. I don't know the Sanhopes well at all, but I've always admired Grace. That woman doesn't need another tragedy!" He stabbed viciously at a piece of fish. "Just when she straightens up, something comes along again and knocks her over at a fell swoop."

"Don't cry, John. It may not be quite as swoopy as you think." I washed down a fry and took a bite of sandwich, while they looked at me expectantly. At last I swallowed and told them Dr. Gloetzner's information. They were as taken aback as I had been.

John announced that he wanted Mary and Maureen in his office as soon as they could be reached, but Trish disagreed. "Wait until Alex talks to Jack Sanhope," she suggested. "Right now we don't know whether Maureen just acted foolishly or with an agenda. We don't know that the baby is Jack's or what she plans to do about it, although if she's going to have an abortion, she better get moving.

Even if the baby *is* Jack's, that doesn't mean he couldn't have raped her last Sunday."

I took another bite and mumbled around it. "I think she's right, John . . . we know s'more about Lothario, it may explain more 'bout M'reen."

John frowned but agreed, and waved for the check. Second rounds or dessert were not included. He pulled out the charge card carbon and carefully wrote "Delaney conference" on the receipt and shoved it in his shirt pocket. "Get all this written up and call me tomorrow the minute you finish with young Sanhope," he instructed. Trish gave me a pat and followed him out.

"Will do. And thanks for lunch," I called after him. I finished mine more slowly.

On the way out I stopped and paid for Fargo's stew. I collected Fargo and picked up his Styrofoam dishes.

At home I changed into jeans and a shirt and took the walk-around phone into the backyard where Fargo was patrolling for heffalumps and tiggers. I slumped into one of the yard chairs and dialed Cindy's direct number.

"Cynthia Hart, may I help you?"

"Will you accept charges for an obscene phone call?"

"Certainly not! I get plenty of lovely ones for free. Why should I have to pay for this one? Is it better than the others?"

"Smart ass! I'm home."

"I certainly hope so. I'd hate to think we were having this conversation with you on an open phone at the Wharf Rat Bar. How's your day going, darling?"

I laughed and propped my feet up on another chair. "It's been a doozey. I'll tell you when you get home. I just called to see if I'm supposed to do anything about dinner."

"No. I was going to call you in a bit. Your mom called. She and Aunt Mae sent a bunch of fried chicken and what not all over to the Rev. Bartles' place for some occasion. But they made extra, as usual, and invited us to eat. I said we would, if that's okay with you."

80

"Sure. Where? When?" I swallowed a yawn.

"Your mom's, sixish. I'll probably come straight from work. It's been Monday all day," she sighed.

"Okay, honey, I'll let you go. Thank you for flying Sky-High Airlines."

"Idiot."

I stretched. We were guaranteed a good dinner. I don't know who was the better cook, Mom or Aunt Mae. It must be somebody's birthday over at Bartles' place. He was a youngish, born-again preacher, and he and his prune-mouthed wife ran a sort of shelter for teenage strays. He and I had crossed on several occasions but had more or less declared a truce. My mother and aunt ignored his religion, but praised his efforts with kids and contributed to his larder. So I shut up.

And I awoke at a few minutes after five.

Chapter 13

As I prepared to meet with Jack Sanhope Tuesday afternoon, I recalled part of the conversation last night at my mother's. We were eating at the picnic table in the backyard of the house I had called home for many years. It was a straight up-and-down two-story house, a type seen often in Ptown, painted a pale yellow with maroon shutters. A white picket fence set off the small front yard, and a driveway led along the house to a separate garage and fairly large backyard. By Provincetown's scrunched up standards, it was considered a sizeable piece of land.

Sonny had joined the four of us, late, and was still addressing smother-fried chicken, pasta salad with diced green peppers and carrots, and coleslaw, while the rest of us progressed to Aunt Mae's fresh peach cake with caramel drizzle and pecan pieces on top. Oh, Lord, how did she do it?

Mom interrupted a silent moment with the question, "How's the poor Delaney girl doing? Has anyone seen her? Would it be a kindness to stop by and visit her, or better to let it be?"

Cindy, Sonny and I flashed sly grins, and it appeared I was the one elected to answer. "Well, Mom, since it's supposed to be a deep, dark secret, it might be best to let it be. On the other hand, so many people seem to know about it, there may well be a line of well-wishers around her house as we speak. How did you hear of it?"

"No special way." Mother spread her hands. "One of the Bitter End waitresses warned Betsy Raymer to be careful. Betsy told her mother and she told me at work."

"I wonder if it really is Jack Sanhope?" Aunt Mae interjected.

This time there were no grins. Sonny parted with a drumstick to ask sharply, "Now how the hell did *that* get out?"

Aunt Mae looked smug. "Through your front gate, Mr. Grumpy. Elena Madeiros stopped by your place of business to pay a traffic ticket."

We all smiled at that. Mrs. Madeiros looked like a grandmotherly pouter pigeon with thick glasses, but drove like a graduate of Demolition Derby in an old gray Escort that had left its spoor on most every phone pole, parking meter and fireplug in Ptown. And the mechanically challenged Mrs. M. also managed to park frequently in crosswalks, or with one wheel on the sidewalk or snuggled up to a fireplug.

"Anyway," Mae continued, "There was no one at the front desk, so she went through the little gate into the back to look for someone. She overheard Mary O'Malley and Alex talking about Mercedes cars and rapes and Jack. She ran into me later at the store and told me."

Sonny shook his head in annoyance. "Dammit, that gate is supposed to be latched, and there's a bell on the desk to ring. Nosy old biddy!" He turned to me. "Too bad you and Nacho weren't talking about that slimy son-in-law of hers."

"Oh, dear," Mom sighed. "I really hope it isn't Jack. That family has had its share of heartbreak."

"So I keep hearing," Cindy said. She looked at Mom. "Is it all true?"

"And then some." Mom nodded. "An infant dead of SIDS, Robert killed in Vietnam. William by a heart attack . . ."

"Jeanne, you dated Robert for awhile, didn't you?" Mae asked.

Mom looked slightly wistful and I wondered if it had been more than casual, but she answered easily enough. "Oh, a bit. It was nothing. I wasn't in his social or financial league, and Grace made sure he remembered that."

I heard a hint of bitterness, and Aunt Mae's next comment underscored it. "Maybe Robert wouldn't have dashed off to fight in Vietnam if she had kept her mouth shut. She should have concentrated on keeping her husband in line." She closed her mouth primly. Apparently neither of them knew how Robert really died, thank goodness.

"Peter got out of line?" I asked, amused. I snitched another small piece of cake.

"With everything that wore a skirt," Aunt Mae snapped. "And then there was that poor girl who worked there as a maid, getting her pregnant."

My ear pricked up. "He seduced her?"

"That was the word usually used," Mom said with a heavy dollop of sarcasm. "But when the seducer is your boss, how can you call it anything but a different form of rape?"

Memory of those words took me through getting ready for Jack Sanhope's arrival . . . setting out a pitcher of iced tea and fixings, putting my notebook and pen on the table, along with an ashtray, a bowl of nuts and coasters. A car door slammed in the driveway, and I walked around the side of the house. A Mercedes convertible sat in the drive and a young man, tanned, with dark curly hair walked toward me. I'm not an investigator for nothing. It took me no time at all to figure him for Jack Sanhope.

I extended my hand. "Hi. I'm Alex Peres." His grip was firm, but held no attempt to be a bone-crusher.

"Jack Sanhope."

"Come on around back, it's cooler out here. Have a seat." I poured two glasses of tea and looked up to see him still standing, looking mildly distressed.

"Gee, Ms. Peres, I'm sorry you went to the trouble. I really can't stay. Pete said there was some thought my car might have been in an unreported accident. I just came by so you could look at it and see for yourself. There's not a scratch on it."

"Call me Alex and I will call you Jack, if I may?" He nodded. "Good. Now sit, Jack, I want to talk to you about Maureen Delaney." He sank into the chair with a face so full of guilt, I wondered if it were necessary to continue the conversation.

"Let me explain to you that I am a private investigator, employed in this instance by attorney John Frost." I passed Jack sugar and lemon, and he absently accepted. "Ms. Delaney is his client. She has asserted that she was the victim of date rape, a week ago Sunday, June fourth."

"Rape! Oh, no, the poor girl. What a terrible thing! Is she all right . . . I mean . . . she's okay physically and all?" I nodded and he looked relieved.

Then his face clouded. "No, wait, that's wrong. You said June fourth. No, that Sunday she was with me, she was fine. Somebody's got their dates mixed. I met her about . . . oh, ten o'clock and she was perfectly okay. And about one o'clock I took her home, right to the door of that old lady she's moved in with. I saw her go in."

I looked down at my notepad and scribbled a note, so he wouldn't see the grin on my face. Mary would love that one. I wondered how he had me catalogued? At thirty-two, I probably rated late middle age. "You picked her up at the Bitter End?"

"Not exactly." He shook his head. "Out in back of it. On the wharf, so I could double park if she were late."

"Then?"

"Then we drove up to my house. Grandmother and my brother Richard and his wife had gone back to Boston. Nobody to bother us, so we had a couple of drinks in the library and I took her home."

"Jack." He looked up at me and I stared him down. "At this point, it's the truth or the cops. It may be the cops anyway, but let's try the truth first. When you drove to your house was the top on your car down?"

He looked at me curiously. "No, it wouldn't have been. It was misty, I think, almost a rain. Why?"

"No big thing. Maureen thought she remembered it as down."

"She's probably thinking of another time. Wait a minute . . . just wait one minute! Is she trying to hang this rape thing on *me*?"

"Yup."

His laugh was bitter. "Alex, if anybody got raped in this deal, it was me."

"Tell me about it. From the top."

"Yeah, all right. About three months ago, I met her at the Bitter End. She was beautiful, fun. She knew how to dress. She liked to dance, liked good food. We were having a ball. After maybe three dates, she came back to the house, back to my room with me and we made love. Let me tell you, she was *good* at that! She yanked me every which-a-way but up!" He looked as if he'd like to say more, but was trying to be at least fractionally gentlemanly.

"You use any protection?" I asked.

"Yes, the first time. Then she asked me if I'd been tested. I said yes and she said she was clear, too, and it would be a lot more fun with nothing between us. She said she was on the pill, so I put away the condoms and we had one grand time. Every time. She was wild, that one, wild to try it all, invent new ways. She was a tiger in heat." He sipped his tea and shook his head.

"But," he continued, "She sort of changed. She was still great in bed, but very critical otherwise. Like, *the table is lousy, Jack, can't you speak to the maitre d'?* And, *don't drink your beer out of the bottle, Jack, it looks common.* Or, *I don't care you've got a paper to write, I want to see the new act at the Poly/Cotton Club.* You know?"

Actually, I didn't know. This was a side of Maureen I hadn't seen. I thought of her and Mary. Two control freaks together. It could make for an interesting relationship. "I understand," I said. "So what happened?"

"I was going to ease my way out of it." He grimaced slightly. "I wanted to do it nicely. Gently. But the next time I saw her, she dropped a nuke on my head. She says she's pregnant. She screwed the pills up somehow, it's all her fault, and she's so sorry. She's sobbing, she's so upset. Well, I tell her not to worry. I've got enough money to cover the abortion." He paused and looked embarrassed. "I don't have much cash ever, Alex. Grandmother controls the money, and she's not overgenerous. But I had enough for this. I even said I'd go with her, but she said she'd handle it. So I gave her most of what I had . . . eight hundred dollars. I knew it was more than enough. I know because I drove my cousin Pete and his girl down to a clinic last fall." He looked suddenly stricken. "Please don't mention that to anyone. I should never have said that. Oh, God, what was I thinking of?"

I patted his hand. "Not to worry. My lips are sealed. So, did Maureen get the abortion?" In a pig's ear.

He looked at me with eyes that reminded me of a deer caught in the headlights of a car. "No. I don't know. Maybe." He laughed at himself and fished a cashew out of the nut dish. "I saw her the next week and she was all lovey-dovey. Sexy, but sweet and almost cloying, actually. I asked her if she had had the abortion, and was it safe for her to have sex so soon. She laughed and said the sex was perfectly all right. She had not had the abortion, she'd had a wonderful idea instead."

I lit a cigarette I was pretty sure was number seven, but this was no time for a lecture. Instead, I gave Jack a wry smile as he said, "She wanted us to get married and have little Whosis and be the happiest family in the whole wide world. I told her no way! First of all, I have law school to get through. I want to do well and get all I can out of it. That does not include a wife and family. It particularly does not include Maureen. I guess I was stupid to stop using condoms, but, frankly, I don't feel solely responsible for this pregnancy. I'm quite willing to fund an abortion. I am not willing to spend the rest of my life with Maureen. So I told her to get the abortion and be done with it." He drank some tea, but I think it could have been saltwater for all he tasted.

"Is that how you left it?" I asked.

He nodded. "For then it was. Then she called me at school, in the middle of finals, and said she had to see me. I came up on the third and saw her on the fourth, on Sunday night. And damned if she wasn't still stalling! We went back to the house. We'd both already had a bit to drink, I guess, and we had more and started to argue. She was still talking marriage and really came on strong to me, really dialing up the sexy approach. She was getting to me sexually, but I was also getting angry about . . . about everything, I guess. So I went along with the sex. I told her if she wanted jungle sex, I'd give it to her. And I did. But it wasn't rape. She was as aggressive as I was. She kept laughing like everything was a big joke, and the madder I got the more she laughed. Jesus."

He had his hands clasped in front of him, and I could see they were shaking. "I don't mean to be crude," he said. "I don't doubt she was bruised. So was I. But there was nothing sensual about it . . . or even personal between two people. It was just . . . rutting." He took a deep breath that was very nearly a sob.

"That's all interesting and plausible, Jack. It's too bad there wasn't a third party eavesdropping so we could prove who's telling the truth. But I don't think an abortion is in the picture now, and for reasons we needn't explore at this point, I don't think she wants to marry you now, if she ever did. But I have a strong feeling she may have decided to have the baby and hit you for the biggest child support payments in history."

He turned pure white, buried his face in his hands and muttered, "I'm finished. Completely finished. That does it." He gave a half sob. "I'll kill her."

Chapter 14

I got him into the house and pointed him toward the bathroom. When I heard water running, I poured both of us a good splash of bourbon into rocks glasses and added ice. I sat at the kitchen table and waited.

In a few moments he came into the kitchen, still pale but under control and looking very young with droplets of water still along his hairline and a damp spot on his shirtfront. He was filled with apologies, but I raised my hand and pointed him toward a chair and his glass. "Please. Don't apologize. You're understandably upset. It's bourbon," I added.

"Thanks. I never quite got the hang of scotch."

"Me either. If I may ask, Jack, what got into you all of a sudden?"

He sipped his drink and set it back carefully in the same spot on the coaster, as if testing the steadiness of his hand. "All of it, I guess. I could have dealt with an abortion okay. It's done. Over.

You move on, even though you didn't really like doing it. But if Maureen is going to have it—have the kid . . . my kid . . . God, what a can of worms *that* will open up!"

"Such as?"

"Okay." He started ticking points off on his fingers. "In a nutshell, marriage is out, and I don't want Maureen raising a kid of mine. Nor do I like the idea of adoption, no matter how fine and caring the adoptive parents might be. If I'm to have a child, I want to be involved in his or her life, and I don't believe one should try to do that if the kid's adopted. Not fair to anybody."

"You're assuming it is yours." I made it a statement.

"Yes. More and more, I'm getting the feeling the whole thing was planned. If it had worked, we'd marry and she'd be set for life. If not, she'd sue for big bucks and still be set for life, and you wonder how much of the money the kid would see. And you wonder what kind of life Maureen would lead." His eyes were a very bleak, cold blue now and his face no longer looked so boyish. I wouldn't want to face him in a courtroom in five years.

"And," he continued, "From a purely selfish point . . . this is going to mess up my life big time. You see, Grandmother didn't mind my going to law school when she thought I was going into the company business at the end of it. Hey, every banker can use a good lawyer, right?" He smirked.

I nodded. "So what's the problem?"

"The problem is, I'm not going to specialize in corporate law. I'm going for environmental law, and I will not be practicing that at Lanham and Sanhope Securities. Amazin' Grace thinks I've chosen a pointless career filled with a bunch of bleeding heart pinkos and pansies . . . her words." He grinned and then sobered. "It's far from pointless! We're killing our world so fast I don't know how we can turn it around, even if everybody tries. And the second half of her opinion is just silly. *But*, she has already threatened not to pay my law school tuition and expenses and not to come up with any money at all for me. I get an inheritance when I'm thirty, that she has no control over, but that's light years away! This Maureen thing is going to send her right over the edge. When she finds out about it, she won't even give me a sandwich and coffee at the back door."

I leaned back in my chair. "I can understand her point, even if I don't agree with her, on your choice of careers. It's an uphill battle with few victories. But what is so awful about your not joining the family firm?"

"Aha." He pointed his finger at his chest. "I was to be the great white hope. You see, my brother Richard is the only family male at L and S, and he and Lillian apparently can't have kids. My sister has two airhead daughters. I was to keep the line and the business going." He laughed ruefully. "Well, if the DNA checks out, I'll have proved I'm not sterile! I'll assume I can produce an heir and a spare or two in a more conventional manner at some point. Maybe one of them will like finance . . . or the ballet . . . or roping cattle. *My* kids will be whatever they want to be."

"But first, how do you get through law school if grandma locks the cash register?" I looked at him closely, wondering just who, in this entire mess, was telling the truth.

"Well, all may not be lost. My mom will try to help if necessary. She's in England now, married to an old sweetheart. Bruce is a nice guy, and I think maybe they can afford it . . . just. My sister Francesca might help, and so might my brother Richard, but it would cause an awful family row if they did. I don't want that. I'd pay everybody back, in time. I get that money when I'm thirty that Grace can't touch. Damn her, this is plain spite."

His eyes got that bleak look again. "She and Maureen make a great pair. Do it my way, or else! I'd like to strangle them both. Well, the hell with them! I'm accepted at Georgetown for late September, and to Georgetown I'll go. Lots of things can happen in three months." He drained his glass and set it down hard. "What do you suggest I do for now?"

I thought for a moment. "Wel-l-ll. I think you can forget about being charged with rape. Ms. Delaney has some questions to answer there. But she will want—and get—some kind of money. If it's your kid, it's your bill. Maybe you'd better alert your grand-mother that Attorney Frost will be in touch with you. And don't see or talk to Maureen."

"Yeah. Maureen may be in for a surprise. My net worth right now is about two hundred bucks plus a maxed-out credit card. Jeez, I dread this. Grandma will go ballistic."

I finished my drink and spun the ice cubes in the glass. "Not a great deal of love lost between you and Grandma?"

"That's not a word I frequently associate with Grace. Responsibility, duty, focus . . . even admiration, but not much love, I think. Well, it will work out. There are always ways to get around things. I just need to think clearly. Too many thoughts bubbling around just now, but I'll settle down. Those two charming ladies will not ruin my life, no way. I'll do what I have to do." We both stood and shook hands and I walked him to the door. "Thank you, Alex. You've been a great help. I owe you a big one. Anytime."

"You don't owe me a thing, but thank you. By the way, your cousin Pete was mad as hell I made him help me con you into this little meeting. He swore up and down you would never rape any woman under any circumstances."

"Pete's a good man."

"He is that."

Before Jack even got his car started, I had John Frost on the phone. It was not a pleasant conversation. It ended with John saying, "Be here at eleven in the morning. I'll have those two crazy women in here if I have to pull them off a phone pole." Somehow the words sounded familiar.

I don't know how long I sat at the table wondering what on earth Maureen was up to, and if her story was true, then what was Jack's about? Suddenly Fargo scrambled to his feet and trotted to the back door, tail a-wag. A moment later Cindy came in, carrying her shoes. How that woman did hate shoes . . . and walking. She'd drive from the kitchen to the pantry if she could get her car in the house.

She kissed Fargo's head and stroked his ears and neck. "Poor baby, have you been locked in all day with this grouchy-looking barfly? Give me a minute and I'll go out with you. Hello, darling grouchy barfly. I'll change and be right back . . . just time for you to make me an apple martini." I got a pat on the head as she passed. What was wrong with this picture?

As we made and then ate dinner, I recounted my visit with Jack Sanhope. When I told her what he said had transpired with Maureen, Cindy managed not to say *I told you so*, but just barely.

She completely sympathized with Jack. "Well, as he said, many things can happen over the summer. Let's just hope one of them isn't that he tosses grandma off the cliff. Or walks Maureen off the end of the pier late some foggy night."

I laughed and added my plate to those already in the dishwasher. "Oh, I think Maureen is safe enough. She's carrying a Sanhope, no matter what everyone may think of her. And grandma's got the whole clan too intimidated to do anything to her."

"Don't be fooled by his cute grin," Cindy warned. "The more intimidated he is, the more he may see no way out but . . . *mur-dah!* What's on TV?"

We adjourned to the living room and Cindy opened the TV guide. She scanned the program lineup and made a face. "Nothing, nothing and worse-than-nothing."

"Check the History Channel," I suggested. "They're usually okay unless they've got secrets of ancient Egypt and the damn pyramids on again. Someone in their programming department has a fetish for pointy buildings with secret rooms."

She flipped a page and ran her finger down the listings. "You're in luck. It's half a world away from Egypt."

"Good. What is it?"

"Secrets of ancient Mexico and the Mayan pyramids."

Chapter 15

Fargo and I strolled up Commercial Street to keep our eleven o'clock date at John Frost's. I deliberately concentrated on tourist watching to keep from thinking of the ensuing conference. I was trying very hard to keep an open mind.

Many of the town's visitors were trying very hard to deal with mouths full of saltwater taffy as they walked, looking like cows working their way through tough forage. Others were heavy laden with plastic bags—smiley faces and *Thank You* stenciled on the sides. Some slurped at cold drinks, others looked hopefully for an empty bench, still others dragged fussy children behind them, and some actually limped as they walked and stared vacant-eyed at crowded window displays. All were on vacation and, if asked, would assure you they were having fun. And the natives smiled and smiled as they listened to the joyous muted bell-song of their cash registers.

Arriving at John's office, I found him, Trish, Mary and Maureen gathered in the conference room ahead of me. John was definitely not in a good mood. "We were about to start without you," he snapped. "I want this situation clarified here and now."

"Sorry," I muttered, and slipped into a chair at the other end of the table, Fargo by my side.

John turned to Maureen. "Ms. Delaney, I confess to total bewilderment. We now have so much conflicting information about your situation, I hardly know where to start." He consulted his notes and made a good stab at it. I didn't envy Maureen's position here.

"For example, Ms. Peres has come up with some rather astounding facts. You didn't bother seeing a doctor until Wednesday after the Sunday you were presumably raped. You are two months pregnant, quite probably by the man you accuse of raping you last week. He allegedly gave you eight hundred dollars for an abortion, but is not sure you had it—."

"Attorney Frost." Mary Sloan leaned forward on the table. "This all sounds very convoluted, but let me tell you how it came about." She looked at Maureen questioningly, received a slight nod and continued.

"Maureen met Jack Sanhope in March. He seemed very nice, and she simply thought she was making a new friend in a new country." She glared at John. "Things are a bit simpler where she comes from, you know? Well, Sanhope *did* rape her, and got her pregnant, after drugging her and taking her back to his house in early April. She was too frightened then to see a doctor or tell anyone. She didn't really know the girls she shared an apartment with, had no nearby relatives, no close friends. So she told the only person she could. Jack Sanhope. He insisted on an abortion. She couldn't bear the thought of an abortion but didn't know what else to do."

I poured a glass of water and watched Maureen. She seemed deep in thought. Mary went bravely on with her tale, which seemed no less convoluted than the earlier one.

"Maureen and I were becoming . . . quite close, and she finally told me what had happened. We talked it over. Maureen really didn't want to give the baby up for adoption, either. She really wanted the baby and, frankly, I was quite pleased at the thought of helping her raise it."

"Did she happen to mention the eight hundred dollars for the abortion she had agreed to have?" John's tone went well with his surname.

Maureen spoke at last. "Indeed and I did," she said defiantly. "And, yes, I knew I wouldn't use it to commit that terrible sin. I'm Catholic. You think I want to burn in hell? I agreed to anything, I was so afraid of Jack. So I took the money. I knew I might need it when I had the baby. He said it was all he had, so I knew he'd give me no more. Mary agreed that I deserved it."

She dropped her head again and spoke softly. "Dear, dear Mary. What would I have done without her? I'll love her past death, I will. She took me in, cared for me, advised me. She told me to keep the money, that I'd have expenses. And bless her forever! She told me not to worry, that we would keep the dear child and raise it and she would help me. Surely the good Lord sent her to me."

All Maureen needed was an organ playing softly in the background. Trish looked as if she'd swallowed a spoonful of vinegar. "There's a bit of discrepancy here, Maureen. Jack Sanhope says you leaned on him to marry you. Did you love him?"

I wondered how Maureen would answer this one. If she said yes, Mary would surely be bent out of shape. If she said no, it would look like all she wanted was Jack's money and social position. She surprised me by giving Trish a sweet smile and saying, "No, of course I didn't love him. After all he had done to me? But I thought of the baby . . . needing a name, needing a father. We shouldn't punish the child for our sins. So I mentioned—I did not demand—marriage. That's the way it usually works at home, you know? Even feeling the way I do about him, I'd have married him for the baby's sake. But Jack did not want marriage, he didn't want me to keep the child or even give it up for adoption. He wanted abortion." I wondered why Maureen was bothering with the Sanhopes. She could make millions in Hollywood.

Trish muttered, "Uhmm," and wrote something down as Maureen continued. "I was afraid of going to the police and having Jack arrested. I thought he might kill me, with his awful temper. So after Jack got me drunk, or maybe he even drugged me again, and forced himself on me last Sunday . . . all right, Mary and I did a foolish thing. We thought making the rape more recent would sound better than it having happened back in April." She shivered slightly in the warm room. "And I desperately wanted enough money to raise my baby properly, send it to university and all. So, Mr. Frost, we turned to you for your help."

She flashed another sad smile, which Frost now returned warmly, while Trish added another "Uhmmm." I was glad Trish was making notes. Personally, I was lost.

Mary tapped a pencil on the table, as if calling us all to order. "Now, here's the way Maureen wants it set up. Mr. Frost, you'll have to make it all sound legal, but here it is. Maureen naturally doesn't want to go to court, but I don't think the Sanhopes would, either. They'd look pretty bad. And I happen to know they don't like that. So, Maureen will get all her medical expenses paid during and right after her pregnancy. She's not trying to take them for anything, but when she has to leave work she'll want the equivalent of her salary while she's on leave."

She looked around the table to make sure our attention hadn't wandered . . . fat chance. And how did Mary know the Sanhopes didn't like court? And had John and Trish realized that all the "ideas" here seemed to be Mary's? I went back to listening.

"Naturally, Maureen will want provision for the child's college to be guaranteed, and private high school, should that seem advisable, plus any medical or dental expenses not covered by her insurance. And she will need three thousand dollars a month for expenses like clothing, someone to watch the child while Maureen is at work, school incidentals, all that sort of thing . . . until the child's twenty-first birthday. And Maureen should get twenty thousand dollars up front for pain and mental anguish. That's all she wants and it really isn't much, considering."

Whatever Mary's "pleasure" in helping to rear the child, it did not seem to include financial donation or baby-sitting chores. And Maureen's contribution to this entire situation would seem to end with giving birth. Thirty-six thousand a year for twenty-one years. Plus twenty thousand for your piggy bank. Not bad if you could get it!

John cleared his throat and looked a little dazed. "Well, all right," he said heartily. "That's very straightforward and, I believe, complete. Let's get some coffee in here and see if we can't get all this down in order to present to Jack Sanhope and perforce, I imagine, his grandmother." He picked up the phone, pushed a button and asked for coffee.

John and Trish compared notes and spoke softly to each other, while Mary, Maureen, Fargo and I looked at each other across the table. Finally, I couldn't resist.

"Hey, Mary, how do you know the Sanhopes are allergic to the courts?"

"Oh . . . my . . . mother . . . she worked for them briefly. There was a . . . uh, disagreement. They settled out of court. That's all."

At that moment the door opened and a young woman brought in a tray with a coffee service and cups.

Right behind her came a rather tall, slender woman wearing a faultless blue-and-white seersucker suit, with dark blue shoes and a matching handbag that simply screamed "*Coach!*" Her hair was silvery white and perfectly groomed, and a large sapphire ring glinted on a manicured hand carrying a pair of spotless white gloves.

She extended her right hand. "Hello, John."

John scrambled to his feet. "Well! Hello, Grace, what a pleasant surprise!"

Chapter 16

"Mr. Frost," the secretary was babbling, "I'm so sorry. I told her you had clients and she said she would wait, but I didn't realize she was right behind . . . I'm so sorry . . ."

"It's all right, Doris. Thank you, now just run along, it's all right."

"Poor John." The woman smiled. "I'm sorry to discombobulate you. I was downtown and just took a chance you might be free. I had no idea my visit would be so opportune."

"Er, yes. Let me introduce you. My assistant, attorney Patricia Woodworth. Mrs. Sanhope."

They exchanged greetings and John turned toward me. I was already on my feet, Fargo standing alertly beside me. It had been drilled into me since I could walk, to always stand up when an older person enters the room. And so I had done, and would probably still be doing when I was sixty, if the person entering were sixty-one.

"Mrs. Sanhope, Alexandra Peres, my investigator."

I extended my hand and she took it in her cool, dry, firm one. "Hello, Alexandra. You look just like your mother. I remember her from years back."

"Thank you for the compliment. And I'm sure Mother will be thrilled by your recollection."

Grace Sanhope uttered a genuine, full-throated laugh. "Ooh, the cub has teeth! Good. I like that. I like it when people stand up for their families." She looked down at Fargo. "And I assume this handsome animal is yours? May I pet him?"

I liked that she asked. So many people meet an animal and just maul the hell out of him, never asking if that's agreeable with owner or pet. "He'll be disappointed if you don't. His name is Fargo."

She let him smell her hand and then stroked his head and neck around his ears. I was proud that he stood so straight, not wiggling and nudging for more, tail moving in a slow, regal sweep. This was royalty greeting royalty here and they both knew it.

"Oh, Fargo, you are just fine, aren't you?" She gave him a smile several watts warmer than any of us had gotten, and before John could continue his litany, she turned to Maureen.

"And you must be the dear little mother-to-be." She did not offer to shake hands. "I must admit you're a pretty thing even if you are missing a brain under that beautiful hair. And if it is any comfort, Jack will be paying heavily for his equal stupidity." Maureen never looked up, never said a word.

Amazin' Grace moved her eyes to Mary, and for the first time, her composure slipped.

"Mary Sloan! What in God's name are *you* doing here? Is there no end to your meddling?"

Maureen spoke at last. "She's my friend! You leave her alone!"

"Your *friend?*" Grace asked. "I'd heard rumors you were a lesbian, but I never dreamed . . . you do have a bent for forming catastrophic relationships. Well, Mary, your presence is neither needed nor wanted. Please leave us."

"I want her *here!*" Maureen almost screamed.

"And I do not. Mary, either leave, or this meeting is finished and we will see you in court."

Finally, John found his voice. "Ah, Ms. Sloan, perhaps it would be best if only the principals remained . . . and my staff, obviously . . . if you would be so kind."

"All right, Mr. Frost, I'll go. But be careful, she's a slick one." Mary gave Grace a look that would disintegrate Mount Rushmore and walked out.

Mrs. Sanhope slid into a chair at my end of the table and took an envelope from her bag. "Would you pass that to John, please?"

She leaned her elbows on the table and pushed an errant ashtray away. "You don't need to read that right now, John. It's just for reference. I'll tell you what we're going to do." Oh, goody, someone else to tell us what to do! She folded her hands on the table and began calmly. "I am assuming the child is Jack's and that it is normal. In that case, Maureen will have the baby, but will straightaway sign an agreement forfeiting all custody rights. Immediately after the baby is born, we—my attorney—will take over any adoption proceedings."

"I'm keeping the baby." Maureen sounded firm.

John patted her arm. "Let her finish, my dear, then we'll talk."

Grace gave him a tight smile that said, *Like hell we will,* and continued. "We will pay all medical expenses surrounding the pregnancy and birth. A few weeks before the baby is due, Maureen will check into an excellent private maternity hospital of our choice in New Hampshire, where she will have the baby."

She turned to Maureen. "Whenever you go on maternity leave from your job, Maureen, if it is unpaid leave, we will pay whatever salary you currently make. When the baby is born, you will receive five thousand dollars when you leave the hospital, minus the eight hundred you extorted from my grandson." Without a pause, she asked, "John, do you know Jake Raymond, my attorney in Boston?"

"Quite well. We both clerked for Judge Allsworth."

"Fine." Grace collected her bag and gloves and stood. "Get together with him and get that written up so everything reads right." She pointed at the envelope. "Jack will sign it. So will Maureen. Good to see you, John, nice to meet you, ladies. Good day."

"Wait!" Maureen sounded desperate. "I want to keep that baby, and I won't sign this thing."

Grace answered her with a mild tone and deadly words. "That is certainly your right. If you elect not to accept our offer, you will have to go to court to get child support. Jack has a very small income. You will not be awarded much. We will make sure that you have nothing resembling a reputation left when the trial is over. We will prove you a crook and a dubious mother. It will be widely publicized because of who we are. I do not look forward to that, but we will survive it. You will look like the Whore of Babylon." She nodded once more to John and strode through the door.

We sat as if posed for an artist. Stiff, expressionless, silent. Maureen recovered first. "That terrible old woman! Can she do that? Can she get away with it?"

Trish shrugged. "Could and probably would. Actually, she's offered a lot of what you wanted anyway. We can hopefully get you some more cash. As for the rest of it, they'd probably drag in six guys to swear they slept with you, and Jack just had the bad luck to get you pregnant. They would question your late report of one rape and the good possibility that the other didn't happen at all. They would ask why you took the abortion money when you had no intention of actually having one. When her bunch of lawyers got through with you, you'd be a basket case and you'd be lucky to get a hundred dollars a month in child support . . . if the State let you keep the baby at all."

"Then I really want that twenty thousand. I'll need every penny." Maureen was hanging tough. Where had the happy couple bringing up baby gone?

"You won't get it," John supplied. "I'll try for ten plus attorney's fees. Let me talk to Jake Raymond, he's a reasonable guy. Now try not to be upset." God, I loved it when people said that. "I'll be in touch." We dispersed.

Fargo and I hid in the ladies room for a while until we were pretty sure neither Maureen nor Mary might still be around. We went down the back stairs and out through the alley. And then we practically ran to the Rat.

Chapter 17

Fargo flopped in the shade while I looped his lead around the anchor outside the Wharf Rat door. I told him I'd be right back and went inside to fetch him a bowl of water and a slice of Billie's meatloaf. She asked about the family. "How's Mae? Still growing all those herbs you mostly wouldn't know whether to eat or drink or rub 'em on? And Jeanne, still working for the Catholics though she isn't?"

You had to get used to Billie's speech patterns, but after many years practice, I answered easily. "Aunt Mae stays busy, though mostly she grows herbs for cooking, not for medicinal purposes. And Mom still works at the church office. They're both fine, and ask about you often."

"Give them my regards. Got some good crab cakes the way you like them on special without much breading. Want a plate?"

"Sure."

Fargo's lunch delivered, I went back in and looked around for a table. There were none, but I spotted Pete Santos again at the little table by the kitchen door. I hoped he'd give me a chance to apologize and maybe buy him lunch at last.

He accepted my apology with frigid courtesy, and coolly declined my offer of lunch and a drink, which I could understand. I'd make it up to him someday when it didn't seem like a minor payoff.

"So the girl dropped the rape claim?" he asked.

"It seems so. I hope so. You know how it is, Pete, everybody tells the same story with a different slant. Maybe nobody's exactly lying, but nobody is exactly telling the truth either."

He warmed up a bit, grinning slightly. "Story of the world, I guess. Well, now I'll have to make my peace with Jack for roping him into going by your house."

"I don't think it will be too hard. I told him it was my idea, and that you said all along he didn't do it. Aha! At last!" My crab cakes and a cold Bud had arrived. For the rest of the meal we chatted of nothing special. The Yankees. Would Jeter kindly break another small bone or so? The Red Sox. The curse had finally ended! Pete finished lunch first and left to go back to work.

I finished my filling lunch and went out to find Fargo dozing happily away, now in the warm sun. I had a great desire to join him, but thought it might look a little odd. So I picked up his dishes, unhooked his leash and we started home, where it wouldn't look odd at all.

By the time we walked the several blocks home, I felt a little less like one of Billie's clams and a little more awake . . . which was just as well, for parked in front of my house was Mary's truck. Shittay! As we say in old France. I went around the back of the house and there they were, comfortably ensconced at my outdoor table.

"Oh, hi, Alex." Mary didn't seem the least ill at ease. "We figured you'd be at the Rat, but when we got there, you were with Pete Santos, and we didn't want to interfere, so we just came on over here to wait."

"So I see." I sat down and didn't offer refreshments. I had some hope of making this visit brief. "What can I do for you?"

Maureen answered. "Oh, Alex, you're so clever! Surely you can figure out a way I can keep my baby and not go into court against Jack and that awful woman."

"Easy," I answered. "Just have the baby, keep it and raise it."

"But to do that, I need money." She gave a sweet, pouty smile.

"Work." I could see my gentle nap fluttering away across the treetops. Fargo didn't help by yawning cavernously and collapsing noisily by my side.

Mary tapped her finger imperiously on the table. "Grace Sanhope should *not* be allowed to get away with this!"

Feeling a little imperious myself, I tapped right back. "*Grace* isn't getting away with a thing. She didn't do anything. Jack has already paid, quite generously, for an abortion. Or they will pay you to put the baby up for adoption. If you want the baby that much, either support it yourselves or go to court. And I personally think the last is a very bad idea. You will both come out looking like a couple of opportunistic blackmailers."

"Well, really . . ."

"Alex!"

"Look." I tried to be patient. "You've both lied about when Jack was supposed to have raped Maureen. I can understand, Maureen, why you didn't go to the cops back in April if . . . er, when he raped you, but I cannot understand why you didn't go the night in June, when you say it happened again. You say he either got you drunk or drugged you. Well, the way to prove that would have been blood tests right away. Now it boils down to *he said . . . she said*. And Jack may possibly show up with friends who'll say they had sex with you, too. It will be perjury, but who will prove it? And now you're asking the Sanhopes to support a child being brought up by two lesbians, which might not sit well in court, either, depending on what judge or jury you get." I lit a cigarette and blew out a vicious cloud of smoke.

"Either do as John Frost suggests or don't. But don't ask me to do the impossible or fabricate something to make you look better." I stood up. Startled, Fargo lunged to his feet and growled. I didn't even correct him, I just laid my hand on his head to quiet him.

"I would never ask you to lie, Alex." Mary sounded hurt, and I was sorry for that, but Maureen was her problem, not mine. "I guess we'd best be going," she added lamely.

"Indeed and we might as well," Maureen snapped. "You see how it goes, don't you, Mary? Her mother knows Grace. Grace likes her dog, the big spoiled lout. Her brother and Pete Santos are both coppers together. Alex and Pete just had lunch together. So you and me, darlin', we're outside and lookin' in."

I was stunned at the words and the vitriol they held but tried not to show it. I did not appreciate her references to my mother and Fargo! Mary and Maureen walked across the lawn toward the driveway. I took a couple of steps after them and called, "Mary!"

She turned back to me, and I said softly. "I'm sorry about all of this, Mary. I know you have a heavy emotional investment in this situation, but I really cannot help you. I know you wouldn't ask me to lie. I hope you also know I would never slant information in someone else's favor, either."

"I trust you, Alex. I don't always like you, but I trust you." For some reason we shook hands, and she left.

I hoped I was finished with Mary and Maureen. I wished them well, but I wanted no part of it anymore.

I seemed to have been granted my wish. The following days went quietly. I got some dawn runs with Fargo and a few photos that I liked. Then I got carried away and decided to put up a couple of badly needed shelves in the garage. I actually got them installed, and damn near level, with but one small bruise on my thumb and one close call when I nearly put a board through the garage window.

Saturday afternoon I was allowing myself to be cajoled by Cindy into putting some shelves in the tiny back hall of the cottage. They would provide some very welcome storage space for canned goods and extra pots and pans. We were now deciding exactly what I would charge for this service. We had about agreed on Sunday breakfast in bed and whatever might follow, and I was now trying to explain that some down payment was customary in these cases, when the phone rang.

It was Sonny. He and Trish had been fishing and caught a bunch of nice flounder. Would we be interested in a fish fry? I asked Cindy. She said she'd agree to a postponement of down payments if Sonny and I would clean the fish outdoors where she wouldn't see or smell them, so I told them to come ahead.

Sonny, bless him, had already cleaned and filleted the fish when they arrived. He and I made dinner, dipping the flounder fillets first in an egg wash, then in cornmeal and dropping them into a skillet with hot olive oil for a fast brown and flip. We made french fries and a big salad with four—count 'em, *four*—gorgeous radishes right from my garden, thinly sliced as garnish. A dash by Sonny to the store for tartar sauce . . . and dinner was served.

And it was good. Afterward we lounged around the outdoor table with coffee and a B&B liqueur and I felt very rich.

"What's the latest on Jack the Raper?" Sonny asked.

"Don't look at me," I replied. "I hope to God I'm not in that mare's nest anymore."

He turned his head to look at Trish, who shrugged. "Fairly quiet. John talked to the Sanhope attorney and got Maureen an extra four thousand in cash plus attorney's fees. She was not happy, although I don't think anyone could have done better. At any rate, the papers are signed."

Sonny shook his head. "I don't know Maureen, but can't you cut her a little slack? She's only a kid. She's a million miles from home. Pregnant and dealing with a bunch of lawyers . . ."

"And doing quite well, thank you." Trish grinned sourly. "I think you can put away your armor and white horse. Maureen will not lose in this."

"So now," Cindy asked, "When Maureen has the baby, is it immediately available for adoption? Or is an adoptive family found in advance? Just how does that work?"

Trish poured herself another B&B, unusual for her. "I can tell you how I think *this* one is going to work." She looked at me. "You say Jack told you his brother Richard and wife can't have children, right?"

"Right. I think her name is Lillian."

"Okay. And the papers Maureen signed state that she's to check in the Mountain View Maternity Hospital, just outside that town in New Hampshire, no later than November seventeen. Her due date is December tenth. Keep that in mind." She sipped her drink and went on.

"Right about now, Lillian is telling a few close friends that she is at last pregnant, but that she must be very careful if she is to carry full term. She's going to stay down here in Ptown and be super quiet. While she would enjoy e-mails, phone calls and cards . . . visitors and visiting are a no-no. But she will keep them apprised of her progress by letter and phone. On or about November seventeen, Lillian will check into Mountain View."

Sonny was scowling. I looked at Cindy, and she seemed as bewildered as I was.

"Trish," I said, "Why would Lillian say she's pregnant if she isn't? And why check into Mountain View Maternity Hospital?"

She laughed shortly. "Because big money lets you do a lot of things the rest of us can't. Follow me closely. On or about December tenth at Mountain View, a baby will be born to Lillian and Richard Sanhope. That is the way the baby's birth certificate will read, *Parents, Richard and Lillian Sanhope*. Then one other thing will happen. Maureen Delaney will be told her child was stillborn. Oh, she'll still get her money because the Sanhopes feel sorry for her loss, but she never had a viable baby."

"My God," Cindy nearly whispered. "So the baby is 'born' a Sanhope, not adopted at all!"

Sonny couldn't stay quiet. "This is all highly irregular! They should be stopped. Trish, as an officer of the court, you have to report this to the proper authority." Sonny was sounding pompous again.

"Yes, possibly and no. Yes, if I am right, it is illegal. Possibly it should somehow be stopped. I'm not so sure. You seem to have forgotten the child." She looked at each of us in turn and, in turn, each of us looked away.

"This is the only scenario where the child does not suffer. If it were put up for adoption, who is ever absolutely certain it will be a good match? Adoptive children sometimes have more emotional problems. No one is sure why, but they do. If Maureen keeps the child, do you really think she's parent material? I don't. And I doubt she'll stay with Mary, who would at least provide some stability. And no child in the country will be more loved, I'll bet, or have more advantages, than little Whosis Sanhope. An abortion, obviously, is self-explanatory. So, no, Sonny, I have no intention of propounding this theory to John or anyone else 'in authority.' It's unprovable, for one thing, and reporting it would simply alert Mountain View and the Sanhopes to do it some other way, for a second. Not to mention getting me fired as a meddlesome big mouth, for a third. Case closed."

"Boyohboy," I breathed. "The child is half Sanhope anyway. Now he or she suddenly becomes *all* Sanhope and Jack becomes the loving uncle. He said he wanted a role in his child's life. Well, he'll have it. One thing for sure, it ought to be a gorgeous kid. But, really, what about Maureen? She could be deeply grieved over her presumed loss."

"I seriously doubt it." Trish smiled wryly. "You were there, Alex, in John's office. After a few little maidenly squeaks about love and religion, Maureen hunkered right down to hard money. A damned lot of money, if you recall. She will mourn the 'lost baby' all the way to the bank and then get on with life, probably in a large city sans Mary . . . who will, unfortunately, probably be the one who gets hurt in this."

Sonny was still frowning, but brightened visibly when Cindy said, "Who wants chocolate ice cream and who wants butter pecan?"

It looked as if the case were indeed closed.

Chapter 18

It's funny how you feel that Monday is a work day, even when you're someone like me, who doesn't work a steady schedule. You have to *do* things. So, after Cindy left for the bank, I did some laundry and some housework . . . vacuuming myself into a fairly foul humor. I think people who are always telling you what *satisfaction* they get from doing household chores have some terrible guilt about something and use the dirty work to assuage it. Me, I don't get no satisfaction. Does that mean I have no guilt?

It was nearly noon when I sat down to a second cup of coffee and cigarette number three. Fargo came in to get a drink and stretch out on the cool tile. He had spent the morning outdoors, being no more enamored of what I was doing than I was. I suggested that when I finished my coffee, we take a run down to the hardware store and pick up the boards and brackets for Cindy's shelves. That would put us near the Wharf Rat Bar just in time for lunch. What a lovely coincidence!

He agreed, with a tail thump and a roll onto his back for a tummy scratch, and the phone rang. It was Trish, asking if I could stop by sometime during the afternoon.

"Oh, God," I moaned, "What have they done now?"

"Nothing," she laughed. "This isn't about them. Remember an old man named Erno Malik?"

"Sure." I took a sip of coffee. "He ran that beat-up auto repair shop until he died a few months back. But he was good. The two young guys who have it now are good, too, if you're looking for a place to go."

"No, no. It's not that. Those two young men have been just sort of running the place since he died. They want to buy it, but we seem to have misplaced May and June."

"Strange," I replied. "I can see them right here on my kitchen calendar." Fargo moved to the door to let me know he was ready to leave any time.

"Very funny. May and June Malik are his nieces and his only heirs. They moved to Louisiana some time ago, and now we can't find them. John hired a local PI down there last month, who says they've disappeared. At first the PI said one of them had died. Then he said, no, they had just up and driven into the sunset. John thinks the PI is simply a dud who did nothing and sent a big bill. Now he wants you to find them."

"So he wants me to do something and send a small bill?"

"Something like that."

"I'll see you later." We hung up, and Fargo and I went forth.

The shelves at the cottage would perforce be short, so I had no problem getting boards, brackets and screws into the car's trunk. Convincing Fargo to move out of the driver's seat took a little longer. Finally, we edged into Commercial Street's endless stream of summer traffic, falling in behind a giant camper whose driver should have known better than even try to navigate in town.

We inched forward toward a cross street where I could go over to Bradford, which would be marginally faster. Then an ancient but beautifully kept station wagon in front of the camper pulled to the curb and stopped to discharge passengers. The camper tried to ease around it, decided he couldn't make it and stopped halfway. I eased up behind the station wagon to give the camper some wiggle room, and that allowed me to watch the wagon. I saw Grace Sanhope, in the front seat, say something to the chauffeur, open the passenger door and get out. Two younger women in the back seat began to move, leaving two men waiting patiently, perched in the third bank of seats.

At that moment I saw Mary Sloan break through the crowd of pedestrians on the sidewalk, pushing people aside, headed for Grace Sanhope. Then we all went into slow motion. The chauffeur was yelling at the camper to move so he could get out of the driver's door. The two men were climbing clumsily across the women trying to reach a rear door. I turned off my ignition, grabbed the hand brake and started climbing across Fargo to the only door I could exit.

Mary moved faster than the rest of us. When I got to her, she already had Grace up tight by the collar of her dress and was screaming into her face and shaking her like a bobble-head doll.

"You will *not* do this again! You cheapskate, meddling bitch, you will *not* ruin my life a second time! Maureen is beside herself! She could lose the baby over this, all because you have to run the world! So help me, I'll kill you first, you miserable—"

"Mary! Let go!" I yelled. I grabbed her arms and saw Grace's collar rip, but I kept pulling till I could get between them and pin Mary's arms at her sides. "Stop it! Mary, damn it, can you even hear me?"

At last I felt Mary's body slump and eased my grip. "Mrs. Sanhope, are you hurt?" I asked over my shoulder.

"Not fatally, I think." She fingered the collar of her dress and managed a smile. "Thanks to you."

By now her family and friends or whoever they were had crowded around her, making soothing murmurs and glaring at Mary.

"Madam, shall I get a policeman?" The chauffeur put his oar in our roiling waters.

"No, Tom. That won't be necessary. Alex, can you keep that woman under control until we can escape into the restaurant?" She moved her hand again. I could tell that collar was bothering her.

"With a one-two punch if necessary." I gave Mary a glare of my own. "Probably somebody in the restaurant has a safety pin," I continued. "The tear really isn't all that bad." I don't know why I was trying to comfort her. Maybe because she looked shaken and frail, maybe because she appreciated Fargo, maybe because I'd had it to the eyeballs with the Bobbsey twins. "And a shot of brandy wouldn't hurt you."

She momentarily rested her fingertips against my cheek, and I felt an almost sexual frisson. It was not an old woman's touch.

"Well, the cub is not only brave, but kind." She smiled. "My hero." She turned and walked steadily up the shaded walkway to the elegant restaurant where I assumed they had luncheon reservations. I felt something for the woman. I didn't even try to figure out what it was.

One of the men, who looked like an older Jack, thanked me also, as did one of the women, whom I presumed was his wife Lillian. The chauffeur and I returned to our respective vehicles, to the irritable horn blowers and the probably five-mile traffic jam we and the camper had caused. I still had Mary firmly by the arm and shoved her unceremoniously into the back seat, which seemed simpler than convincing Fargo to move from the front. She appeared spent and subdued as we drove to her house.

Once there, I followed her inside and sat at the kitchen table. "For God's sake, give me a beer. Then I want to know what gives between you and Grace Sanhope. And if I hear the phrase 'little misunderstanding.' I'll crown you." It was indicative of both our states of mind that I wiped neither Fargo's feet nor mine, and that Mary did not comment on the omission.

I waited quietly while Mary uncapped two bottles and placed them on the table without even the offer of a glass. Finally she sat. "She likes you."

"I'd like me, too, if I rescued me from some raving lunatic trying to choke me."

"I'm not a lunatic, and I doubt I would have choked her." Mary spoke softly, tiredly. "It all kept building up . . . until, I guess, when I saw her, so hoity-toity in that antique station wagon with her chauffer, I just sort of blew. It won't happen again."

"Gee, that's good to know." I stood and took a saucer from the dishrack to use as an ashtray. Mary didn't seem to notice. "Twice now, you have said something about Grace Sanhope ruining your life for the 'second time.' What were you talking about?"

Mary gave a big shuddery sigh. "Years ago, when she was a young girl, my mother was a maid for the Sanhopes. First in Boston and then here in Provincetown, when they came out for the summer. Late one summer or maybe early fall, Mrs. Sanhope went to Europe with some lady friends for a couple of months. Old Peter—well, he wasn't so old then—hit on my mother. She was lonesome, he was still pretty good-looking, and Mother hadn't had much to do with men."

Mary took a sip of beer and looked at the bottle as if she weren't sure what it held. "Well, Grace was away, and he told my mother it was a legal separation, convinced my mother he loved her and intended to marry her and, wouldn't you know? Managed to get her pregnant."

I shook my head. "What a nice guy! But then, what? Grace came home?"

"Yeah, and blamed the entire thing on my mom. Fired her on the spot and sent her back to Boston."

"Couldn't your mother do something? Was she a minor?" I couldn't believe this.

"No, she was nineteen. All she knew was *fired* and *pregnant*. She went back to my grandmother . . . who was Irish, widowed and Catholic. Grandma was mortified at what people would think. They came up with some story that Mom had been engaged to a young Marine who went to Vietnam and got killed. I guess it was the best they could do. It's what they told me, too, when I got old enough to ask questions. When they got a letter from the Sanhope's lawyer a little later, they just took what was offered. I doubt either of them had a thought of getting their own attorney."

I could understand that. An unsophisticated immigrant woman alone, now with a "fallen" daughter. And the daughter, still a teenager and probably still wondering how it had all happened so quickly and so disastrously. Then it hit me. "My God, you're old Peter's daughter?"

"In the flesh. And isn't that a barb in *Grace's* flesh! Damn them all, anyway!" Mary continued. "So, Mother and my grandmother went to see this Sanhope lawyer and signed a bunch of papers agreeing never to file any claims against the family or contact them in any way. The Sanhopes paid for my mother's medical bills during pregnancy and provided a hundred dollars a month, paid through the lawyer, until I was eighteen." Mary looked across at me with a wan smile. "Believe me, Alex, even back then you couldn't raise a kid on a hundred a month!"

"No, I guess not." I tried to smile back, but it didn't work too well.

"Anyway, we lived with Grandma, who had a small pension, and Mom waitressed and we limped along until I graduated high school. I tried waitressing and store clerking and didn't like either. I had just gone with the telephone company, when Mom got the flu. She kept trying to go to work and got sicker and sicker. Finally, she collapsed at work and died of pneumonia some days later. Grandma didn't last a year. I think she had really loved my mom an awful lot. So had I. She was nice and warm and fun and funny. She should have been married and had a big family. She would have been good at it." I saw the tears come up and reached across the table to take her hand.

"You poor thing! What terrible losses! What on earth did you do?"

"Some soap opera, huh?" Mary was trying to hang tough, and I couldn't help but applaud her for it. "Let me get us another beer." She stood and swapped new bottles for old, this time remembering to add napkins and glasses.

"Well," she said, wiping her mouth, "After Mother and Grandma died, I was cleaning out the papers in the desk when I found the legal file and learned the truth about my father. Strangely enough, the phone company had just offered me a transfer for continued field training in Ptown. I jumped at it. You know why? Talk about simple! I thought it would be nice to be near my remaining *family!*"

"Oh, no."

"Oh, yes. After I got here I did a little homework and discovered that Grace had lost all three of her kids. I thought she might be glad to see her husband's offspring, and I figured Richard and Francesca and Jack would be happy to have an aunt, although I'm only a year or so older than Richard and actually younger than Francesca. So one fine day, I simply arrived on their doorstep."

"Oh, no," I said again. I couldn't help grinning, and Mary didn't miss it.

"Yeah, you're right. If my childhood was a soap opera, this was some kind of sitcom. A maid answered the door and I said, 'Hello, I'm Mary Sloan, here to see my step-mother and my niece and nephews, Richard and Jack.' The maid looked kind of funny and said she'd check if they were 'receiving.'"

Mary pushed her beer bottle in a little circle, looking embarrassed. "I didn't know what that meant, so I just followed her into the living room, where she made her little speech to Mrs. Sanhope and Richard. Lillian was there, too. Jack, I learned later was away at boarding school, and Francesca had married and moved away." She stopped, as if her story were complete.

"So," I prodded, "What next?"

"Richard and Lillian obviously hadn't a clue, but asked me to sit down, just trying to be polite, you know. Amazin' Grace popped up and said that wouldn't be necessary, I wouldn't be staying. She told me I had no legal right to be on their property and I could be arrested for trespassing and she was gonna sue my mother . . . she was really raving."

I ground my cigarette out angrily. "What a terrible reception!"

"Yes, I got kind of mad, too, although I was humiliated in front of Lillian and Richard and the maid, who just kept standing there like a dunce. I told Grace my mother was dead and that *I* hadn't signed anything since I wasn't even born yet. I said I lived here now and had just thought it would be nice for us to get to know each other. She really blew when I said that. Kind of incoherent, you know. Something about shanty Irish bastards daring to move here to bother them, probably for money, and trade on their name and I don't know what all. I just finally backed out and left, and she started screaming at the maid for letting me in."

"Whew," I exhaled, now realizing I'd been holding my breath. "That's unbelievable."

"The end of it is even weirder. A few days later Richard came by my apartment, all apologies. Said he had never known anything about me even being alive, said he had got part of the story from his grandmother and part from her personal maid who had been there at the time it all happened. He felt I had been badly treated, start to finish." She sipped her beer and gave a short, bitter laugh. "He handed me one of those 'don't ever bother us' releases to sign, along with a check for ten thousand dollars. He said he had convinced the old lady they owed it to me."

"Did you take it?"

"You bet your butt. They *did* owe it to me! I used it to help buy this house. Even so, you can see why there's no love lost between her and me. Or any of them for that matter. Uppity bunch!"

"Yes." I could see how she felt humiliated and resentful. Paid off. Condescended to. Not accepted. And none of it her fault. But I could also see why, from their point of view, the Sanhope Clan didn't want still another illegitimate child swelling Ptown's population, and being raised by the first one. It would become a tasteless joke all over town . . . that every generation begat a little Irish bastard whose real last name was Sanhope, no matter what it was actually called.

I realized Mary was speaking and tuned back in. " . . . and now they're doing it again. Maureen is a wreck over this." Mary sighed and blew her nose. "Dammit all, we were both so happy! You know, Alex, I really was looking forward to having a kid around." There didn't seem much more to say.

On the way out I glanced around Mary's neat, spotless kitchen and wondered if she had any idea what a kid could do to it in thirty seconds. I wondered if Maureen really wanted the child, too, or if Trish was right. I wondered how Amazin' Grace could be so appealing and yet so cruel. Obviously, as a judge of people, I was hopeless. I probably would have told everyone that Caligula was really a lovely boy with a slight attitude.

I mentally drew a line through my leisurely lunch at the Rat. Fargo and I each had a fast hot dog at a crowded stand. As he and I stood and ate, I thought of Mary and what a god-awful time she had had of it. No father. Mother dead at a wrenchingly early age, and Grandma—the last bastion—dead of grief shortly thereafter.

Perhaps Mary's overneatness and emotional neediness were less a matter of control and need*ing* than they were of the very human desire to be need*ed* . . . by something . . . by someone. And maybe being such a control freak was because she was afraid that if she ever *wasn't* in control . . . well, we had just seen what that brought on.

Chapter 19

Trish and John were waiting for me, complete with a little package of all they thought I might need: map of Louisiana, last known address of May and June Malik, plane ticket to New Orleans, rental car reservation, three hundred dollars in cash, the special credit card they kept for me to use on trips, etc.

"Where the hell is Haute Bayou?"

"Out near Morgan City."

"Where the hell is Morgan City?"

"Out in the bayou area."

"Well, that's helpful. Still in the United States, I assume. John, do you realize somebody has me on a seven a.m. flight out of Boston? Do you know what time I'll have to get up?"

"Well," he shuffled papers importantly, "I figured it would give you time to find the place before dark."

"Just how far out in the boonies is this bayou? Maybe I should stay over in New Orleans and drive over the next morning." I looked at the map. I would not have been surprised to find areas marked "Here be dragons."

"Oh, I think you can do it in one day." God forbid I should have a night in New Orleans. "Now, before you leave, take some color shots of the old garage and the cottage behind it. I want May and June to realize how run-down it has become. And show the Police Impound Lot on the one side and that 'adult' film rental place on the other. I don't want them thinking that property is worth a bag of gold as a B&B or restaurant or cutsie little boutique. Here's the sales agreement. And here are your figures to deal with."

He handed me a slip of paper. "The two prospective buyers will pay this much maximum, but start twenty thousand lower. And here's a check for the binder. The bank will honor your signature on this. Give 'em up to fifteen thousand, but try for five. Now, all set to leave Thursday?"

"I guess so. I hope I can wrap this up and get home for at least part of the weekend. How about leaving Wednesday?"

Trish at least had the grace to look embarrassed. "Er, we couldn't get you a seat on the early flight until Thursday," she said, not meeting my eye.

"Okay," I sighed. "Always a pleasure doing business with you and Ebenezer."

"By the way . . ." I recounted the morning saga.

John shook his head. "This whole thing is worrisome, and the really bad thing is, everyone is *here* and liable to run into each other, and it won't really be resolved for another six months."

"Oh, it may be." Trish gave an acid smile. "Let's see. Jack kills Maureen. Mary kills Grace. Richard kills Mary. Then he and Jack duel over who gets the baby—which has been miraculously C-sectioned into life—and kill each other. Leaving Lillian with all the money and the baby and they live happily ever after."

"I'm outta here."

That evening I recounted my day to Cindy, and no part of it pleased her. She felt that Mary might understandably be cracking up. She didn't trust Maureen.

"You know," she said, "I've heard of women sort of selling their babies before they are born. They go to a large city, get a lawyer to advertise for people who want to adopt but don't want to go through all the rigmarole or have an eligibility problem, and the lawyer sets up a deal where the couple pays expenses plus some cash and gets the baby when it's born." She sipped her Cape Codder and set the glass back on the outdoor table. "I asked Trish about it. She says it's both legal and fairly common. Dear Maureen may just not be here some morning."

It sounded pretty convoluted to me. "Why should Maureen bother? She's already got that set up with the Sanhopes."

"She's already got four thousand in cash out of them, minus that eight hundred Grace is so adamant about. Trish says it's easy to get ten thousand dollars, and sometimes more, for a healthy Caucasian kid. That would make at least fourteen thousand dollars all told . . . and she screws the Sanhopes to boot, which would please her. And she's rid of Mary, who's getting super-intense about this."

I took a belt of Bud. "That's plain dishonest."

An irritated looked crossed Cindy's face. "I don't know what Maureen has done to charm you so thoroughly. She's been *plain dishonest* from the get-go." She stood up and walked into the house.

Finishing my beer and cigarette, I wondered what was bothering her. I hadn't been especially defensive of Maureen. I didn't trust her either. I went inside to find Cindy cutting up a salad. I decided to risk the knife.

"Honey, I don't know why you're upset. I have no great love for Maureen. I'll keep my wallet in an inside pocket when she's around and count the silver when she leaves." I put my arms around her and tried a light touch. "Now Amazin' Grace is the one to worry about. She called me her hero."

Cindy managed a weak grin, gave me a peck on the cheek and returned to the salad. "Oh, darling, don't mind me. I'm just all at sixes and sevens. Bad day at work. And the car is making that noise again. Frankly, I'm not happy with you on an airplane. And I do wish I could go with you. I've never been to New Orleans, and we could have such fun!"

I was getting confused. Did she think I was just whisking off to the Deep South for a few days' vacation? Had she forgotten it was work, not riverboat cruises and love under the magnolias? And I strongly suspected I was less likely to die in a mid-air explosion than I was of indigestion if I ate all the cucumbers she was absent-mindedly slicing into the salad.

"Cindy," I said gently, "I've never been to New Orleans either, and I'll probably spend about forty-five minutes there . . . in the airport. That's if they haven't lost my luggage and the car people haven't mislaid my reservation."

"You mean you won't be dancing through the French Quarter with a beautiful belle on either arm?"

"Not if John Frost has anything to say about it. I'll be slogging through mangrove bogs with alligators in hot pursuit."

"Oh, well, why didn't you say so? As long as it's alligators in hot pursuit I won't worry."

I took a deep breath and grabbed the salad bowl and set it on the table. Crisis past. Over dinner, Cindy told me of her day, mainly centered around a man who had previously bought some mutual fund shares and thought that because he owned a hundred shares of the *fund*, it meant he owned a hundred shares each of every *stock* the fund owned. He had tried to sell one of the stocks in the fund because he didn't approve of its product, and the fun had continued from there. Idiots are found everywhere, I suppose.

Then we talked about what we should do with her hiccupping car. Finally, we discussed where Fargo should stay while I was away. We decided on leaving him with Mom, as usual. It would mean he spent less time alone. Perhaps more importantly, it would mean Mom didn't feel left out.

Later, we made love, and it was warm and satisfying, as it always was. As I was dozing off, an errant thought floated across my mind: it would be nice to be getting out of Dodge for a few days.

I went to sleep.

Chapter 20

I was a stranger in a strange land. It was a long way to Tipperary. There was a long, long trail a-winding. And I had miles to go before I slept. The afternoon sun glared in angry frustration against my air-conditioned cocoon. In the distance, heat waves made me wonder if the concrete of the road might indeed be liquid when I reached that spot.

Inlets of sullen gray-green water showed first on my right, then on my left, a weak wind providing the occasional small, irritable whitecap. Sometimes the trees grew right up to the edge of the road, hung with Spanish moss. In my rearview mirror, I could see the breeze from my car set them to rocking and bending like old, bearded men lounging on a storefront porch and laughing at a dirty joke.

I felt very alone and hoped that Hertz indeed maintained its rental cars as meticulously as it said it did. I did not want a breakdown on this road.

Finally a small sign pointed to the right and said *Haute Bayou 3 mi.* I turned onto a narrower road, where I passed a roadhouse, with a sign reading *Cajun Cuizine Dancing Weekends* atop a sagging roof. I wasn't tempted. Farther on, a twin building had a sign propped out front advertising *Good Drinks, Good Eats, Good Music.* I might have believed them had it not been for a pen off to the side holding two enormous hogs. I had a feeling they got a lot of left-overs.

Then came the strip mall that I am convinced introduces every small town in America. I entered "downtown" which looked older and much more solid, boasting a bank, a post office, a café, a couple of small office buildings and, finally, a gas station. I wasn't especially low on gas, but I didn't want to get that way, either. And I needed directions, so I pulled in.

The young man was pleasant and knowledgeable and informed the city slicker carefully to, "Go straight on down this road for two miles, turn left at a sign that points left and says 'Bayou Fishing Camp' and follow that there road right into th' front yard."

Actually, I stopped a few feet short of the front yard in a neatly raked gravel parking area. I faced a rambling, big old house that looked in excellent repair, with flowers all around, a vegetable garden peeking around the back and a path leading down to a dock and bait shack on the bayou itself. Two other cars and a pickup truck shared the parking area with me. A giant dusty oak lent a suggestion of shady coolness to the porch, where a skinny teenage boy sat on the steps unsnarling the line on a fishing reel.

"Hi," I said. "I'm looking for May and June Malik. Would you know if they're around?"

"Not anymore." He turned and called into the house. "Hey, Mama, somebody's here to see those women who used to have the place."

A pleasant-face woman in her forties stepped onto the porch. "Hello. I'm Edith Martine. May I help you?"

I explained who I was and who I wanted and more or less why. Ms. Martine looked vague. "Well, we bought the place about four months ago, and they left the morning we finished it all up at the bank. My husband got disability from the fire department up in Baton Rouge, you see." She pointed skyward, making me wonder once again where I really was. "We bought this place, and naturally they would leave, you know."

"Yes," I agreed with a smile. "I just wonder if you could give me their forwarding address?"

"Why, no. They didn't leave one with us. Now that was strange, wasn't it?"

It certainly was. "Er, did everything end up all right? I mean, did the sale go through properly for you?"

"Oh, yes, everything was settled that morning at the bank. My husband's cousin works there, that's how we originally knew it was for sale—this place, not the bank, you understand." She laughed merrily.

I smiled weakly. "Well, thank you. I guess that does it. I'll just find a place to stay the night and ask around town a bit tomorrow. Thanks, anyway."

"Oh, right here!" She gave a little bow. "You should stay here. We have a lovely ground floor room available, with private bath. Come, I'll show you." She placed a friendly arm across my shoulder and I was led away.

In fact, the room was quite nicely furnished, the bed looked clean and felt firm, and the bathroom was plain but adequate. A window fan moved the hot air around briskly, and I could but hope it would cool down at night. It was probably as good, or better, than I would find elsewhere, so I agreed to stay, despite a hand-printed "No smoking, please" sign tucked in the mirror. Breakfast, I was told, was served from seven to nine.

But dinner was what my stomach wanted first, so I went back into town and headed for the café, where I had surprisingly good large-mouth bass fillets fried in a spicy cornmeal batter. I asked the waitress if she knew the Malik sisters.

"Sure," she said. "Though I didn't know they was sisters. Julie's name was Harker, I think."

I wasn't surprised at the different last name. After all, one of them could have been married at some time, and the difference in June and Julie could just be a slip in pronunciation. But how could you look at twins and not assume they were sisters?

"Any idea where they moved to? I need to locate them."

"Over Florida-way, I heard. You might try looking over there."

"Thank you."

Back at the ranch, a bunch of people sat in the living room, laughing along with the canned audience at some sitcom. I bypassed them and located Ms. Martine in the kitchen, where I begged a small bowl of ice. I discovered my room was slightly cooler, but the minute I turned on the lights, bugs the size of blue jays began to bombard the screen. Knowing it was a matter of time before they won, I quickly put ice in the bathroom glass, added bourbon and turned out the lights.

I felt my way back to the bathroom where I sat on the edge of the tub so I could flick ashes into the toilet and blow smoke out a small window. The bugs turned to other targets, allowing me to hear more distant night noises. Far away, a boat putt-putted and a bobcat screamed. Closer, I thought, an alligator roared. Then I heard a slow *plop . . . plop . . . plop* nearby in the bayou. At first, I was pretty sure it was fish jumping for the bugs attracted by the night-light on the dock. Then I became absolutely certain it was one of those three-toed dinosaurs that look like giant ostriches with very mean eyes, coming across the bayou. *Plop . . . plop . . .*

I pulled the cell phone from my shirt and called Cindy. "Hi, darling," she said warmly. "I'm so glad you called! I miss you. Where are you?"

"Jurassic Park."

The sound of many feet passing my door woke me at the end of a sweaty, fitful, dream-filled night. Obviously the visiting fisherfolk were filing in to breakfast. I took a slow shower, repacked the little I had taken out for the night and stared out the window until they finished their meal. When I saw them sauntering down the path to the dock where the teenage boy was unfastening boat chains, I went into the dining room.

Mr. and Mrs. Martine were smiling and alert. I felt scowling and logy but managed a smile and nod of thanks for my orange juice. A few moments later a large plate arrived, filled with two nicely cooked eggs, a slice of real country ham, a sausage patty and a spoonful of white stuff I took to be grits with a pat of butter melting in the center. Then came a small basket holding two hot biscuits, and a bread-and-butter plate with real butter and homemade strawberry preserves. Coffee completed the service, and I was left to take a delicate taste of grits. And then a less delicate one. They were really quite good.

Food helped, although the sausage cleared my sinuses a little more thoroughly than was comfortable. I didn't linger over coffee, thanks to another no smoking sign on the buffet. I stuck my head into the kitchen, where the Martines were having a well-deserved cigarette, and asked if we could settle up. We could, and when I was told that the tally was $55, I made myself retract all the snide thoughts I'd been harboring.

I drove into town and started my inquiries at the bank with Cousin Martine. He seemed quite startled that the bank had no forwarding address for Ms. Malik and Ms. Harker. It seemed the waitress had been right last night about the second name. They didn't really *need* an address, he explained. Everything had been settled at the closing, but somebody really should have jotted it down, just in case. He knew they'd gone over Florida-way and was almost certain they were on the west coast thereof.

I moved on to the post office, where I was told it was a crying shame how many people forgot to fill out change-of-address cards. It caused no end of problems for all concerned. It was certainly causing plenty for me.

More with the thought of being thorough than any hope of being successful, I went down the block to a small concrete block building with a drooping flag out front and a sign that read

"Sheriff's Office" above the door. I entered and saw a man whose ID tag said he was Sheriff R. Laurence himself.

"Mornin'. I wondered when you'd show up." He had a sweet, grandfatherly smile.

"Why did you think I would?" I grinned back.

"Oh, you were asking directions yesterday, in a rental car. Your car was at the fishing camp overnight. I just saw you go in the bank and the post office. So I reckoned you'd misplaced somebody, like mebbe May Malik or Julie Harker."

He motioned me to a corner office and to a chair across from his desk. A small air conditioner struggled in the window and I raised my voice to override its growl. "You hit it. They moved, and I can't find anybody with their new address." I showed him my license and explained my mission. "I hope they're just careless. You don't suppose they're some kind of serial killers, do you?" I skipped over the Julie/June submystery. I'd work that out when I found them.

"Haven't had no complaints," he chortled. "I don't know 'zactly where they are either, but maybe I can help." He pulled out an atlas. "May mentioned to Jeeny White—she's the hairdresser—that they had bought another B&B over on an island off Florida. Now there's several islands over there, you'll notice, but Julie had said something about this inn being near Bradenton and Sarasota. Mentioned it to Arthur Parc. He runs Parc's Market, you see."

"I see." I really did. I knew exactly how small towns operated.

"Well, there's three islands it could be. But I know that area a little bit, done some fishin' over there from time to time. And I think it ain't St. Armand's Key. That's way too snooty for your average B&B. Same for Longboat Key, that's gone real upscale over recent years. So that leaves Holmes Beach." He stabbed his finger down on a little blob on the map and grinned up at me over his glasses.

"If I was a betting man, I'd say that is where you'll find 'em."

"That's good enough for me." I felt quite relieved. "Holmes Beach, here I come. All I have to do is figure out how to get there."

"There's probably a flight out of Baton Rouge, just up a ways." He waved vaguely over his shoulder. Haute Bayouites seemed a little fuzzy on the location of their state capital.

"Well, Sheriff, forgive me if I say I'd rather spend a night in New Orleans than Baton Rouge. You've been a treasure trove of information. What's a good place to stay in New Orleans?"

"There's a place the missus and I like, a nice little bed-and-breakfast . . ."

"Again, no offense, sir, but I want luxury for one night. I want room service and valet service and a wet bar in my room, and I want my bed turned down and a piece of candy on the pillow and a concierge panting to make my stay just perfect."

"Le Pavillon. They got all that and then some. Even the lobby *looks* right, not this modern stuff that looks like your dentist's waiting room. Real chandeliers and potted palms . . . the whole nine yards."

"Think I can get a room?"

"One way to find out." He buzzed the front desk and told them to put through a call. When his phone rang moments later, he picked it up and handed it to me. I could indeed get a room. I gave them my credit card number and they told me how much they looked forward to my arrival. John Frost was going to love this bill.

The Sheriff and I bade each other a cordial farewell with those silly comments about, *"If you're ever in my part of the country, etc."*

I took the Interstate back and made better time. I also felt more at ease. The Sheriff's directions had been explicit, and I pulled up to Le Pavillon without a miscue. They took away the car, they took in my luggage, they did everything but dust me off, which might not have hurt. But I was where I wanted to be. My room was Elegant Edwardian, and it seemed almost sacrilegious to be standing there barefoot in jeans and a mussed shirt, slugging down cold tea out of the bottle. The walls had textured paper and even held somebody's early nineteenth century portrait. There was a gas fire-place that looked workable and an enormous testered bed with a carved headboard.

I flicked back the bedspread and stretched out. I don't even remember setting down the tea.

Chapter 21

Walking through the long lobby of Le Pavillon that evening, I was glad I had worn my cord slacks and navy blazer. Most people seemed pretty much dressed up. Of course, I was going out, but I had to traverse the lobby to *get* out and jeans didn't seem to hack it here on a Friday night. Was it only Friday? I felt like I'd been gone a month.

Quite a few people were sitting in the comfortable chairs and settees, having cocktails or coffee and listening to a woman serenading the guests with a harp. It was charming and timeless and I very nearly sat down and joined the listeners. Then I decided: if you had only one night in New Orleans, you probably would not wish to tell your friends later that you had spent it in a hotel lobby listening to a harp.

I walked across St. Charles Avenue, listening to and watching the antique trolley cars clang and rattle by, expecting a raucous *Stel-l-l-a* to accost my ears any moment. Just before St. Charles became Royal Street, which meant it was now the French Quarter, I saw a small haberdashery store with a crowded single-window display and a neat sign reading, "We cater to the *elite*." I always wonder about signs like that. If you have to tell the *elite* you cater to them, *do* you?

But in the display I saw something this *elite* had always wanted. A derby hat. They had one in navy, in my size, and I told them a hatbox was unnecessary. I would wear it. They also had a silver-tipped cane that I suddenly coveted, but thoughts of trying to get it on an airplane in today's world discouraged me, so I left without it. On the street I pushed the derby rakishly forward over one eye and sauntered into the French Quarter like the *boulevardier* we know I am.

A zydeco band played in Jackson Square and I stopped to listen. The music was catchy and fast and hard and seemed a sort of bastard combination of Cajun and bluegrass with—I swear—a touch of a Yiddish *klezmer* band. The group had two fiddles, a concertina, a clarinet and a washtub bass plus a rub board, which looked like an old-fashioned washboard, strummed with both hands, fingertips covered by sewing thimbles.

After a while, I'd had enough and dropped a fiver into the upside down top hat provided for such gifts. The bass player yelled his thanks, and I waved without turning back. I looked in store windows and restaurant windows and walked quickly by a voodoo shop with a courteous tip of my hat. I passed bar after bar with strains of New Orleans jazz floating out. It was like an appetizer to me, causing me to yearn for the sounds of Coltrane and Baker, Rich and Parker.

I reached the Court of Two Sisters restaurant and decided to give the famous eatery a try. Ordering a Ramos gin fizz because I thought I should, I then wished I hadn't. I'm not crazy about licorice flavor . . . Pernod or whatever it was. I ordered a shrimp cocktail, with the biggest shrimp I've ever seen, and seared redfish which was splendid. A cup of New Orleans coffee, rich and bitter with chicory, gave me the jolt I needed to move on.

Dependent upon the kindness of strangers, I asked the waiter if he knew any nearby lesbian clubs. He did and I gave it a try. It was loud and crowded, and I no longer felt like a *furriner*. I was glad to find a seat at the bar, my Italian wingtips were not quite as comfortable as my usual sneakers. I ordered the familiar Bud and settled into my hobby of people watching. Later I noticed a young woman across the corner of the bar looking in my direction. She gave a tentative upturn of the mouth, and it was nice to receive a smile from a person not in the tourist business. I returned it with the full Peres wattage.

It was late when I returned to Le Pavillon. Cleaning people were at work, placing chairs back in proper positions, clearing the night's accumulation from the tables. The harp slept silent and shrouded in a nearby corner. Faint noise reached out from one of the bars off the main lobby but I was not tempted. The *boulevardier* was beat.

The next morning I enjoyed breakfast in my room, roguishly attired in pajamas and derby, which seemed to please my waiter no end. Several floors down, the concierge beavered away, getting me a flight to Sarasota/Bradenton, a room at the Golden Sands Motel and a car rental. I didn't have a great deal of time to kill, and all too soon I had lavishly tipped my way downstairs, through the lobby, across the steaming sidewalk to my car . . . and back into the real world.

Bradenton's Golden Sands was not Le Pavillon. It was, however, clean and cool, and pleasant in a paint-by-numbers sort of way, and what was a little walk down the hall to the ice machine? It was, like the man said, a reminder that the rich are different.

The motel did at least have room service, and I munched at a club sandwich with lukewarm french fries and a lukecool Diet Coke as I contemplated the Yellow Pages holding listings for

Holmes Beach. Nine bed-and-breakfast inns were listed. I figured I could safely cross off Betty and Bob's B&B, as well as Harriet's Hostel and Pete and Paula's Place. Alliteration is so twee, isn't it?

I started down the remaining six listings. The Castaways answered with a tape, so I'd try them again if need be. With the Fair Weather Inn, I got lucky. When I asked if this were the inn owned by Ms. Malik and Ms. Harker, the woman who'd answered said, "No, I'm afraid you have the wrong . . . oh, I think I know the place you want. It changed hands not long ago, and I know two women have it now. But they kept the name. It's the Sandy Dolphin."

Thanking her kindly, I hung up, ran my finger down the page, and redialed. Since I still wasn't certain if Ms. Harker was *née* Malik, I asked for May Malik when the phone was answered.

"This is she," was music to my ears.

After introducing myself, I gently gave her the news of Erno Malik's death, and she sounded genuinely grieved. "Poor Uncle Ernie! All he ever did was work in that garage! We tried to get him to come South and visit, but he never would. And . . . oh, dear . . . what with moving over here and getting settled, I haven't been in touch the way I should. I feel awful about that, I never even knew he was ill."

I was dying to ask why there was no address at which she could have been informed of his brief illness, but I figured that could wait. I explained that I was here in connection with the inheritance Erno had left to her and her sister June, and that I needed to meet with them to explain some options and complete some paperwork. At this news she became quite flustered and began to babble on about Uncle Ernie's generosity and my kindness in coming all the way to Florida to bring the news. Apparently it had yet to dawn that the cost of my kindness would be deducted from Uncle Ernie's generosity.

I interrupted the flow to ask for a definite appointment, and she got flustered all over again. Finally, we settled on eleven the next morning, when they would be finished serving breakfast. The fact it was Sunday, fortunately seemed not to matter to the gushing May.

Now that I had cornered my prey, my next move was to find a way home as early as possible Monday. I found no joy in flights out of Sarasota/Bradenton and moved my inquiries on to Tampa, some forty miles north. There I was told I could take the early bird flight at 6:05 a.m., land briefly in Cincinnati and wing on, non-stop, to Boston. I'd have to get up about 2:30, but by now that seemed a minor inconvenience.

Advising my employer of my success in his behalf struck me as wise, so I called John Frost at home to update him. He was pleased and even asked if I had enjoyed my evening in New Orleans. I assured him I had.

He said, "I meant to tell you about a very decent little hotel I stayed at once down there, but it slipped my mind. Did you make out okay?"

"I stayed at Le Pavillon."

"*Le Pavillon!*" There was a lengthy pause I made no effort to end. Finally he almost whispered, "My God! I had drinks in there once and was afraid of what it would cost to use the ashtray. Are you crazy?"

"Listen, John, I spent Thursday night in a fishing camp on your damned bayou, where the mosquitoes had bills like swordfish and an alligator spent the night burping up nutria under my window. *That* luxurious little inn cost a whole fifty-five bucks including a breakfast *I'm* still burping up, so just knock it off. I am tired. The temperature and the humidity are stuck at a hundred down here. The food varies between superb and causing terminal acid reflux. The people are mostly charming but weird. I have located the Bobbsey Twins at great personal sacrifice. I do not wish to see another lizard in this life and I am sick of palmetto bugs stuck in the car grille. I'll be home sometime Monday and see you Tuesday. Goodbye."

I should have stayed off telephones that evening. I called my mom and was told that everyone was fine. Fargo was also fine, but jumped up eagerly when anyone came through the door, and then went back under the table and flopped with a large sigh. That made me feel just swell.

Cindy was cool . . . I mean, chilly cool. She asked about New Orleans and wondered why I hadn't called. She asked where I had stayed and said I was definitely treating myself okay when I told her. She asked if I had seen anything of the town and commented that I had certainly had a full evening when I described my dinner and the derby and the zydeco. Thank God, I had the sense to leave out the jazz and the gay club.

I told her where I was now, that I had found the Maliks and that I hoped to be home Monday afternoon. She said she would try to leave work a bit early on Monday, but now had to run, she was meeting Lainey and Cassie for dinner. I asked her to tell Cassie to meet me at Logan Airport Monday around noon and she said she'd be happy to save me a phone call. On that note, we both said, "Love you," very fast and hung up.

My trio of calls sent me stomping to the Golden Sands Bar and Grill and into a bourbon old fashion. After the first gulp, I made myself calm down. John was just being John. He was not a penny-pincher at heart and always okayed expenses in the end. Mom had not meant to upset me. She probably thought she was just reassuring me that, while Fargo was really fine, he was still *my* dog.

Cindy, on the other hand, had been spoiling for a fight. I wondered why. Surely she knew airplane travel was no thrill these days. Driving an unfamiliar car over unfamiliar roads provided no particular pleasure. Louisiana's and Florida's west coasts in late June were simply miserable. And a pleasant evening in New Orleans really didn't make up for all the rest.

I didn't usually travel on business very far or very often, but I hoped this wouldn't happen every time I did. Sighing, I ordered another drink sent to my room, along with a steak and salad, and went back outside for the sweat-popping hundred-foot walk. Inside my room, the phone message light was blinking. Now what?

"Hi, darling, it's me. I'm sorry I was so bitchy before. It's just, well, I really miss you. More than I thought. And I guess in my mature, sensible way I just wanted to make sure you were miserable, too. Forgive me, love. I miss you. I really want to see you and touch you. Till Monday. I love you."

Well. Okay. I could deal with that. I immediately called back, though I knew I'd get the tape. "Hi, there, Culpa. Put away the sackcloth and ashes and hang on for forty-eight hours, and I guarantee we'll touch! I miss you too, despite the madcap nightlife here in Bradenton. And I love you lots. Bye."

The steak was surprisingly good, and I watched with mild contentment as the Braves stomped the Marlins

It was just before eleven Sunday morning when I crossed the causeway over the bay and turned left for the Sandy Dolphin. As I pulled into the parking area and exited the car, a red-throated lizard hissed hysterically from a nearby palmetto palm. I stared back with similar displeasure.

"Don't worry, he won't hurt you. It's just their way of establishing territory."

I turned to face the pleasant voice and encountered the strangest looking woman I have ever seen.

She was a good six feet tall, without an ounce of excess poundage. She had on light blue denim pants ending about halfway down her calves, and a ghastly bright pink rayon blouse with even deeper pink embroidery around the sleeve cuffs and collar and down the front. On her head was a black curly wig, ill fitting and obviously cheap. And she peered at me through little round spectacles that seemed to have been made for a much smaller person.

"Hi, I'm June Malik."

"Alex Peres." Whoever she was, she had a good, firm handshake.

"Come on in, May's in the kitchen."

We walked around to the back porch and she kicked off her gardening clogs to reveal feet that might have prompted the ancient joke about throwing out the shoes and wearing the boxes they came in. She opened the screen door and I entered to see another woman with real black curly hair, about five-foot-three and quite appealing in a well-rounded, butterball way. She, too, wore the pink and blue get-up and the round glasses, although they fit her face.

Now, I had seen twins dressed alike as small children, but never as adults. And, anyway, if these women were even sisters, I'd have that lizard for a sushi lunch.

We all sat down at the well-scrubbed pine kitchen table, and May poured wonderful-smelling coffee into three mugs. After a few moments of chatter regarding the fine character of Erno Malik, the heat and what a long trip I had made, I opened my briefcase and pulled out papers.

I explained the inheritance—the garage and a small insurance policy. I told them of the two young men who wished to buy the garage, their offer, and approximately what the women would receive. "June" said nothing, and May seemed pleased with the amount, actually uninterested in details, glancing quickly at the photos and passing them on to "June," who simply pushed them aside. "And now," I looked up. "There's the matter of some ID for the two of you."

I expected confusion, but May simply reached behind her to the counter. She picked up two pieces of stiff paper and handed them to me. "Yes, I assumed as much. Last night I dug out our birth certificates."

She was going to brazen it out. Looking down at the two documents, I was struck by the tiny footprints at the bottom of the pages. "Look at those tiny little feet!" I blurted. "You'd never believe . . ." I stopped. I had been about the say, "You'd never believe those teensy baby feet would grow into such big adult feet." I had stopped mid-sentence, not wanting to hurt "June's" feelings. But I got an amazing reaction, anyway.

"June" leaped up, yanked off her wig and glasses, slammed them onto the table and began to pull viciously at her clothing.

"Godammit, May, I told you these crazy costumes wouldn't work! She knows by the footprints it isn't me!"

"Well, they were the best clothes I could find at KMart late on a Saturday night in sizes to fit us both. You were no help, pacing around and moaning we'd be arrested as murderers!"

I looked longingly at the back door, but both women were closer to it than I was. So I tried a little brazening of my own.

"You are Julie Harker, aren't you? Where is June Malik? Is her disappearance why you left no forwarding address from Haute Bayou?"

They both looked startled. "Didn't you fill out the card?" May queried.

"Yes, and you said you'd drop it off that day you went to the hairdresser."

May put a hand up to her mouth. "You know, I completely forgot. It's still in my handbag. Oh, my God." I believed her. I also needed a cigarette. I had the feeling today I wouldn't be counting.

I lit one, and May got up and handed me an ashtray and freshened our coffee. Maybe they weren't planning my demise after all. She sat back down and covered her face with her hands for a moment before she spoke.

"This sounds silly, but in high school June and I had both read this wonderful romantic book about New Orleans and sworn we would someday live there. When we graduated, we just got on a bus and went. No plans, no knowledge of the town, little money. But teenagers are omnipotent, you know, and so were we. And in the beginning it worked." She pulled out cigarettes of her own and I pushed the ashtray to the middle of the table.

"We got an apartment," May said. "I got a job in an insurance company. June had never been a nine-to-five drudge and got a job as a waitress in a bar and grill. Before long she was drinking a lot and was—I was pretty sure—taking drugs. She got fired and got another job in a really rough bar and just went to hell in a hand-basket. Booze, drugs, slimy men . . . you name it." She shook her head in remembrance.

Julie took over the tale, revealing that I was obviously a solid blip on her gaydar. "By then May and I had met and fallen in love." She gave May a smile of such warmth, her face looked actually beautiful. "We wanted to live together in the house I'd inherited from my parents, but what to do with June? We really didn't want her living with us. Finally, we agreed to go on paying half the apartment rent till June could find a roommate."

She reached for May's cigarettes and swore. "Dammit, every time I think I've quit, I haven't. Anyway, June found a roommate, and then another roommate and then another. Finally, there were just a series of various men and women 'crashing' in the apartment for a week or a night. We cut the money. Would you like a beer?"

"I'd kill for one," I answered, startled by the change of subject, and then thought there might have been more tactful ways to phrase that. "Er, yes, please. It's a really hot day."

Julie grinned and May headed for the fridge. "Cutting June off may have been a mistake," she said over her shoulder. "It might have been better to just keep paying the rent. June started showing up at our house drunk or stoned, sometimes with one or more of her so-called friends. They were loud. June always wanted to 'borrow' money and picked arguments with anybody—her friends or us. The neighbors began to give us funny looks. We got her into a rehab, but that didn't take. Finally, we told her if she came back, we'd call the police. That got to her. She stopped coming. We lived in glorious peace." She smiled wistfully and set the drinks on the table.

"But not for long?" I guessed.

"Bingo." Julie took a healthy swallow. "One night we came home from a movie, and there was June on the chaise on the front porch, passed out."

"Alone?" I asked.

"Yes. I shook her and called her name, but no results. Finally, I gently slapped her and she raised her hands as if to protect herself. That's when I saw both her hands were bloody."

"My God!" I exclaimed. "Shock time. What did you do?" I found myself lighting another cigarette and grimaced.

"I ripped her blouse open, but there was no wound. Not there. Not anyplace on her body. We practically stripped her right on the porch. We were debating what to do when she halfway came to. She muttered something like, 'Bastard tried to get me with bad stuff. Well, maybe he did, but I got him first. I got the bastard.' Then she passed out again, and it dawned on us that the blood wasn't hers. She must have been in a fight and had cut or stabbed or even shot someone." Without asking, she stood and went for refills.

"This may sound cold and callous," May put in. "But when we thought of calling 911, we suddenly pictured an ambulance and police cars and flashing lights and a lot of questions we couldn't possibly answer. I mean, what if there was a body somewhere? Then we thought of newspapers and TV cameras . . . the neighbors and our jobs. What if people thought *we* were involved? Or worse, what if one of the stabbed person's friends thought I was June and killed me in some kind of revenge?" May's voice had become shrill and loud with remembered fear.

"So what did you do?" I asked quietly.

Julie answered for her. "We decided to drive her down to a park near the hospital, put her on a bench and call 911 anonymously. Okay, we were not thinking too straight, but it might have worked. We half-carried, half-walked her to the car. May got in the back with her and I drove. Just as we reached the park, June made this funny noise . . . like a car revving its motor sort of. And then May yelled that she couldn't find a pulse."

"What the hell did you do next?" They must have been approaching hysteria by then.

"We just kept driving," May answered. "Past the park, on by

the hospital. We knew she was beyond help. I can't even remember what we talked about, if anything. Finally, I realized we were way out on Route Ninety, but we still just drove. It was like, if we didn't stop, we didn't have to decide anything. God knows where we would have ended up. Baton Rouge, I guess. But finally, of all the mundane things, I had to go to the bathroom. So Julie turned off onto this little dinky road and we ended up by the water. We both got out and peed, and I noticed a dilapidated old dock nearby." She paused and took a shaky breath.

"I knew what we had to do. You know, I'm still not sure we said anything. But we got out the spare and took the tire off the wheel. There was some plastic clothesline in the trunk and we tied June to the wheel and the jack and a bag of pebbles for my plants. And we just eased her off the end of the dock. And she was gone." May began to cry, and I felt like putting my arms around her.

"To wrap this up," Julie said harshly. "We found a motel out near Morgan City. Next morning we saw a notice in a café that the fishing camp in Haute Bayou was for sale at a good price. The owner was unwell. We bought it, sold my house in New Orleans, and that was that. We made a new life, and I don't believe we did anything wrong." She raised her chin defiantly.

Frankly, I agreed with her. They'd been through hell with June. She was beyond human help, and my not entirely impious thought was that God could find her in a bayou as easily as a hospital morgue. I took an oblique approach.

"Why did you later sell the fishing camp?"

Julie looked startled at the change of topic, but answered easily. "It was a big rambling place, as you saw. Lots of work, indoors and out, for two women. And no great income. You can't charge much in the boonies. To top it off, the man who ran our dock and took care of the boats announced he was going to retire soon. We saw this place advertised in a trade magazine, and it seemed perfect."

I nodded, and May solved another little mystery I'd been contemplating. "Another thing appealed to us," she said. "There's a fairly active gay community here. We're actually making a few friends. We'd spent over fifteen years in isolation in Haute Bayou, infrequent trips to New Orleans was about it."

I nodded again. "So June's . . . uh, body was never located?"

"No. Alex, it's been so long. Who would care anymore? I mean, I will always care, in a way, but couldn't we just forget this whole sad mess? I mean, we virtually *had* forgotten it." May sounded plaintive.

I sighed and took a sip of beer to gain a moment. I was about to ruin their day. And mine. I felt terrible for them. In my mind they were probably at least as much victimized as June had been. Certainly, they had not harmed her. She would doubtless have died anyway, if not that night, then another one soon, and possibly in a truly horrible way. On the other hand, they'd broken a handful of laws, a couple of them serious ones. It wasn't like I could pretend I never saw the fireplug they had parked beside.

"I'm afraid not. There are laws about reporting deaths and the . . . ah, disposition of bodies. There's the blood on June's hands. It could have been evidence in another crime. And, we want you to get what's coming from Erno's estate. For that we need a death certificate, so you will get June's share." I didn't even want to think how complicated *that* had become.

May let out a sigh that moved the kitchen curtains. "So now what?"

"A good criminal lawyer," I replied. "Hopefully, the State of Louisiana will give you a little wrist slap and that will be it. Some kind of fine and maybe some community service to be performed here in Florida. With any luck, they'll figure the blood is too long gone to matter. Get the Haute Bayou sheriff in on this, he likes you both. I'm sorry, I really can't ignore this. And God knows my boss wouldn't."

We chatted quite awhile longer, but nothing changed, and finally I left.

I was having another lukewarm room service dinner and making myself eat slowly. Neither May nor the lawyer had called, and I was wondering if I was going to have to call the Bradenton cops and be stuck at least one more day in their charming environs. I had told myself the phone would ring before I finished dinner and was now reluctantly dipping the next-to-last fried shrimp in the sauce. It rang.

A soft, deep-pitched southern voice inquired, "Is this Miz Alex Peres?"

"Yes, it is."

A deep sigh. Relief? Despair? Resignation? "Lordy, ma'am, what a can of worms you have gone and opened up!"

Chapter 22

Even at 1500 feet the air was warm in the lovely little Beechcraft, and we had the side vents open. Warm or not, the air had the clean, salty smell of the North Atlantic in it, with none of the fecund, slightly overripe heaviness I'd been getting used to. I sniffed appreciatively and Cassie laughed.

"Smell like home?"

"Yeah. And I'm ready for it. I've flown and driven a million miles. I've slept about fifteen hours in four nights. And John Frost will be in cardiac arrest this time tomorrow when he sees my expenses."

I'd given Cassie a brief recap of my trip as we flew toward Provincetown Airport. Like May and Julie, she couldn't understand why I didn't just develop sudden acute myopia and "believe" the two women were twins. Obviously everybody's sympathy was going to be with them, and I just hoped it carried over to a New Orleans prosecutor. It would not carry over to John Frost.

I sighed and changed the subject. "Anything new here at home?"

"Nah. We're tripping over tourists. It's going to be a good season. Oh . . . yes . . . I almost forgot. Lainey has a big, important case for you."

Cassie's lips were twitching, and I went along with whatever the joke was going to be. "Oh. I'll get right on it. What's up?"

Cassie cut the throttles slightly and began to lose altitude. "Well, it seems Lainey walked down the ER corridor the other night and saw a laundry cart parked there, with some soiled linen in it. Not sanitary, not good for the morale of incoming ER patients. So she told an aide to take it to the laundry room."

"And the aide tried to kill her and then disappeared?"

"Close. A little later, Lainey saw the cart was gone and thanked the aide for acting promptly. The aide replied she hadn't moved it at all, that it was already gone when she got to it. But . . ." Cassie waggled her finger to indicate more mystery. "Just before quitting time one of the laundry workers reported that the inventory check indicated a couple of sheets and pillow cases, a blanket *and* one of the new laundry carts were *missing!* No one can account for them. So, Sherlock, get with it!"

"You might remind Lainey I'm not the one she wants snooping around looking for a bunch of icky sheets. When it comes to hospitals, I'm the one who gets sick while I'm still in the parking lot."

"I know. Well, I tried."

Fargo managed to knock me down in Mom's backyard and then nearly licked me to death. I was never so glad to be attacked. When I managed to get inside the house, Mom's greeting was more restrained, but equally welcoming. So was her question, "Have you had lunch?"

When I told her I'd had a doughnut about five a.m. and a sausage sandwich about nine, she gave me a raised eyebrow look and turned to the fridge. While she fixed a plate of cold sliced chicken, tomatoes with oil and bleu cheese and got out some potato salad, I called Cindy. She was delighted I was safely home and would see me at the house as soon as she could wrap up her business day.

I ate quickly, interrupted by frequent begging nudges from Fargo, to let me know he had been cruelly starved in my absence. Between bites, I told Mom of my trip and got the expected response.

"Those poor women! Really, dear, it would have been so much simpler just to let those birth certificates do their job. John Frost will have a fit."

"Mom," I yawned. "You can't just pop the odd body into the bayou for convenience, and apparently she *had* been in some sort of stabbing party, and John will just have to be brave."

"Yes, well, I hope you can work it out so you don't have to go back."

"Oh, God, I hadn't thought of that." I yawned again. "Sorry. Not much sleep."

"Go home and get some rest, dear. You look exhausted. I'll talk to you tomorrow."

"Yeah. Thanks for everything, Mom. Sorry to be so deadbeat."

Fargo almost knocked me down again, jumping into the car. I was glad he didn't. I think I would just have gone to sleep there in the yard.

Pulling into my driveway moments later, I clicked the garage door opener on the visor. As the door went up, I pulled forward and immediately stomped the brakes. Something was blocking the entrance.

I got out and Fargo ran past me, sniffing and whuffling excitedly. I grinned as I walked toward the object and wondered what joke Cassie and Lainey were pulling on me. It looked suspiciously like a laundry cart.

I heard a faint, low hum, like some low-powered electrical appliance. As Fargo circled the cart, his shoulder bumped its corner, and at least a thousand flies swarmed upward in a buzzing cloud so black, at first I thought it was smoke. Before I could turn away, I glimpsed a yellow-green, bloated face, with one eye half closed in a grotesque leer and the other wearing some kind of *outré* monocle with red and green trim.

Screaming, "Run, Fargo, *run!*" I pelted down the driveway, slapping and brushing at the flies I was sure were all over me. "Run . . . run . . . run!" I panted with every footstep. I made it to the end of the drive before my stomach gave a horrendous wrench, and I bent over, grabbed the corner of the front wall, and lost my lunch. I crept along, leaning against the wall, to the end of my property. I had to get far away, I thought, far away. But I didn't think I could walk much farther, so I sat down on the last large flat stone, and Fargo jumped up beside me.

I shivered and brushed my hair, certain there were flies in it. There were not. Fargo and I held no interest for them, they had immediately returned to their feast. I put my arms around the dog. He felt wonderfully warm and real. Help, I had to get us help. I had called Cindy on my cell phone . . . had I put it in my shirt pocket? Yes! Thank God. No way could I have returned to the car for my handbag, or gone into the house.

I flicked it open and called 911. Twice I hit wrong numbers. Finally, I propped it on Fargo's sturdy, steady back and managed to punch in the correct call. I must have been coherent in whatever I said, for it seemed only seconds before I heard the approaching whoop of sirens.

Sonny was in the first car, and was out of it before it stopped. I felt his very welcome arms go around me and started to cry. "It's okay," he said. "It's okay. I'm here, I'm here."

"You're being repetitive," I hiccupped.

"Well," he managed a small smile, "I guess you're going to live if you can bitch about my speaking style."

"I'm freezing. It's boiling hot and I'm freezing."

"I see that." He turned away and called, "Medic! Medic, please bring some oxygen and a blanket here. The garage can wait."

One of the EMTs trotted down with the items, tucking the blanket around me and handing me the oxygen cone.

Sonny asked, "Will you be all right? We need to see what's going on up there." He jerked his chin toward the garage.

"It's a body, an awful body, with this crazy monocle. And flies, Sonny, you've got to do something with the flies."

About that time I heard some sort of ruckus out in the street and looked up to see Cindy out of her car and actually wrestling with some young cop who was trying to stop her. Sonny yelled, "Let her through, she lives here!"

She ran over and pulled me almost roughly to her breast. "Are you hurt? Darling, what happened? Tell me! Tell me what's wrong!" I couldn't. She was pressing my mouth and the oxygen cone so tightly to her, I couldn't speak. I couldn't breathe much either. Finally, she let me go.

"I'm okay," I managed. At least I had quit crying and shaking, though I was still weak and my stomach was far from settled. The EMTs came out rolling a gurney with a body bag on it. I looked away, although there was nothing to see, except Pete Santos throwing up in the gutter.

Fargo moved to go investigate, and Cindy grabbed his collar. She turned to me, shocked. "A body? You found a *body?* Good God, who is it?"

"Who knows? I'm not sure if it was male or female. I'm barely sure it was even human."

"I'm almost certain I know who it is." Sonny had rejoined us, looking pale himself. "Grace Sanhope disappeared Friday night. I think she was your weekend visitor."

Chapter 23

The sound of voices outside the window woke me. It took me a minute to remember where I was. Too many strange beds lately. Then I reached out and felt Fargo and remembered. I was at the cottage in the familiar bed, sheets smelling faintly of the fresh lavender Cindy always kept in the linen closet. Home . . . or the next thing to it.

Slowly I identified the speakers: Mom, Sonny, Trish . . . then Aunt Mae and Cindy. The family had gathered, I grinned, to support the shell-shocked cub . . . who had slept soundly through most of their rescue mission. I felt much better, I realized, having had a shower and a long nap. It was after six as I got up and doused my face in cold water and swished some Listerine around.

Going out on the deck, I was greeted by hugs and commiserations on my horrible experience. I appreciated them, all of them, and the fact that they cared. As I accepted a beer from Sonny, I couldn't wait. "Well, was it Grace?"

"Yes. Her grandson Richard came down to ID her. Poor bastard almost fainted. Fortunately we convinced Lillian to wait outside."

"Good. Nobody should have to look at that. Er . . . Sonny . . ." I couldn't think of a casual way to bring up what was bothering me. "Uh, well, those flies . . . my garage . . ."

"No flies within a mile. Garage and driveway are all disinfected, hosed down and there's a big fan blowing in the garage to discourage any strays. You're okay."

"Thanks, I think that was the worst of all. But what happened? Did you say she went missing Friday? Was it kidnap?" I lit a cigarette, surely I was still under five for the day . . . in a pig's ear.

"She went missing sometime Friday between five and nine p.m. Right now we know very little. We aren't sure whether it was a kidnapping, although no one called or left a note that we know of. It could be she was murdered at home. Or she could have left under her own steam. Her car is missing. There's jewelry and cash missing, lots of jewelry, everything but some *really* valuable pieces kept in the bank, plus five hundred to a thousand dollars she kept in the jewelry box. And Richard told us that an opal ring she usually wore, was missing from her finger. Strangely, the thief left a gold locket and her diamond wedding ring on her body." He put out his hands in a *who knows?* gesture.

"Sentiment," Aunt Mae stated firmly. "Whoever did it knows her and respected the sanctity of the ring and emotional importance of the locket."

Trish nodded her approval. "Good point."

"Yeah," Sonny admitted, as he reached across the table for my cigarettes. "And we can use all the points we can get. They didn't report her missing until late Saturday morning, when her maid finally got worried that she hadn't rung for her breakfast and entered her bedroom to find the bed had not been slept in. Frankly, we're still trying to sort out their cars and who was in which one, when."

"Why?" Mom asked. "Do they have that many? And why do you care?"

"I care because murder usually begins at home and I can't seem to nail down who was where during the critical hours. Look . . ." He used his fingers to tick off family members. "Richard worked late in Boston Friday night, he says, and caught the last flight over, rather than drive. That left his Lexus in the garage at home in Boston. Presumably."

"Excuse me," I interrupted. "I want to hear all this, but I am starving. My breakfast was sometime last week and lunch—ah, didn't stay with me. Could we order pizza or something?"

There was a babble of agreement and a gush of suggestions. Cindy finally stood up and went inside to phone in an order before discussions continued through the night.

"Okay," I said. "Now what about the Lexus?"

"Yeah," my brother grunted. "The butler/chauffeur drove Richard to work Friday morning and took the car home. In the summer, there's only the butler and a maid in the Boston house, and they only work Tuesday till Friday noon, because none of the family is there weekends. So, we can't call them, but we *assume* the car is there."

"Now, over here," he continued, "We have one confirmed activity. Lillian left the house in her Saab around two, to play golf at Hyannis with a girlfriend. The golf club confirms that the two women indeed played golf and had dinner, with the dinner check signed by Lillian and time-stamped eight eleven p.m. That put her back here about nine, some twenty minutes before Richard arrived, by cab from the airport."

"And where was Grace at that time? I'm confused," Mom admitted.

I could tell from various expressions she wasn't alone. I stood up and took a drink order. Cindy came in with me to help, and we managed our first real hug and kiss, and looked at each other with regret. So much for romantic homecomings.

"We don't know for sure where she was." Sonny shrugged. "They didn't see her that night. Both said Grace sometimes went to bed early and watched TV or read. It's a really big house, you know, you don't hear noises much. They assumed that was where she was."

"Lots of assumptions going on." Trish reached unerringly for her Scotch highball on the tray I extended. "Any other facts?"

"Oh, yes, it's a fact that we haven't the slightest idea where Jack—or his car—may be." Sonny favored us all with a sour smile.

Hungry or not, that got my attention. "Do we know where he is *supposed* to be?"

"More or less," Sonny grumbled. "It seems that early Friday morning Jack was out in the yard barefoot and somehow managed to step on a nail. Lillian says it bothered him all day, but not enough to cancel his weekend plans." He began his fresh beer.

"Which were?" Cindy asked, as she stood and looked down the drive. Surely it was pizza time.

"He was going to pick up a friend in Newport, and the two of them were going to take the ferry across to Montauk, Long Island, and attend a house party at Sag Harbor. By the time Lillian left, he was limping and the foot looked inflamed, so Lillian made him promise to stop in the clinic. He said he would and they confirm that he did. After that, however, we can't seem to place him."

Headlights appeared and Grace Sanhope would no doubt have smiled ironically to know plebian pizza immediately took precedence over the tale of her aristocratic demise. There was a great, semipolite scramble for the food, and our little crowd took on the look of the zoo at feeding time, jaws grinding rhythmically, conversation in abeyance.

Finally, pizza diminished and salad demolished, we started talking again. "Why is Richard a suspect?" Aunt Mae asked. "I thought he was the goody-goody one in the family."

Sonny swallowed manfully. "Well, I hear from Pete Santos that Richard was supposed to become head of the firm on his thirtieth birthday. That didn't happen. His thirty-fourth birthday was last week. It didn't happen then, either, but I understand he and Grace had quite a set-to about it. She won't—wouldn't—give up the reins. Well, she has now."

"So Richard has motive," I mused. "If he wasn't in his office, he could have driven over here Friday afternoon late, killed Grace, driven back to Boston and flown over, leaving his car at home in Boston. But—and this makes no sense—he would have had to go to the clinic right before or right after he killed her, conveniently spotted a laundry cart, stolen it, jammed it in the back of his car, put Grace in the trunk, and driven her to my garage and placed her there in the cart." I stood up to dump my paper plate in the trash. "Is he familiar with the clinic? He certainly isn't familiar with my garage."

"Probably no to both," Trish agreed. "And a look at the Lexus, wherever it is, would show any clothing fibers or blood."

"There wouldn't necessarily be any blood," Sonny disagreed. "And since she used the car frequently, hair and fibers will be in it anyway, and that type of wound doesn't bleed much."

I'd been avoiding that topic, but now I had to ask. "Exactly how *was* she killed?"

Sonny gave me a dirty look, as if he wished I had waited till we were alone for that explanation. But it was too late now. Every face was turned toward him. He got his pedantic look and spoke as if he were reading from a case notebook.

"The murder weapon was a standard-type kitchen meat thermometer. It was shoved through the victim's left eye, into the brain, and wiggled around." He took another of my cigarettes and slowly lit it, giving his audience more than enough time to assimilate his news. Continuing, he said, "The victim would have been immediately unconscious, although she might have remained technically alive up to several hours."

We were all silent. Then my mother got up and began to clear the remains of our meal with quick, nervous movements. Trish

155

began to help her. Cindy moved over into her chair and took my hand. "Try not to think about it, darling. At least she was unconscious. She didn't know . . . all the rest of it."

I nodded, unable to speak. Aunt Mae had reached for a tissue. Sonny glared.

Aunt Mae pulled it together and said, "Sonny, you didn't say why you can't find Jack. You believe he has run away?"

"We don't know. Neither Richard nor Lillian know what friend Jack was picking up, nor who was giving the party in Sag Harbor. At least that's what they say. They are contacting some other people who 'might know.'"

He stood and turned to Trish. "I'm going back over to the Sanhope place and then to the office. I want to see if Lillian has heard from Jack. And I want to talk to the cook and maid again. They were so busy crying Saturday, they couldn't remember their names. And I'm hoping the old station wagon may have been found. Maybe we can figure out if Grace drove somewhere herself—either to meet someone or maybe running an errand. Or maybe the killer used it to transport her body. God, what a screwed up mess!" He turned and shook my shoulder gently. "Take it easy, Alex. I'm sorry you had to find her, but don't worry, we'll sort it out."

"I know you will. It just saddens me to think of her dying so horrifically. I know she was selfish and stubborn and sarcastic, but she was vibrant and smart and brave and humorous, too. And I'll bet in her day, she was sexy as hell." I don't know why I said that. It earned me a bunch of very strange looks.

But Aunt Mae bailed me out. "Indeed she was, my dear. Grace had a good twenty years on me, but I can remember looking at her when I was a young woman and being grass-green with envy."

Sonny yawned and stretched. "Tell me, Aunt Mae, where were you between five and nine o'clock Friday night?"

Chapter 24

Walking into John Frost's reception area at nine sharp on Tuesday, I handed my expense account to his long-time secretary to be typed up in legible form. "Be sure to give that to him when he's had a good lunch," I suggested with a smile.

She looked back at me with a sour grin. "I'll give it to him on his way home, so he can yell at his wife, not me," she said. "He and Trish have been here since eight this morning, and I haven't heard any gales of laughter. And he won't be thrilled to see Fargo. Yesterday some woman's Yorkie peed on his oriental rug."

"Oh, God. Well, into the valley and all that."

I tapped on the door and entered. John looked up and questioned, "Is Denver housebroken?"

"Good morning, John. Good morning, Trish," I caroled. "How nice to see you both. Yes, I am glad to be home, thank you. And his name is Fargo, and his manners are impeccable." I hoped they were. I had visions of Fargo sniffing where the Yorkie had gone and feeling the necessity to prove his superiority.

"Yeah, yeah," John grunted. "Whatever. Sorry you had such a bad experience yesterday. Trish has been filling me in. Anyway, what the hell is the story on those two birds in Florida? I got a call from a lawyer in Bradenton, said they dropped the sister in a bayou, tied to a tire jack? And now the lawyer and some sheriff over in Louisiana are trying to say they really did nothing wrong and we should have looked the other way and given them the money?" He looked at me wonderingly. "What kind of people did you get mixed up with down there?"

"Different. Nice, but different. I need some coffee. This won't be short."

It wasn't. It was a long and unhappy tale, unhappily received, and I was relieved when it was finished.

I decided to check on the other long, sad tale I was involved in. Fargo and I walked over to the police station, pausing en route while Fargo, gentleman that he was, paused at a handy maple, having bypassed John's carpet.

The station was more heavily manned than usual with people on phones, on computers, on the fax—all too busy to more than nod a greeting. Pete Santos looked up from his desk, his face strained and tired.

"Hiya, Pete. I'm sorry about all your troubles. How's your mom holding up?"

Scowling, he answered, "About like yours would, I imagine, if she'd lost one relative and had another suspected of murder."

"Oh, come on, Pete, have a little faith. Jack may walk in any minute with a logical explanation."

Standing, Pete slammed some papers into his desk drawer and snapped, "Yeah, you really believe that? You were ready enough to nail Jack for rape, why not murder?"

"Pete, I really—"

"How do you know the same person who kidnapped and killed Grace hasn't kidnapped Jack? Maybe killed him, too? Well, I'll tell you one thing, if Jack is alive, he's innocent!"

He walked away, leaving me embarrassed and speechless. I'd been so busy thinking of Jack Sanhope as a suspect, it had never occurred to me he might be a victim. Suppose he and Grace *had* been kidnapped together. Why hadn't the kidnapper demanded a ransom? No phone call had been received . . . at least not after the police got the tap on the wire. What if it had come through earlier, or in the mail? What if the Sanhopes had been trying to deal directly with the kidnapper?

I found Lieutenant Peres behind the door that said I would—feet on desk, coffee mug in hand, squinting at a blackboard across the room. The board had two columns, one headed *Long shots*, the other *Short shots*.

Under *Long shots*, Sonny had listed the caretaker/chauffeur as being at his daughter's wedding in Worcester. The maid and cook were marked as being together downtown for most of the critical time and having paid for their dinner by credit card. Lillian Sanhope carried the notation: "At country club 3 till 8:15 p.m." Finally, Richard Sanhope was noted as being "Barely possible, unlikely. Hired a killer? Unlikely."

Under *Short shots*, were the names I expected. Topping the list was Jack Sanhope with the succinct statement: *missing*. Following Jack was a notation of unknown kidnapper and/or robber. Lines three and four were dedicated to Mary Sloan and Maureen Delaney, with no descriptive notes.

A second blackboard, angled off from that one was headed *Facts about Grace*.

One section headed *Friday* had several entries.

"*Friday approx. 12:30 p.m.* lunch w/Lillian, in good mood, no sign of distress."

"*Friday approx. 5:15 p.m.* told cook to leave cold dinner in fridge and then she and maid could have evening off. This was the last time Grace was seen by any household member.

"*Saturday approx. 8 a.m.* cook and maid came on duty. Grace's dinner plate, etc. in sink. No other sign of disturbance.

"*Saturday 11:27 a.m.* Call by Richard to Ptown police. Grace missing. Lt. Peres notified. Sgt. Mitchell and two officers conducted search. No clues. Ground slightly disturbed near telescope, but rain late Fri. night and Sat. morning destroyed details, if any.

"*Saturday approx. 2 p.m.* Phone tap arranged. Officers at house from then till midnight Sun. No unusual calls.

"*Monday approx. 2 p.m.* Grace's body found by Ms. A. Peres in her garage."

"Nothing new on Jack?" I asked.

"Nothing new on anything." Sonny put his feet down and sat up straight. "No report of the station wagon sighted. We've got a three-state alert out on that. And we're getting photos of the jewelry from their insurance company so we can put an alert out on the jewelry, in case somebody tries to hock it."

"So what's next?" I sipped delicately at the coffee I had poured myself. It was industrial strength.

"Mary and Maureen. I've got to see what they were up to over the weekend. Trish doesn't trust Maureen worth a damn, and, as you know well, Mary attacked Amazin' Grace in broad daylight. It should be a fun day."

Before I could tell him of Maureen's verbal attack on me, his phone rang. Sonny picked it up, listened a second and said, "Put him through." At the same time, he switched the phone to speaker and turned on a tape, and I heard Richard Sanhope's voice.

"Good morning, Sonny. Richard here. I've got some news for you."

"That's good to hear."

"Yes and no." Richard sighed. "Well, first of all, I just spoke to the butler in Boston. The Lexus *is* there. You can have someone look at it anytime."

"Thank you. I'll take care of that." Sonny made gestures of smoking a cigarette. I took the hint and lit one for him.

"And . . . well . . . the old car has also turned up and so has Jack. Now don't go riding off in all directions, Sonny. It's really all quite simple." Richard was speaking very fast, as if to keep Sonny from interrupting.

"You see, Jack stepped on this nail Friday morning—"

"I know all about that—"

"No, you don't." Richard sounded irritated now. "Let me say this my way." Sonny looked at me and shrugged, as Richard continued. "Okay, he stepped on this nail. He was supposed to pick up a friend in Newport and the two of them would continue to Sag Harbor to some party. As the day went on, the wound bothered him a lot, and Lillian insisted he see a doctor. He agreed and Lillian went on to her golf game."

"Yes, Richard, we have this." Sonny sounded bored.

"Yes, but what you don't *have* is this. Jack started to leave, planning to stop at the clinic and go on to Newport. His car wouldn't start. The battery was okay, but it wouldn't start. He called the garage and they came out but couldn't start it either. They towed it away. So, figuring nobody would need the old station wagon, Jack took it." He stopped, as if he had explained everything.

Sonny ground out his cigarette and signaled me for coffee. I gave him a dirty look as I complied, Cinderella never being my favorite role.

Sonny's boredom had ceased. "Really! Okay, so he took the wagon, went to the clinic and then what?"

Now Richard was speaking slowly, picking each word as if choosing melons in a market. "Yes, well, at the clinic they dressed the wound and gave him tetanus and antibiotic shots plus antibiotic pills for later. He left and headed off-Cape. By the time he got to Buzzard's Bay he was feeling nauseous and headache-y. He stopped for coffee. It made him worse, and he says he really didn't feel like driving all that way to a party he felt too sick to enjoy. So he called his friend, cancelled and . . . uh . . . went on home and went to bed."

Sonny frowned. "Home, where? What home?"

"Uh, Boston. The house in Boston."

"To Boston." Now Sonny was talking fast. "He went all the way to Boston, to an empty house with no one to feed him, no one to take care of him if he got really ill, no company. He sat all weekend until Tuesday morning in a big empty house all by himself? Come on, Richard, does that sound sensible to you? Why would he do that when he could drive about the same distance back to Ptown where there were people to care for him?"

"Oh, really, Sonny, it's not so strange. He wasn't all *that* sick. He just felt lousy. And things had been a little tense in Ptown. He just wanted to be alone and think things out, he says. And there's loads of food in the house, and TV and the DVD player and films and books. Oh, there's a pool table and hot tub." Poor Richard sounded as if he were a real estate broker touting a really badly over-priced house.

"Where is he now?" Sonny asked coldly.

"On his way here." Via the car wash, I added silently.

"Well, thanks for calling, Richard. Have Jack phone me when he gets here."

Sonny hung up and looked at me. "So, what are you thinking?"

"First of all, things have been 'tense' at Sanhope-ville for weeks, but this is the first time it's been mentioned by anyone but Jack." I put Sonny's coffee on his desk with an ungracious slop. "Second, that busted Mercedes sounds very handy. It gave Jack the perfect excuse to take a car he could carry a corpse in . . . although I suppose the laundry cart was just luckily available. He probably just planned to wrap the body in a blanket."

I held up three fingers. "Third, Jack was not entirely happy with our conversation last week. He would have been a logical person to hide Grace in my garage . . ."

"But how did he know you were out of town?" Sonny asked.

I shrugged. "It was no secret. Cassie and Lainey knew. Frost's travel agent knew. The dry cleaners. I think I mentioned it to Nacho and Pete. Joe at the Rat knew. Hell, I don't know . . . anybody, everybody . . . plus whoever Mom and Aunt Mae told. That pretty well covers the eastern seaboard. Jack, however, probably didn't know I'd be back so soon."

"Yeah, I see. Well, I'll be interested to see what Jack has left for forensics to turn up in the station wagon. He had all weekend to vacuum and scrub."

I laughed. "He'll miss something, never fear. Well, we'll get out of your hair. Good luck with Jack, whenever he shows up."

"I hope it's fast and simple. Chief Franks and the prosecutor are getting edgy for an arrest. See you later." He gave Fargo an ear tousle and a tired smile as he turned back to his blackboards.

Chapter 25

My watch said noon. Time for all good workers to break for lunch. I didn't have to tell Fargo, he had already pointed us toward the Wharf Rat. We pushed and edged our way down the crowded sidewalk. We dodged around a large family group, only to bump into the back of a slowly moving woman ahead of us. I muttered an insincere, "Sorry," and received a good-humored, "Oh, you're forgiven, Alex," in return.

I looked up to face Lillian Sanhope, laden with shopping bags and looking pallid and tired through her perfect makeup.

"Well, hello," I said. "You seem a bit burdened. Let me carry something. We seem headed the same way."

She thanked me and handed over a shopping bag and an explanation. "I hope this doesn't look uncaring—my doing a bit of shopping—but I just had to get out of that house for a few hours. I walked all the way down here, but now walking back seems beyond me. I think I'd better call Richard and have him come get me."

"Sounds good to me, and I can well understand your need to get out in the world for a while." We were walking slowly on as we talked. "And I must tell you how distressed I was by Ms. Sanhope's death . . . and the manner of it. I didn't know her well, but I . . . I *liked* her."

Lillian smiled. "She liked you, too. She mentioned you several times, said she liked your spirit."

I was strangely moved and had to clear my throat as I spoke. "Look, we're almost at the Wharf Rat. Fargo and I were going to have a bite to eat. Can I buy you something cold while you wait for Richard? You really do look a bit wiped out."

"What a nice idea! I think I'll join you for a bite if I may. Breakfast was early and small."

"Great. Oh, I don't know where my mind has been! I should have told you right away. Jack has showed up safe and sound in your Boston house. Richard just called my brother." I began tying Fargo to his familiar anchor.

"*Boston!* What on earth is he doing in Boston?" She didn't look happy.

I told her what I knew and left her at the phone booth, calling her husband as I went in to get Fargo's sliced chicken and water.

A few minutes later, we had a table and Lillian had ordered a Caesar salad with seared scallops and a glass of iced tea. Feeling I should perhaps forego my plebian pastrami and fries, I had duplicated her order, except for a beer.

Lillian sipped her tea and settled back in her chair with a sigh. "This was a wonderful idea, Alex. I thank you. I've just been unbelievably stressed, I guess. I'm so glad Jack is all right. Richard and I were getting frantic that something awful had happened to him, too."

A second reminder of my callousness. "I'm glad he's safe. At least that's one thing off your mind."

"Yes. And Lord knows there are plenty of things *on* my mind lately." She looked longingly at my cigarettes and I pushed the pack toward her, but she shook her head.

"You know," she sighed heavily, "this has been a terrible spring. The whole family has been at sixes and sevens. And now, finally, when everything was going to be just fine, all settled and friendly again . . . Grace had to go and get herself killed. And she was so excited and happy! And no one knew but me, which is so sad. She wanted to tell them herself, wanted it to be a real occasion."

I was totally confused, but not too confused to wolf down a bite of the salad placed before me and wash it down with some beer. Then to complete the interruption of Lillian's already disjointed monologue, a wave of beer and garlic fumes enveloped the table and Harmon stood before us.

"How do, ladies," his raspy greeting strengthened the aroma.

"Hello, Harmon," I replied. "This is Mrs. Sanhope. Lillian, Harmon Killingsworth."

"Yes, I know." He nodded. "Alex, I need to see you when you finish your meal. It's really important."

"Okay. I'll catch you before I leave."

"Don't forget." He started away, then turned back. "Miz Sanhope. My sympathies on yer loss." He gave a strange, formal little bow and left before she could answer.

"He means well," I started to explain, when Lillian raised a hand to stop me.

"I know. Oddly enough, he and Grace were rather good friends. He does little jobs for us once in a while. You know," her eyes glistened slightly," his comment means more to me than a lot of the fancy calls and e-mails we've been getting from the rich and famous who hardly know us."

"I can see how it would. But to get back to what you were saying. What was Grace so excited about?"

"Oh, she told me all about it at lunch last Friday. She told me she'd been awake half the night, thinking about things. Said she realized she'd been running not only the business, but all our lives

. . . and for too long. She said she was really going to bow out and let the younger generation have the world, as she put it."

Lillian waved to a waiter and absently ordered coffee for two when he approached. "She had spent that morning talking to her lawyer and various board members of the company, getting it all set up to turn the business over to Richard. She was late enough coming to that action," Lillian added. "But it was wonderful news, all the same. And she was going to clear up the trouble with Jack. Of course she would pay his tuition, had meant to all along. And if Jack was heart-set on environmental law, so be it. There were many years to worry about Richard's successor."

She stirred milk into her coffee. "Finally, she said she was going to have some fun for herself. She was going to England to see Jack's mother, whom she said she had not treated very well in the past, and then onto France where some old schoolgirl friend still raised racehorses. She said she had never met a real live racehorse, and might even buy one herself. Who knew? Oh, Alex, she was so *happy!* She was like a girl!" The tears spilled over.

I took her hand. "I'm sorry. So sorry. No wonder you've been so upset. Her timing was really tragic, wasn't it?"

"Oh, it gets worse." She dabbed at her eyes with a tissue. "She made me promise not to say a word to Richard or Jack. She wanted to tell them herself. She had her little speech all planned for Monday night when we would be together for dinner. Naturally, I agreed, but now they'll never hear it from her. Most of it will happen, but it won't be the same."

She reached up and unconsciously touched the pearls at her neck. "Grace nearly always wore a gold locket Peter had given her. It held two photos, one of her as a young woman and one of Peter with their baby girl who died. She had taken those out and put them in an album. Now the locket held a picture of Francesca and Richard with Jack as a toddler. The other side was empty, waiting for a photo of Jack's baby. She said it was part of 'updating' her life."

I sipped my coffee and lit a cigarette. "Well, Lillian, at least you knew her wishes and plans and how happy she was. Fortunately you can pass that news along to the others. At least they'll know her last day was a happy one."

She nodded, still teary-eyed. I took a plunge. "Lillian, speaking of babies . . . there was a rumor that you'd be going up to that fancy maternity hospital along with Maureen in the fall, that somehow the record would indicate that her baby was stillborn and that you had a healthy child the same night. In other words, adoption wouldn't be necessary. Would you continue with that plan, now that Grace is gone?"

Lillian's eyes looked like saucers. "Are you crazy? Where the hell did you get that idea?" She was furious. "That would be morally and legally outrageous! I can't imagine any hospital allowing it even if we were so brazen as to suggest it! And to tell Maureen her baby died? Such cruelty! It's monstrous and completely untrue. Who made that up?"

I was getting a little angry, too. At myself for listening to Trish and Cindy's wicked-witch fairy tales. "It doesn't matter, Lillian. Lots of crazy things come up in a murder investigation," I quibbled. "I had to ask. I apologize. Forget I ever said it. But let me ask one other question that may be touchy. Do you think Maureen will go through with this adoption as planned?"

Lillian's light blue eyes had calmed and she smiled slightly. "You think she may try to pull a fast one? I doubt it. I believe Grace's lawyer 'counseled' her about the difficulties that would cause her. Then, too, she pretty much got what she asked for. No, she won't scarper." She actually twinkled. "Alex, if I tell you a secret, will you keep it absolutely?"

"If it has no bearing on this murder, yes."

"Okay. As Jack may have told you, Richard and I haven't been able to have a baby. We have tried absolutely every avenue. I seem to be all right, but Richard has a low sperm count. God, don't *ever* tell that to anyone, he'd kill me. Well, we finally just gave up. You can imagine, we were heartbroken. Actually, Richard's count isn't all *that* low. Technically, we *could* produce a child. Maybe giving up was a very good thing and we both just kind of relaxed or something, for I missed a period three weeks ago. It's awfully early but I *think* I may be pregnant. I haven't even seen a doctor yet. Oh, and I haven't told Richard, I don't want to disappoint him if it's another failure. But I just *feel* that I am."

She looked as if she could levitate and fly around the room. I could feel my own face split into a wide grin. "Hey, that's great! How marvelous for you to have some *good* news right about now! I'll cross my fingers for you."

I did so, and she reached across the table and grasped my hand. "Thanks, Alex. I really appreciate that. My only regret is that I didn't tell Grace."

"Lillian," I paused and then managed to ask, "now that you are, we hope, pregnant, will you still adopt the other baby?"

"Sure! It's Jack's baby. It needs a loving family, like any child. Maybe it will be like raising puppies. Two won't be much more trouble than one." We both laughed, and I guessed that with enough nannies and maids, maybe that was true.

She glanced at her watch. "Oh, my God, Richard will be parked out front in someone's yard waiting for me! He'll be seething!" She yanked some bills from her wallet and put them on the table. "I must run. Forgive me."

I sipped my coffee and smiled as I watched Lillian hurry out. These Sanhope women indeed had charm. Which was more than I could say for the dusty figure now seating itself at my table.

"Hi, again, Harmon. What's up?"

"Sonny's been so busy I can't reach him," Harmon explained. "But I seen somethin' really important last Friday afternoon. I seen th' killer leavin' the Sanhope place."

"Really?" One didn't get too excited with statements like this from Harmon.

"Yup. I'd been out to the beach, seein' what the morning rain stirred

169

up." I understood this. Harmon combed the local beaches and sold any interesting flotsam—driftwood, lobster markers, even firewood.

"I was comin' down Bradford when I saw this little blue car parked at the foot of Sanhope's driveway. A feller was walking down the drive, carrying a case."

"What kind of case?" I asked.

"Hard to say. It was smaller than a suitcase, but kinda fat. And bigger than them apache cases. It were black leather."

I bent over my coffee cup to hide my smile. "Uh-huh. What did this man look like?"

"He was maybe thirty-five or forty, kind of average, you know. Oh, he wore glasses and a kinda light blue suit. I noticed it were the same as the car, like he was color-coronated."

"Right. What made you think the car was his?"

Harmon tipped up his beer bottle and leaned back expansively. "Well, now, Alex, you know I ain't a stranger to crime. So I just casually pulled over and stopped and got out like I was checking something under th' hood."

Given the condition of his truck, no one would be suspicious of that move, I thought. Harmon continued, "The man got in the car and drove away. Here's his plate number." He handed me a smudged scrap of paper with a Massachusetts license number carefully printed.

"Good for you! Harmon, they should give you a badge! This really could be important, and I'll make sure it gets through to Sonny!" I turned. "Waiter! Bring this man a nice, cold beer."

"Thanks, Alex. Y'see I figure it was this way. This feller in the blue suit was a drug dealer, of course, and he'd been there making a sale. Probably with the cook, never did like that woman. Now, accidentally, Miz Sanhope walks out and sees what's going on and they kill her. And just to make the p'lice look bad, the cook hides the body in your garage."

"Gotcha." I nodded. It made about as much sense as anything else. And just by the law of probabilities, one of these days

Harmon was going to spot a real drug dealer. "I'll get right on this and let you know what happens."

On the way to pick up the car downtown, Fargo and I stopped by the police station. Sonny was out, but Nacho ran the plate number for me. It came back as a blue Saturn registered to a William Whitmire in Eastham. Thanking her, I left and on a whim, decided to go say hello to Mr. Whitmire.

Traffic was moving, but not very fast, and I had ample time to wonder whom I was on my way to see. The "case" Whitmire had been carrying sounded like one of those old satchels doctors used to carry on house calls . . . I'd seen old Doc Marsten's many times as he made his way around Ptown's ill and injured, surely the last doctor standing who made such visits.

But maybe you could get a doctor to come out if you had lots of the ready . . . although bringing one all the way from Eastham seemed a little inefficient if the patient were badly injured. Why would you need to call a doctor from far away with a clinic nearby and EMTs available for emergencies? Well, I supposed, if you wanted the treatment kept secret, it could be very handy.

Suppose Grace did not die right away and someone found her? Or maybe it was even a terrible accident. Could Whitmire be a friend who was a brain surgeon? Or even someone on their payroll who would keep his visit quiet? Of course, one always got back to the damned laundry cart. But first things first. We had arrived.

The small house was set back from the road, with generous flower beds that raised my envy level with every step. We reached the door and I rang a bell. A man about my age answered.

"Mr. Whitmire?"

"No." He smiled. "Just a moment." He turned and called, "Billy! A visitor."

A slightly older man appeared and identified himself as Bill Whitmire. I showed him my ID and asked to come in.

171

We went into a pleasant living room, sat down, and both men looked at Fargo quizzically. He sat beside me as he always did in a strange place, looking benignly bored. Oddly, most people thought he looked protective and ready to charge. Personally, I think he was just wondering where he was and when he could leave.

"As you probably know, Grace Sanhope was murdered last Friday in Provincetown. We are just checking out some details." Okay, so I made it sound like I was working for the cops. "Since you were there around five p.m. that day, we'd like to know why, and if you saw anything unusual."

"Good God!" Whitmire looked shocked. "I heard something on TV, but I never made the connection. Yes, I was there . . . got there about three thirty and finished up, I'd guess, shortly after five."

"Finished what?" I asked.

"Oh. Tuning the piano."

Tuning the piano. Of all the jobs in the world, piano tuner may be the one I would have thought of last. Whitmire's companion, who had been introduced merely as Walter, took pity on me. "How about something to drink? Maybe a beer, or if you're on duty . . ." He let it trail.

"A beer would be really welcome."

Whitmire continued his account. "Part-time piano tuner. I'm music director at the middle school and do piano tuning in the summer. It keeps me as busy as I want to be. Anyway, I didn't see anything strange at Sanhopes. The maid let me in and kind of fussed around the room most of the time I was there. Making sure I didn't steal anything, I guess."

"How come you parked on the street?" I nodded my thanks to Walter and accepted a beer and glass from the tray.

"Oh, yeah. I started up the drive in the car, but a big old station wagon was at the top, starting down, so I just backed out and parked. Walked up."

"Did you see who was in the wagon?" The beer tasted marvelously cold.

"Some young man. He waved thanks. I really didn't get a look at him."

"Hah," said Walter.

"Well," Billy then admitted, grinning, "he was dark with curly hair and had on a blue polo shirt."

I made a note of the shirt, grinning myself. "Did you see Mrs. Sanhope?"

"I think so. In the house, I mean, not the car. You see, when I finish tuning an instrument, I always play a piece or so to make sure it sounds as good being played as with individual notes being struck. I'd just finished a couple of short Chopin *etudes* when there was applause. I turned around and there was this elderly lady, clapping. She said it sounded great and that she would enjoy the piano again herself although her fingers weren't so limber anymore. She said that her grandsons both played better than she and would be pleased it was back in tune. Then she handed me a check and I thanked her and left."

"Did you by any chance notice if the wagon had returned when you left?"

"No, I don't think it had. There was a three- or four-car garage, I recall. Doors open. But the only car I saw was a little tan one, an old Civic I think." That was the cook's, I knew.

Then he asked if I knew Jeanne Peres, adding that he took care of her piano. I said she was my mother, and conversation turned away from murders. By the time I left, they had made friends with Fargo. And it turned out they knew Lainey and Cassie well, so we agreed to make a date with them to go to the Poly-Cotton Club next weekend. At least the drive had been worth it.

Chapter 26

Or I guessed it had been worth it. Traffic had gotten heavier and slower. I knew there was not a damn thing I could do to speed it up, so I tried to think of pleasant things.

Lillian Sanhope's news was good, assuming she was correct about being pregnant. I smiled. Perhaps at a later date she would give me permission to mention her condition to Trish and Cindy. It would be fun to ask them if they ever heard of a woman "giving birth" in December and then again in April.

I hoped Lillian was being truthful about Grace's last day. I wished she had lived long enough to buy her racehorse. I'd have bet on it to win, hands down.

Pleasant thoughts completed, I wondered if I should go to the cottage or the house. I had to go home sometime. Today was as good as any, but that brought up the matter of dinner. Sighing, I turned off Route 6 and went over to Bradford and my favorite little store. I picked up half a roasted turkey breast and two sweet potatoes for the micro and some frozen spinach. I knew you were supposed to have yellow veggies and also dark green ones . . . together? Well, I was on the safe side. I grabbed a melon for dessert, knowing there was ice cream in the freezer. Oh, yes, milk. Gosh, I was getting to be quite the little homemaker!

Preening myself, I drove home and was fine until I made the turn into the driveway. I started to shake and Fargo gave me a concerned look. Obviously he'd forgotten all of yesterday's trauma. Well, I could do that, too, dammit! I parked in the driveway—garage tomorrow, maybe—and got out the groceries. I walked nonchalantly to the back door, unlocked it, and we went in.

Fargo made his usual tour of every room, whuffling and sniffing for any signs of invasion during our absence. Fortunately, there were none. By the time I had opened windows, put away groceries and given Fargo fresh water I was pretty much back to normal and called Cindy to tell her I was in residence. She was delighted and volunteered to pick up dinner. I was delighted to tell her it wouldn't be necessary.

Fargo and I repaired to the backyard for a check on the garden and a brief game with the hose. I popped the Bud I had taken out with me, lit cigarette number four—I think—and settled into a chair. The Baroness Peres and her trusty hound were back at the manor and all was well.

Cindy came through the door, petted Fargo, poured herself a glass of wine, unbuttoned her blouse and threw it on the floor. Taking a few steps toward the hall, she removed her bra and tossed it to the floor. A couple of steps farther and her skirt followed suit. I sat staring. Was this my neatnik Cindy?

"I'm making it easy for you to follow my trail," she explained. "And you had better not get lost." She kicked off her panties and ran for the bedroom. I was now in hot pursuit, adding my spoor to hers.

I did not get lost and we fell across the bed, laughing. We

kissed, and laughed some more. We murmured endearments and muttered profanities and then everything came into that perfect focus that was just us. Out there somewhere together. Beyond place, time, thought. Just . . . together.

We wandered around the kitchen, ineffectually putting dinner together, pausing for quick kisses and pats, laughing as Fargo pushed between us to claim his share of the affection. I was not thrilled when a movement outside the window showed Sonny trudging up the walkway to the back door. He did not look happy himself.

So my opening words were, "May I assume a beer is in order?"

"I'd rather have a bourbon if you've got any."

I nodded toward the dining room. "It's in the cabinet. Help yourself." I heard the bottle gurgle . . . and gurgle again, and Sonny came back with a rocks glass nearly filled with liquor. He plopped in a couple of ice cubes and then plopped himself at the kitchen table.

I saw Cindy's eyebrows rise slightly, and she asked, "Will you have a little dinner with us?"

"No, thanks, I'll have something later at home. You two go ahead and eat. I just figured I'd let you know, the plot thickens."

Cindy looked at me and I gave a slight shake of the head. I wanted a leisurely intimate dinner with her, not one gulped down while Sonny talked and probably picked bites off my plate. A brief smile and nod showed me she read me and agreed. She poured us both a glass of wine and made a threesome at the table.

"What's up?" I asked.

"Well, Jack Sanhope is looking less and less like the killer."

"Oh?"

"Yep. We have the old station wagon. Jack was either too smart or too dumb to try to clean it up. Forensics says there was everything in it but mud from the Mississippi River. They made a cursory inspection . . . more detailed later." He took a gulp from his drink that would have choked me.

"What turned up?" I sipped my wine delicately, and Cindy laughed.

"No blood anywhere that they found so far. Fibers all over the place, which doesn't mean much, even if some of them belong to the dress Grace was wearing. They could easily have gotten there some other time when she had on the same dress. Some coarse cotton fibers that could be from the laundry cart, or could be from some dropcloths the handyman had brought over to use in a bathroom he's going to paint." Sonny reached in my shirt pocket for cigarettes, and actually remembered to offer me one.

"That's all kind of iffy, isn't it?" Cindy spread her fingers and tilted her hand back and forth. "Could be yes, could be no."

"Absolutely," Sonny agreed, "But there's more. Jack thinks the waitress in the café in Buzzard's Bay will remember him. He says there was some conversation about his not feeling well and she acted 'very motherly' toward him. Then later, when he got to the house in Boston, he called the girl who was giving the party in Sag Harbor and told her he would not be coming. The call will show on their bill, assuming he made it. He says it would have been around seven thirty or eight o'clock. We will check all this out, naturally, but I imagine it's true."

"Well," I said, "I can add a little weight to Jack's innocence, I think." I told them of running into Lillian and our luncheon together, carefully avoiding the topic of pregnancy. Then I added Harmon's information and my follow-up visit to the piano tuner. "Please remember to compliment Harmon," I reminded Sonny. "He actually did come up with some worthwhile information. We know Grace was alive and well for at least a couple of hours after Jack left. I really can't say I'm sorry," I said. Sonny glared and I raised my hands. "Don't shoot. I know you need an arrest, but I kinda like Jack. You sure it couldn't be the cook? Harmon can't stand her," I added.

"Now *there's* a recommendation if I ever heard one!" Sonny

walked into the dining room to freshen his drink. He was putting away an unusual amount of liquor. I got up and explored the refrigerator. Locating a chunk of blue cheese, I put it on a plate with crackers and placed it convenient to Sonny's reach.

He returned to the table. "That's about as good as Captain Anders' idea. He says it's a transient thief."

"Anders always thinks it's a transient thief. He probably thinks Jack Ruby was a transient thief after Oswald's Timex."

Cindy shook her head. "I think Aunt Mae was right the other night. It was someone who knew her well and, believe it or not, respected her or cared for her in some way. Leaving her wedding ring and that locket was a definite clue. Well . . . I mean, that's how it looks to me." She looked down, embarrassed. "You two know more than I."

Sonny patted her hand and nodded. "You make a good point. You know, Lillian's jewelry wasn't touched, nor were a lot of valuable antiques, nor the TVs and such. Almost as if the killer had a purely personal grudge. Of course, he/she could simply have run out of time. Thought he heard a car or something."

"Maybe we shouldn't blow Anders off," I laughed. "You're running out of suspects." I lit cigarette seven and mentally gave my wrist a resounding slap.

"No-oo," Sonny said slowly. "Actually, I've now got one too many. Friday afternoon seems to have been a very popular time with the damned clinic. I think half of Ptown must have been there. And driving vehicles that could have carried that laundry cart. You're not going to be happy about this, Alex."

"What do you mean?"

"I knew I'd be tied up with Sanhopes all afternoon, so I sent Mitch to chase down Mary Sloan and Maureen Delaney and have a little chat."

"Oh, God."

"Oh, yeah." He gave a tired smile. "In a nutshell, here's what he learned. Mary had driven a phone company truck on a repair call to . . . yep . . . the clinic. There she spent most of the afternoon on some intermittent problem with the fax machines, that took her forever to locate, though I guess it was simple enough once she pinpointed it. And to slow her progress even more, she was coming down with some stomach virus. Cramps, dashes to the bathroom, etc. She finally finished up at nearly six o'clock. I don't know why she didn't call in sick and have them send a relief person."

"Because," I sighed heavily, "Mary wouldn't admit there was something she couldn't finish, even if she broke her leg." I wished I hadn't said that. It triggered a shrewd look from Sonny.

"Hmmm. Anyway, Maureen was *also* at the clinic, for a scheduled checkup, driving there in Mary's SUV after she got off work. On her way out, she ran into Mary, who told her she was feeling like hell and would be home as soon as she could finish up, return the company truck to the office and walk the several blocks to her house. Maureen was worried and waited for Mary to finish the repairs, so she could follow her in the SUV and drive her home after she turned in the truck."

I spread some cheese on a cracker and asked, "Did Mary have to sign the truck in at the phone company?"

"Yep. Logged in at six-ten p.m. So their stories add up. And, just as an underscore, Pete Santos was at the clinic visiting Juvenal, who's there with that pin in his ankle, clumsy oaf. Anyway, Pete saw the two women talking on the delivery ramp near Mary's truck about six. He thinks he may have noticed that laundry cart nearby, but isn't sure."

I took a sip of my wine and could almost feel it splash into my empty stomach. "Well, at least he ought to feel better, with Jack looking more and more angelic. I ran into Pete early today, and I think he's mad at me forever."

Sonny shrugged. "I wouldn't worry. He's been indulging himself in a first-class guilt trip. He's going on vacation Saturday to Portugal to see some relatives and go on to Spain and somewhere else, and he's been feeling guilty about leaving, with his family still mourning Grace's death, and feeling guilty about leaving us short-handed, with Juvenal out with a busted ankle. He got mad at me when I told him *not* to rearrange his plans and blew up at Jeanine when she said Jack's problems weren't Pete's problems. He'll get over it. He's just not himself right now."

"Sounds as if he needs the time off," Cindy put in, nibbling a cracker. Times were indeed desperate if Cindy was noshing.

"He does. He's been working hard. Anyway, to complete my sad tale, our two lady friends got home six twentyish. Maureen got Mary into bed with a bottle of Pepto-Bismol and a cup of tea. Then she got herself some dinner and went in the living room to watch TV. About seven thirty she went in to check on Mary and found her sound asleep. She figured sleep was good for her and quietly left the room. But Maureen was bored, it was Friday night, and what the hell? She showered and went out around eight to look up her friends at the Bitter End, returned home around eleven thirty, found Mary still asleep and went to bed herself." He tipped back in the chair. I hated when he did that.

"What was Mary doing all this time?"

"Sleeping, she says. She awoke around one, felt hungry and got up to make some toast. Maureen was asleep in her room at that time. Are you beginning to see a picture here?"

"I'm seeing that Heloise and Abelard are not sharing a bedroom. And you missed the third and fourth possibilities," Cindy added. "That only one of them is lying, and *she* committed the murder."

Sonny gave an irritable growl. I laughed. He growled again.

"Well, actually, I'm seeing a double exposure," I said placatingly. "One is that they are both telling the truth and are innocent. The second is that they are both lying, and conspired to kill Grace. And, neither Mary nor Maureen are in a good mood when it comes to me. I think I'm right up there with Grace." I told them of my last encounter with the twosome.

"Right!" Sonny thumped the chair back onto all four legs and stood up. "Now all I have to do is pick a number between one and five."

"Four," I corrected.

"No, five. Don't forget the transient thief." He giggled and placed a hand on each of our heads in blessing as he left. "Sorry I screwed up your dinner."

And that he had done. The potatoes were cold, the spinach was soggy, the turkey breast was dry. A refill of wine put Cindy to sleep. I was stuck with the kitchen cleanup. Fargo treed a cat, and I had to drag him barking hysterically into the house.

I opened a beer and turned on the TV. The channel was set on Animal Planet and I left it there, too discouraged to check the program guide. *Crocodile Hunter* was on, so I watched him flop into mud holes and wrestle alligators for no apparent reason with no apparent results. I knew sort of how he felt.

Chapter 27

Fargo and I snuck off to the beach about six on Wednesday morning. I think Ptown is getting like New York. We never sleep. And the tourists are never quite out of sight. This morning a family of four was having breakfast on the tailgate of their station wagon. Three surf fishermen were packing up their gear and divvying up their catch. A pair of lovers seemingly welded together came slowly up the beach. A lone middle-aged woman was building a quite lovely sandcastle while her Boston terrier explored treasures caught along the high tide line.

Fargo went over to say hello, and the terrier emitted one loud, shrill, teeth-bared yelp. Fear? Challenge? Overactive thyroid? Fargo looked at him as if he just exited a flying saucer and walked on. The woman and I laughed, the terrier looked insulted, and the day looked to be a good one.

When we got home Cindy was having her grapefruit and cold cereal breakfast. I explored the refrigerator and found that I, too, would be having a healthy morning meal. For the moment I settled for coffee and the first cigarette. I told Cindy of our meeting with the Boston terrier, and she smiled. "I like that breed."

"They're cute," I agreed. "But I've heard they're manipulative."

"I've never seen a dog that isn't," she laughed. "What's on your schedule, my early riser?"

"Fargo's not. Manipulative. Not a lot on my sked. I've got to go to the store. The refrigerator looks neglected, and we're low on Fargo's food." Hearing his name and the word *food* in the same sentence, he immediately nudged Cindy's arm and looked meaningfully at her cereal bowl.

"You're very large for a Boston terrier, but apparently you are one." She set her cereal bowl on the floor, as I continued my calendar.

"I've got to write a report on the southern trip for Frost. It's going to read like a script for *Saturday Night Live*. He's going to just love it. The yard needs some work. You know, puttery stuff. Why?"

"I'm just glad puttery is on your agenda. I think you need it. A tiring trip with a ghastly homecoming, puttery is good." She picked up the now-empty bowl and put it and her other dishes in the dishwasher. "I, on the other hand, must go and slave for the betterment of mankind. See you tonight."

"I'll be here."

Wednesday puttered to a close and must indeed have been what I needed. I slept well and awoke early Thursday, refreshed and ready to go. So we went to the beach, Fargo and I, where a cloudy sky and choppy sea made it entirely ours. Returning home, we found that Cindy had left for work, so I munched a scone without guilt, but then felt I should do at least a few indoor chores before moving on to the outdoor ones. Funny, outdoor work equaled fun. Indoor work equaled drudgery.

Speeding through the indoor tasks, I moved outside and spread around some dehydrated, deodorized cow manure, thinking that was a good, farmer-like move in case it rained. I hoped it wouldn't. Today was Grace Sanhope's funeral at noon in Boston, and funerals were bad enough without slogging through rain to get to them. The sky continued to darken, but my mood lifted yet again when I discovered that two of my tomatoes were turning pink. And then I spotted a tiny green pepper about the size of a cherry. My day was complete.

Well, not quite complete. Fargo sprang up from his favorite spot under the tree and trotted in his business-like fashion toward the driveway. I followed him and found a young deliveryman about to park a large box on the back steps.

"Alex Peres?" He sniffed.

"That's right."

"Roses for you." He sniffed again. Maybe he had allergies and was in the wrong business. "Please sign here. Sorry to have interrupted your gardening."

I signed. He left. I took the box inside and opened it to find a dozen long-stem red roses . . . lovely! I put the flowers in a tall white vase and left them temporarily on the counter, while I poured coffee and sat down to read the card.

"Safe at last and mainly thanks to your good advice! Now you all be sure to come see us any time, you hear? Love, May and Julie."

Well, well, so the master criminals apparently weren't serving five-to-eight. I wished they had been a little more specific, but maybe a letter would follow. Maybe I wouldn't wait. I picked up the phone and called Trish.

"I just got a dozen roses from May Malik and her lover. The card says they are *safe at last* but not much more. Did you hear anything?"

"We did indeed. Early this morning John got a call from their attorney. They followed your advice and all three went to see this Sheriff Laurence over in Haute Bayou, told him the whole story. He called up a judge he fishes with plus the county court clerk.

They went into a confab. Then the judge gave May a slap on the wrist with a four thousand dollar fine, which he said would buy Laurence new air conditioners for his headquarters. Then he gave Julie a kiss on the fingertips with a five hundred dollar fine which he said would paint their little juvenile detention quarters. The tame clerk issued a Replacement of Lost Death Certificate and they all went to dinner. I understand several cases of Kentucky's finest also changed hands."

I could not believe it. "Is that all legal? What about New Orleans?"

Trish giggled happily. "It is if a judge says it is. There was no New Orleans. So now, the Albion brothers get their garage, May gets her money, and justice triumphs once again." She giggled again. "And John just got an enormous bouquet of truly appalling pink gladioli. His office looks like he won the Derby . . . or died."

"Damn! These southerners can certainly be efficient when it's called for!"

"Honey, doncha know! Sorry to run, but I've got a client waiting. I'll let you know if I hear more details. Bye."

So! There was only one thing to do in a case like this. Fargo and I saddled up and headed for an early lunch at the Rat.

I anchored Fargo to his anchor and brought him some water and pulled up at the bar for some liquid refreshment of my own. Joe whisked the bar cloth in front of me and leaned down. "Yes, ma'am, your pleasure?" His nose wiggled and he sniffed. Was it ragweed season or something?

"A Bud, please."

He brought it up from the ice chest below without even looking down, and placed it in front of me with a glass. "So, Alex, how's your garden coming?"

I was explaining in vivid detail about the bounteous harvest I anticipated, when I noticed the regulars from the front table, led by Harmon, were gathering at the bar, looking at the TV. I looked up myself and exclaimed, "Oh! It's Amazin' Grace." It must have been a slow news day, and/or Grace must have been a bigger fish than I realized. She was getting full local cable TV coverage for her funeral, after which there would be a private interment.

The imposing, elegant Episcopal church was packed with imposing, elegant people, all looking properly solemn and important, with the exception of the small group of Provincetown relatives. They sat together in forward pews, looking unhappy and ill at ease in their seldom worn suits and ties and obviously bought-for-the-occasion dresses and hats.

All except Pete Santos, that is. Pete was with Jack Sanhope, and looking as if he'd just stepped from the pages of *GQ* in his well-tailored gray suit with a muted blue shirt, matching blue and black regimental striped tie and black wingtips. As they came down the aisle behind Richard and Lillian, Pete was close beside Jack and beside him as they knelt briefly in front of the coffin. Jack sagged a little, and Pete's arm was immediately around his shoulders. It occurred to me that maybe there was a little more love between Jack and his grandmother than either had ever vocalized. Or maybe Jack was feeling guilty, after all. The Sanhopes and Pete took their seats in the family pew and the service began.

It was the traditional Episcopalian service, direct from the Book of Prayer with Cranmer's ever-beautiful application of our language—mercifully brief, yet eloquent, moving, comforting. The final hymn was sung and it was over. The bishop and the vicar of the cathedral led the exit, followed by the crucifer, then Richard, Lillian—looking sad and tired, Francesca, her husband and daughters and, finally, Jack, white and visibly shaken, with Pete just inches away.

The two churchmen and the three Sanhopes stood on the steps, greeting many of the congregants. Pete, bless him, stood quietly just behind Jack. Right there, if he were needed. The TV announcer came on a few seconds later, and the newscast went on to other coverage.

"Some send-off, wasn't it?" I turned. I had not even noticed Sonny come in.

He ordered a Bud for himself and me, with a sniff. I looked at him sharply. Was he actually crying? No. "Are you coming down with a cold?"

"I sure hope not." He took a swallow of beer and nodded toward the TV. "What did you think of it?"

"Beautiful. And speaking of beautiful, did you notice Pete? That suit must have set him back a good three weeks pay."

"Probably. I imagine Jack was glad to have him there. Jack looked pretty done in. And I'm not surprised at Pete's wardrobe. He's got high aspirations, our Pete."

"What's he going to do? Skip over Mitch and you and Anders and take over as chief? I don't imagine even Chief Franks wears Italian silk suits and Cole-Haan shoes."

"Oh, I don't imagine our Mr. Santos expects leading off the Memorial Day parade in dress uniform to be the high point of his year. I think his plans are to stay here another year or so. Then one of the Sanhopes—Richard, now, I guess—will lead him into a good job with some high class company in the security business, where he will keep Boston and its environs safe from terrorists." He sounded a little bitter, and I recalled a time when Sonny's own menu had read something like that.

"Ah," I said, "I wonder when he'll change his name?"

"The day before it's painted on his office door. Right now I think his driver's license still reads Santos."

"Right." I raised my voice a bit. The regulars were arguing whether one was cremated in or out of one's casket. Harmon was in favor of "in," as being more "honorific to the diseased." Did it for me.

"When does Pete leave for Lisbon?"

"Tomorrow evening. Well, to Amsterdam, anyway."

"Why is he going to Amsterdam to get to Lisbon?"

"He's flying Icelandic."

I occasionally felt that our mother had been frightened by Abbott and Costello during her pregnancies. "Icelandic what? Why?"

"Icelandic Airways," Sonny explained. "Icelandic Airways has for years been a super cheap flight to Holland. I mean, not even half price of the biggies like Delta and British Airways."

"How can they do that?" Somehow one thought of Icelandic travel to be in longboats with square sails.

"For one thing, you stop in Iceland for a nice time shopping in their duty-free airport. I believe dinner is a fish sandwich and a mug of mead. And they are slow. I believe they still fly the old Ford Tri-motors, but they always get there. You never hear of them crashing."

"You never hear of them at all."

"Don't be condescending. Anyway, he'll spend a couple of days in Amsterdam, which I hear is not at all bad for bachelors, then go on to Madrid and finally to the cousins in Lisbon . . . or somewhere around there." He pointed behind me. "There's a free table. Let's get it, and I'll buy you lunch."

I was surprised and pleased. This was indeed a rare opportunity, and my mind leaped toward an old fashion cocktail followed by clams on the half-shell and steak or a seafood platter, but I decided that would be greedy. When the waiter came, I settled for my standard pastrami and fries, and even switched to iced tea so I wouldn't spend a groggy afternoon.

Sonny bummed a cigarette—something new in life—and then fiddled with the ashtray and fiddled with his silverware and finally got it out. "Uh, by the way, Alex, uh, we've made an arrest in the Sanhope matter."

I had an insane picture of Mitch and Jeanine cuffing Jack as he stood on the church steps. "*Who?*"

"Well, uh, Mary Sloan." Our food came and he began to fiddle with putting various condiments on his hamburger. He was beginning to get on my nerves.

"Why?" I asked. "You don't have any solid—"

"Yes, we do. We have good circumstantial evidence. No crime is ever a hundred percent. There's stuff you don't know. And, uh, Chief Franks and the D.A. ordered me to pick her up."

"Why didn't you just say so?"

"They happen to be right, Alex. Look, the meat thermometer came back with a good thumbprint of Mary's and two fairly good partials. There were some cotton fibers in the back of her SUV that could belong to the laundry cart, although there have been some canvas tool holders in there, too. *And* there was a trace of blood in the back. It was so broken down by the heat, we couldn't run a DNA, but it is human blood. And it could be Grace's."

I pointed a french fry accusingly at Sonny. "It could be. Or it could be Mary's from handling sharp tools and wires. Or Maureen's. Hell, it could even be mine. I was bleeding like crazy after helping her get her boat out of the water last fall. The fibers mean nothing. Even the fingerprints. Couldn't Mary have handled the thermometer in a store or a tag sale or something and then someone else bought it? Or couldn't someone have stolen it from Mary? Does she have one?"

He shrugged and swallowed. "That's kind of odd. Mitch asked her about that the other day and I asked again this morning. Got the same answer. Yes, she had one, though she couldn't remember when she last used it. She thought she remembered seeing it recently . . . within the last week, when she cleaned a utensil drawer. But she couldn't come up with it. With her permission, I helped her look all over the kitchen. No meat thermometer."

"Maybe it's in her garage."

"Why would it be there?"

"That's where mine is. In my garage. I meant to give it and some other stuff to the Girl Guides' jumble sale and forgot. Maybe she did, too."

He stopped spreading mustard on his burger and gave me an expressionless stare. "That's a real possibility. We'll certainly check."

"Really, Sonny, you are so unimaginative. All I mean is, people put things in nutty places for what seems like a good reason at the time. Then they forget."

"I'll look around, okay?" Obviously that was the best I was going to get.

"Okay. And you might look at Maureen for the murder while you're at it. She had access to the weapon . . . and the SUV, while Mary slept off her virus. And she certainly had no love for Grace Sanhope. Can anyone place her at the Bitter End Friday night?"

"Yeah. One of her ex-roommates and the bartender saw her—spoke with her—but both of them think it was around ten. A guy she works with thinks he saw her earlier."

"So, it could be that Maureen saw the laundry cart at the clinic and got inspired. She folds it into the back of the SUV where it won't be readily visible. She takes Mary home and tucks her in, possibly adds a little Sominex to the Pepto and waits awhile till Mary nods off. Maureen goes to Grace's house and finds her in her usual evening pursuit of looking through her telescope." I stopped for a bite of my lunch, and Sonny picked up the tale.

"So," he walked his fingers across the table. "She sneaks up on Grace and stabs her. Or, she confronts her, demands more money, is refused . . . and *then* stabs her. Then she stashes Grace in your garage and goes to the Bitter End. It works, but you have to remember, Maureen already got most of what she wanted from the Sanhopes. Sure, she didn't like any of them and probably really disliked the old lady, but why rock the boat?"

He picked up his condiment-coated burger. "And don't forget, Mary has had a beef with that family literally since the day she was born. Add to that, she hates the way Grace has treated Maureen. She also has a history of violence against Grace. Nope, I think Maureen is just a green herring."

"Red herring."

"Green," he repeated. "She's Irish, get it?"

I changed the subject to the elusive rattle in Cindy's car.

I was in the office, matting some prints to fulfill an order from a gallery up in Eastham, when Fargo scrambled to his feet and trotted toward the back door. Cindy was home. "I'm in the office!" I called.

She came in and I gave her a nice hug, and was headed for a kiss when she pushed me away.

"My God, Alex! Have you been mucking out stables? You smell like Hercules after that Augean thing."

I frowned. "Now, come on! I spread a little stuff on the tomatoes early this morning. Anyway, it's dehydrated and deodorized. Aren't you exaggerating just . . . oh." I suddenly recalled all the sniffles and references to my garden.

"Oh, what?" she asked.

"Nothing."

Chapter 28

We hit the beach bright and early, Fargo and I. The air and the water were deceptively calm, and I was betting on a brisk northeast wind as soon as the sun was fully up. An afternoon rain shower might also be on the agenda. I hoped so. The entire backyard smelled humidly of cow manure. A breeze and some rain might cure that and also cure Cindy of referring to me as Hercules.

Fargo ran ahead, nose to the sand, tracking some imaginary sea monster to its imaginary lair. I sat down on a good-sized tree, washed above the mean high tide line in a storm some months back. I spotted a tiny crab claw in the sand and picked it up. Gently, I turned the perfect little ivory and pink shell in my fingers. That was one that rejoined the food chain without ever reaching maturity. Nature was not sentimental.

That made me think of Amazin' Grace. Certainly she'd had good long innings. No one could say she'd been cut down in her youth, although I hadn't seen any signs of her faltering. Thoughts of Grace took me to thoughts of Mary, probably awake by now and wondering how in God's name she'd ever ended up in a jail cell. Guilty or not.

I thought of Mary's upbringing. Raised by a grandmother who was a widow, uneducated, poor and probably never really happy in her new country. And Mary's mother. Again, an uneducated, naïve woman who would have liked a large and boisterous family, but who literally worked herself to death as a waitress to support herself and her only child. It could not have been a very happy household, although I had heard no undertones of violence as Mary had recounted it to me.

Indeed, Mary's mother and grandmother had meekly accepted the little support the Sanhopes had so ungraciously supplied. Even when Mary had learned the truth upon her mother's death, she hadn't gone running to a lawyer seeking redress. And when Mary *had* sought out the Sanhopes in later years, it had been an attempt to join a family, not to hit them up for money . . . or just hit them, period.

I placed the small crab claw carefully on the bark of the tree and lit a cigarette. Fargo stopped by to check on me, sniffed the claw and looked at me quizzically. Was that pitiful shard the best treasure I could find on this wide beach? I hoped he would not be inspired to bring me a nice dead fish. I patted his bottom and he took that as invitation to lie beside me for a while.

Yes, Mary had attacked Grace, and rather viciously. But she had not attacked for herself, but for Maureen and what she judged, erroneously I thought, to be Maureen's distress over having to give up her baby. I had no doubt Maureen would have married Jack in a heartbeat, and for several reasons that made good sense to her. But marry Mary, *de jure* or *de facto*, and raise a child with her? I thought not. She was nowhere near ready to settle down to that life yet, if she ever would be.

Marry a good-looking young man with endless money, at least in the future, and an *entrée* to upper class social life—yes. A forty-year-old, rather dull woman who climbed phone poles—no. I thought Maureen made a much better choice as a killer than Mary. I just couldn't prove it.

Mary's fingerprints on that damn skewer! That was the real rub. No, not a skewer . . . a meat thermometer. Why had I thought *skewer?*

And then I knew.

Suddenly I heard a man's voice near us. "I thought you couldn't have dogs on the beach."

A woman answered him. "It's always the same. Some people pay no attention to the law!"

Oops! We had lingered too long. The daily beach party of tourists was beginning, and we had become a pumpkin and a large black rat. I snapped Fargo's leash on his collar and we scampered for the car.

Catching my breath after our trot to the car (Fargo seemed to require no such recovery), my first reaction was to phone Sonny. My second was to recall that my cell phone was at home, either on the bureau or in the hamper in the pocket of yesterday's shirt. It was probably as well. My thoughts were scattered. I negotiated the early traffic, reached home and we went in to find Cindy long gone. She had left us a note: *Dearest early birds—Remember, tonight we have dinner with Vance and Charles & go to the Art Ctr. for the string quartet concert. Sorry, Fargo, no doggies on this trip. Love, C.*

I groaned. Poor Fargo, indeed! A little string quartet went a long way with me. It was quite magical, really, after ten minutes it turned into a dentist's drill. And I supposed I'd have to dress. Maybe I'd wear my derby. Maybe I wouldn't. New Orleans was still a sort of tender subject. "Oh, hell!" I said aloud. "You are so lucky, Fargo!"

He answered me by collapsing next to his food bowl and nudging it weakly. "Oh, stop it, you're overacting." But I washed his dish, filled it and gave him fresh water and nuked a cup of leftover coffee for me. Was he *really* manipulative?

Finally settled at the kitchen table, I mentally backtracked to the day I had first visited Mary and Maureen to begin investigating her then-presumed rape. I remembered the iced tea and petit fours set out on the tables, and the colorful array of books added to the normally dull-shaded manuals in the bookcase.

I had commented on the new books, and Mary told me she had just bought a bunch that the library was selling, since people rarely checked them out anymore, and the library needed the space. Maureen, she had added, was a mystery buff, so Mary had simply bought a collection of all the English mysteries the librarian could fit into two plastic bags. I had asked Maureen if she were enjoying them.

She said she had just started one by Ngaio Marsh and would let me know. I was certain the book she had shown me was *Death of a Peer*. I had read a lot of Marsh as a teenager and was pretty sure I remembered the plot.

A crotchety, rich old English lord had no children, so the family mansion and money would go to his younger brother upon his death, but for now it was all his. The younger brother was forty-ish, with a wife and I believe four kids ranging from around twenty down to maybe twelve. They all seemed like airheads and couldn't manage to live within the income the wife had inherited. They were always "borrowing" from the old lord. On this occasion they had invited him and his wife to dinner to "borrow" again because they were being evicted from their flat.

The lord refused and stormed out, saying he would meet his wife downstairs at their car. Everyone heard the creaky old elevator descend. The lord's wife finally got into her coat and rang for the elevator to come up for her. She and some of the younger family members stood in the hall and it creaked back up, still holding the lord. He had been stabbed in the eye with a meat skewer and died shortly thereafter. Younger brother was now Lord Whoozit . . . and very rich. Funny, I couldn't remember who had killed the old guy.

I sipped my rapidly cooling coffee and lit cigarette three. My limit of five per day looked doubtful. I might make it, I told myself, if I didn't have to listen to a string quartet.

If I had the right book and the right plot in mind, I certainly had fine inspiration for Maureen. And the book should be covered with her fingerprints. I wasn't the least concerned that Mary might have read it. She never read anything that wasn't technical.

For once, my not having my cell phone in the car had been a blessing. It would be better not to call Sonny until I was sure I was thinking of the right book and the correct plot. Ordinarily, if I wanted information on a book, I'd just go to the library. But it was the library that had gotten rid of it in the first place. Now what? I hated to drive all the way to Hyannis, and while they might locate a title for me over the phone, I doubted they would scan through it to get the plot . . . that's if *they* still had a copy. What was next? Boston? The British Museum? As my Aunt Mae would say, "Oh, fudge!" That's *not* what I was saying.

Adding to my irritation, the phone picked that moment to ring. Sighing, I answered. "Hello?"

"Hi, Alex, it's Jeanine down at the station. I need to ask you a big favor."

I managed not to scream. "Well, sure Jeanine. If I can I will."

"Well, as you know, we're short-handed as hell down here. Sonny's even out investigating a traffic mishap. Anyway, poor Mary Sloan needs some things from home, and I know I'll never get a lunch break today to get them for her, and Trish is in court all day today. I wondered if you possibly could pick them up?"

I managed not to jump up and down and cheer. I sounded mature, understanding, cooperative. "Why, Jeanine, don't even *think* of giving up any lunchtime you may get. *You bet*, I'll do it for you, you poor dear. Just tell Mary to write out a list. I'll stop by later and pick it up . . . oh, and her keys."

"You're a love, Alex, I owe you big time."

I should have felt guilty, but I didn't.

❧

I pulled into Mary's driveway and grimaced. Her SUV was in the garage and the back door was open. Obviously, Maureen was home. I couldn't just stroll in and start searching her bookcase. I did *not* want a suspicious killer on my hands. The last time that happened all hell had broken loose. Well, I'd figure out something as I went along. I knocked on the door and called a cheery greeting. Maureen came, wearing her uniform shirt and trousers and a big smile.

"Alex! What a nice surprise! Come on in."

I entered and followed her into the living room. Sitting down on the couch, I gave the bookcase a fast glance. I wasn't close enough to read titles. Maureen was looking at me expectantly, and I quickly explained my official errand.

"I'll be glad to give you a hand finding things. Then, unfortunately, I have to go to work. How *is* Mary? They wouldn't let me see her yesterday. I called John Frost and he said maybe tomorrow morning would be best."

"I haven't seen her, either. God, she must be feeling deserted by now. Well, I'll see her in a little while. Jeanine says she seems more confused than anything else."

"I don't doubt it." Maureen settled back on the couch, tilting nearer toward me. "Sure and we both know she's done nothing wrong."

Sure and we both did, but did Maureen know *how* I knew? I hoped not. She leaned over and flicked a piece of lint or something from my shoulder, and let her fingers linger there. I looked at her more closely. She had that sexy boyish appeal that feminine women get when they wear masculine clothes. Damn! She *was* good looking!

I guess I smiled. She bent forward and gently kissed me. All I could see was red hair and big blue eyes. I cleared my throat. "That's lovely, but I think it's probably not a good idea." Actually it seemed like a great idea. What the hell was it with me and homicidal women? I made myself sit up straight and blurted out a question I'd been asking myself for a long time.

"Fess up, Maureen, what's your choice? Men or women?"

"Yes."

"Oh." I drew back, startled. "I see."

"Sure it's no mystery. I enjoy . . . the company . . . of both, assuming they are pleasant and fairly bright." She brushed an errant lock of hair off my forehead.

Determined to keep my wits at least somewhere nearby, I said, "So you found both Jack and Mary . . . enjoyable."

She shrugged. "Jack is not as great as he thinks he is, but he's good. Poor Mary doesn't have a clue."

I held up my hand in a *stop* motion. "I don't need to go there."

"And I don't intend to. All I meant was, Mary is more interested in how she imagines things to be than in how they really are. Take this baby." She pointed at her waist. "She has done everything but knit booties. She had visions of us walking in the park with a dear, sweet babe. I have two younger brothers. I know all about smelly nappies, and spit-up milk running down your neck, and temper tantrums and drippy noses. Mary would have lasted about two hours with a baby."

Mary might not be the only one, I thought. Funny, I had cleaned up after Fargo's puppy accidents and upchucks without a second thought, but Maureen's picture did not appeal to me.

"What Mary needs," she continued, as her arm slid back around my neck, "is someone who *cares* about her. A nice lady to have tea waiting when she comes home tired. Someone to fuss over her and scold her for getting her feet wet. That would mean more to Mary than a weekend with Cleopatra. Trust me, I know. I've seen women like that at home, busy doing good works, weeding a garden, brushing the cat, going for walks. Never quite sharing a bed, maybe, but actually, a very loving couple . . . lots of pats and hugs and back rubs. Mary could never keep up with me for two days. Now you, luv . . ." She kissed me again, thoroughly.

I had an extremely vivid scene of an afternoon's delight . . . followed by months, if not years, of twenty-four hour regret. I stood up. "I really can't do this, Maureen. I can't go this route. I'm sorry."

"A fool is more like it," she snapped and put out her hand. "Do you have a list of what Mary needs? I suppose I'd better help you find the things. It's getting late for me."

I couldn't resist. "It would seem the least you can do, after Mary bought you all those nice books." I gestured toward the wall.

"Yes, that was lovely of her. It's part of what I was talking about before. Being thoughtful of someone."

I handed her my now crumpled list. "How did you enjoy Marsh's *Death of a Peer*?" I asked innocently.

"I thought it was quite muddled, actually. I never did figure out what all those charade things were about." She smoothed the list and ran her eyes down it.

"Oh, yes, I remember that part now. I don't believe I ever figured them out either."

"Well, that makes three of us," she answered absently, reading more carefully now. "Pete didn't get it either."

"Pete?"

"Pete Santos. I'd just finished reading it on a lunch break one day in the park by the bank. He came over to say hello and asked to borrow it. When he returned it the other day, he told Mary to tell me he just didn't get it."

"I didn't know you knew Pete." I wondered what chance poor Pete would have had, if she'd turned her sights on him?

"Oh, sure," she answered. "Jack and I went out with him and his girl a few times. I like him. He certainly stuck with Jack through all this."

"Like you're sticking with Mary?"

Maureen let the list flutter to the floor. "You'll find everything in her bureau or closet, or in the bathroom. I'm late for work." She walked out.

I stood until I heard her pull out of the driveway. Then I located *Death of a Peer* and carefully wrapped it in a piece of newspaper and stuck it in the back of my jeans with my shirt hanging out over it, out of sight just in case she came back for any reason.

As I was rearranging the books on the shelf so the lineup wouldn't show that one was missing, I thought I heard a noise and saw Fargo stand up.

I looked around and had a nanosecond to realize we had all been terribly wrong about who had killed Grace Sanhope.

Chapter 29

I smiled sleepily. Fargo was licking my face with great urgency. I didn't feel like waking up, but obviously he really had to go out. I stirred slightly and felt the rug scrape my other cheek. Why on earth had I decided to nap on the floor? Had I somehow rolled off the couch? The dog whimpered.

"Okay, okay, I'm coming." I tried to sit up and realized I had a terrible headache, with a stiff neck to make it worse. I tried again, and felt nauseous. The smell of the rug wasn't helping. It smelled like kerosene. And the air seemed smoky . . . my God, *fire!*

I dragged myself up by the arm of the chair, dizzy and sick, suddenly realizing I was not at home, but in Mary Sloan's living room. I managed to stand and finally to walk to the living room door. It was closed, but behind it I could hear a roaring sound, and smoke was curling under it. The last I knew, it had been open. Probably the draft from the fire had blown it shut. When I touched it, I winced from the heat. Obviously, we could not get out that way. It felt hot enough to burn through at any moment, and if it did, whatever had been poured on the rug would go up like a Roman candle!

That left the window. By the time I walked to it, I thought my head was literally going to explode. I was having trouble breathing and wanted to throw up. And, of course, the screen was stuck. I was beyond subtlety. I picked up the end table, sending a lamp and some other stuff crashing to the floor, and threw the table through the screen.

"Come on, Fargo, we gotta jump." I grabbed his collar. "You have to *jump*, Fargo, *go!*" He looked up at me, confused.

"All right, sweetheart, I'm sorry. Easy now. It's all right." I petted him for a second and lifted his front paws onto the windowsill. Then I grabbed his back legs and heaved him out the window. He landed off-balance, rolled, jumped up and ran a few feet, limping heavily. At least he was alive. I followed him.

That was the last I knew until I awoke to the smell of petunias and the sight of a big yellow rubber boot near my eye.

A deep voice said, "Okay, Les, we'll carry her away from the house and then get her on the stretcher."

"No," I managed to gasp, "I can walk."

"You sure?" One of the two men in fireman's regalia asked.

"Yeah." They got their hands under my arms and heaved me up, and I tried to say they'd better carry me after all, but I couldn't get the words out, so we "walked" about ten miles down the driveway to the back of an ambulance. They sat me on a wheeled stretcher waiting in the driveway and an EMT shoved an oxygen cone under my nose.

I took a couple of breaths and pulled it away. "Fargo, where is Fargo?"

"Who?" One of the firemen grabbed my wrist. "My God, don't tell me someone is still in there!"

"No. My dog, he's out, but his leg is hurt."

"Oh. Here he is, right beside you. He's okay."

And there he was, shivering, with a worried frown, and holding his right paw an inch off the ground. "He's not okay. I have to get him to the vet. Can you move this ambulance so I can get to my car?" I didn't think I'd mention the dizziness and the slight tendency to see two of everything.

The EMT laughed. "Lady, you are not about to drive a car. You have a lump behind your ear the size of an orange. You aren't going anywhere except the hos-pit-tal. Now please lie down."

"No. Not unless Fargo gets in the ambulance, too, and we drop him at Dr. Victor's on the way." Made sense to me.

"Look." The EMT made a good try at sounding patient and reasonable. "We can't possibly do that. Let me get a cop over here to call the dog warden. He'll take the animal and everything will be fine."

"NO WAY!" I shouted, leaned over and then threw up. "No way," I muttered weakly.

A pleasant-looking woman in her mid-forties sat down beside me. "You're Alex Peres, aren't you?" I managed a small nod. "I'm Ann Cartwright. I know your mother. I live right next door here, and I'll be more than glad to take Fargo to the vet and tell him what happened. We'll get this nice fireman here to carry him to my car and it will all work out."

The nice fireman gave us both a dirty look. "Does he bite?"

"No, but I might if you don't get going. He's in pain."

Ms. Cartwright laughed. The fireman picked up the dog. And away they went, my poor Fargo looking back at me, a great black bundle of misery against the fireman's yellow coat.

"Alex!" It was Jeanine, trotting up the driveway, revolver and radio flapping noisily against her generous hips. "Are you all right?"

"No, she's not," snapped the EMT. "She's got a helluva bump on her head and is probably concussed."

"Then for heaven's sake, get her to the clinic!" Jeanine cried.

The EMT took a deep breath and answered gently. "We've been trying to do just that for about an hour. Perhaps you can help."

"I'll certainly try," Jeanine said earnestly. "But just one or two fast questions . . . ?"

"Oh, no rush," the EMT responded. "It's kind of nice just standing here in the hot sun, watching the firemen put out a blaze."

I realized that the fire was pretty well out, although poor Mary's house was not the attractive little bungalow it had been an hour ago. The smoky smell was awful. Rancid and biting, nothing reminiscent of steaks or hotdogs, but sort of dirty and sticky in my mouth and throat. Jeanine cleared her throat and spoke.

"What happened, Alex? The fire chief says they think an accelerant was used, that this was no accident. Did Maureen do this? How did you and Fargo get stuck in there?" I was surprised to see she had a notebook out. This must be official.

I tried to remember. "No-o-o." My mind felt so fuzzy! "No, Maureen went to work. She didn't do this." I shifted on the stretcher. Something was digging into my back. I reached around and pulled out the book I had put there earlier. I stared at it stupidly, wondering how a book had gotten into the back of my pants. Then it all came back with a rush.

"Where's Sonny?"

"On his way. He was down in Buzzard's Bay, checking on that waitress Jack Sanhope said would remember him."

"Okay." I made a mighty effort to concentrate. "Look, Jeanine, hang onto this book. Be careful, it's evidence and should have Pete's fingerprints on it."

"Yeah? Okay. Pete who?"

"Pete Santos. He's the killer. He's the one who started the fire and knocked me out. When I came to, I could smell charcoal lighter fluid on the rug and most of the house was already ablaze. He tried to kill Fargo and me and either get hold of this book or make sure it burned."

Jeanine gave me a long look. "Alex, sweetie, you've had a terrifying, awful experience. Are you *sure* about all this? I mean, Pete Santos? He's one of *us*, Alex. Maybe somebody looked like him? Or maybe you're a little confused. Maybe you saw him earlier today and—"

"Jeanine." I was exasperated. "I am groggy and shaky, but I am not crazy. This book gave him the whole scenario of how to kill Grace Sanhope. Stupid me, I thought it was Maureen, but it was Pete all along. He needed to get rid of it so no one could ever prove he read it. That way, Maureen would be blamed. Now listen to me, when is Pete leaving for Europe?"

Almost grudgingly, Jeanine answered. "I think he's getting the three forty plane to Boston."

I looked at my watch and saw only a blur. "What time is it?"

"Three thirty-five."

"Oh, God. Okay, call the station. Ask them to try and have the airport hold the flight till you can get some people out there to pick him up."

"Alex . . ."

Jeanine's face was anguished, but I had no time to comfort her. "Dammit, just do it! And if they're already in the air, get security at Logan International to pick him up when they land. He'll be headed for Icelandic Airways. Oh, and tell them to watch his luggage carefully. I think he's got a king's ransom of jewelry in it. Now, *call!* If I'm wrong I'll take the heat and I'll apologize on my knees stark naked to Pete Santos at high noon in the middle of town."

She turned away, taking her radio out of its little hammock. One of the EMTs walked to the end of the stretcher. "Santos? Pete Santos? You must have really landed on your head! I went to school with him!"

"Yeah, well, that may account for it. You think we could go now?" My vision must have been getting worse. I could have sworn I saw him make a fist.

I opened my eyes to see Cindy, my mother and Aunt Mae sitting on three hard-looking chairs, and Sonny leaning against the windowsill. Everyone stood, as if I had lifted a baton. They all came to the side of my bed, where Mother kissed the top of my head lightly, caressed my cheek and told me I was going to be just fine. Aunt Mae kissed my cheek, patted my hand and told me I'd be like new in no time. Cindy kissed me lightly on the mouth, patted my leg and told me I'd be home before I knew it.

Sonny held a glass of water and a straw for me, while he advised me that I had a mild concussion, but if things went as expected I'd have no lasting problems and I'd be out by Saturday. Fargo, he continued, had a sprained ankle and would also be released on Saturday, with no serious damage.

Then everybody began to talk at once, and I just smiled and tried not to listen. They were making my head hurt. Finally, Aunt Mae said she'd run along now, but would drop by tomorrow. Cindy said that she had to work tomorrow, but my mother would bring whatever I needed in the morning and she—Cindy—would see me around four. Mother said that since Cindy had to work, she—Mother—would come by tomorrow morning with whatever I needed and Cindy would stop by later. I gave Sonny a desperate look and he herded everybody out.

He stuck his head back in the door. "You want to get some sleep now?"

"No." I waved him in. "I want to know what happened. Can you get me a Diet Coke first, though? I'm dry as hell."

"Sure."

He was back shortly, trailing Lainey, who automatically checked my pulse and then said if I'd like some dinner, she'd have a tray sent up. I nodded gratefully, said, "Ouch," and Lainey laughed and left.

"So tell." I popped the drink and took a long swallow.

"Well, we missed him at the airport. By seconds. Mitch should have told them to have the plane circle the airport and land back at Ptown, and we could have taken him off then and there. I would have assumed he had no weapon that might have endangered other passengers or the crew, and that we could have gotten him off quickly, with no fuss. Hopefully, you can't just stroll aboard a plane with a pistol in your pocket these days. But Dudley Bythebook left it up to Logan security to approach him by surprise."

He pulled over a chair and sat gingerly. "You can kill yourself on these things. Anyway, Logan security was on top of it. They had the plane taxi to an area away from the terminals, boarded and got him and his luggage off without incident."

He looked around the room. "I suppose a cigarette is not a good idea."

I pointed to a little tube taped under my nose. "This is oxygen. I think the Ptown P.D. has given the fire department enough grief for one day." Immediately, I wished I hadn't said it. Sonny sighed and his mouth tightened into a white line. I knew his feelings must be mixed and painful, torn between anger that one of his cops had disgraced his beloved department and sadness that a friend had ruined his life.

Sonny ignored my remark and continued. "You were right about the jewelry. It was in his bag, and he had about fifteen hundred dollars in cash and travelers' checks. That may have been Grace's money, part of it anyway. I wonder why he took the jewelry with him? He had no idea you would survive that blaze. No one would have had any idea he was the perp."

I finished the Coke and set the can on that little table that fits over your bed. "I think I know. Amsterdam is jewelry city, I've read. So even if he popped out the stones and sold them unmounted, and sold the settings by troy weight, he'd have gotten a bundle. And by then they'd have been virtually untraceable. But, God, Sonny, did he need money that badly? And how could he have explained having it? I mean, he could hardly have come home and casually bought a Jaguar."

"Oh, that part is easy," Sonny answered. "All he would have to do is say he had some good nights at a casino in Europe. But I don't know why he 'needed' it, either. I do know Richard would have set him up with a cushy job in Boston. Pete is smart and hard working. He'd have made good, and in a few years the Jaguar could have been his, anyway. There's something we're not seeing here."

"Where is he now?" I was having trouble keeping my thoughts straight.

"In Boston. Cassie is flying Mitch and Hatcher over to pick him up in the morning."

"Hatcher?"

"One of the new patrolmen. Seems bright enough. Anyway, you don't look so bright. You get some rest and don't worry about Fargo. Victor is only holding him so he can keep him caged and pretty immobile . . . probably the same reason they're holding you, come to think of it. I'll see you tomorrow." He paused. "Uh, you done good, Sis."

He only called me "Sis" when he was emotional. I was touched.

As my brother exited, my dinner entered.

A cup of bouillon, four saltines, a watery poached egg on toast left from Tuesday, a little cup of vanilla ice cream. Well, saltines and ice cream weren't bad.

I drifted off to sleep with dreams of pastrami on rye.

My first visitor arrived early Friday morning, bearing the paper, a copy of P.D. James' *The Murder Room* and a container of real coffee.

"I don't imagine you expected me to call." She sounded slightly unsure, not the usual tone for our Maureen.

I waved the coffee. "I'm grateful that you did. Have a seat."

"How are you? I feel awful about what happened. To you and to Mary's house."

"I don't feel too bad, but I don't think you can say that for the house."

"No. The bedrooms and bath are about all that's left. And the garage. Look, Alex." She shifted slightly in the chair. "I know you don't like me much, but I'm really not all that bad. And the good Lord knows I never meant any of this to happen."

She was right. I didn't like her much. But actually, about the worst you could say was she was an opportunist. A beautiful young woman suddenly transplanted from a slow-moving Irish town to the good ol' fast track U.S. of A. Dating a handsome, rich young man. Who knows how anyone might have handled what looked like a real Hollywood script?

"Don't look to me for absolution, Maureen. But if it makes you feel any better, I think a number of people contributed to this mess. You, for one, but Jack was certainly in it. And Mary added to it, and Grace herself was no angel. And then Pete Santos, for some unknown reason."

"Oh," she said. "I think I know what Pete had in mind. He was going to be the hero."

"The *hero?*" Speaking loudly still wasn't a good idea.

"Yes. You see, he adored Jack. Jack could do no wrong. He was Pete's idol. Pete thought Jack was the smartest, coolest guy in the world. Popular with men and women alike, socially very smooth, intellectually bright. Jack graduated Harvard and was accepted at a fine law school, if Grace would just have paid the fees . . . or be put out of the way so Richard could, without causing a ruckus. So . . . Pete killed Grace for Jack, though Jack would never have known it. It would have been enough that Pete knew. Every triumph of Jack's would have been a secret triumph for Pete. And if you had cooperated by dying, too, he'd have got clean away with it."

I looked at her, first in disbelief, then with dawning understanding. It did make sense. I recalled how Pete had jumped me when I even hinted that Jack might have forced himself on Maureen. And how he carried the grudge long after I apologized.

"I have to admit, Maureen, you are one smart woman." I sipped the cooling, but still delicious coffee. "Where are you staying, by the way?"

She grimaced. "I'm spending a few days with my old roommates, in that closet. It won't be for long. I've asked for a transfer back to Boston and been assured it will go through. They're going to put me in a training program for a corporate job. Thank God,

I'll not be climbing phone poles all my life! And sure, I'll be glad to be out of Provincetown." She flashed that smile that made my heart quiver. Or made something quiver. "And I'm thinking there's a few who'll be glad to see me go."

I didn't try to answer that, and Maureen stood. She walked over to the bed and gave me one of those kisses. "We'll never know what we missed, luv." She reached the door and turned back. "May the wind be always at your back."

She left, and I felt strange.

Lainey picked that moment to come in and check my blood pressure and temperature. "Both slightly elevated," she announced wryly. "But doubtless they'll be back to normal before Cindy arrives, and you've plenty of time to get that lipstick off your mouth."

I grabbed a tissue and rubbed. "It was nothing, just a friendly farewell."

"Sure."

"Hey, you and Trish and Cindy are always taking shots at the girl. She's okay. *I* had no trouble handling her," I said, coolly tossing the tissue into the wastebasket.

Lainey let out a guffaw that resounded down the hall. "You? Handle Maureen? Sweetie, she would have you for breakfast and spit out the seeds."

I picked up another tissue.

Chapter 30

Friday morning went quickly. Shortly after Maureen left, Mom came by, bearing a little kit of what I needed, including fresh clothes for tomorrow's journey home. Aunt Mae stuck her head in to bring some beautiful fresh apricots. Cindy came in around noon, as I was having lunch. I was delighted to see her. After a favorable report on Fargo, we spoke of ordinary things: the need of a new shower curtain at the cottage, a TV biography of Fred Astaire that she'd enjoyed . . . comfortable things that reminded me I liked being with her. And she took my mind off what I was eating. I took a nap.

Finally, midafternoon, Sonny arrived bearing a pastrami sand-wich and fries and Diet Coke, and I loved him. "Close the door," I instructed sharply, as I graciously ripped the paper away and tore off a large bite of the sandwich. "They're liable t'take it 'way 'f they smell it," I muttered between chews. "You are a doll!" I shoved a fry in my mouth.

"Jesus, Alex, slow down. I don't want to have to explain why you choked to death in a hospital room."

"Okay, okay. I'm good. Did Pete get back? What did he have to say for himself?"

"Yes. Quite a bit to say. Nothing especially sensible, but I guess it's true. None of this whole incident has made sense. Why start now?" He sat down and popped his own Coke. "I thought about beer, but I was afraid Lainey would kill us both if I brought that," he apologized.

I felt suddenly wistful. "Probably. Anyway, about Pete . . ."

"Yeah. Well, Pete said he originally had absolutely no reason even to think of killing Grace. He was actually quite fond of her. Then he read that stupid book of Maureen's . . . what was it?"

"*Death of a Peer*," I filled in.

"Yeah. I tried to read it myself. Maybe it's because it's so old, but I found it hard to follow. I did get the gist of it, I think. Pete said it got him thinking how unfair Grace was to keep Jack on tenterhooks all the time about money, making him beg for every penny, just like the old lord in the book. So he went to talk to her."

"Pete went to tell Grace she should pay Jack's tuition? Wow! Give him credit for being ballsy."

"You better believe. However, it got him nowhere, as one would figure. I guess Grace thanked him for his interest, but told him she was quite capable of taking care of family matters without his assistance and just blew him off. He came away angry and hurt, he said, but not at all thinking of harming her."

Sonny leaned over and hooked a couple of fries. I didn't have the nerve to move them out of his reach. "Anyway," he continued, "A few days later, Pete finished *Death of a Peer* and went to return it. Maureen wasn't there, but Mary was home, cleaning out some kitchen utensil drawers."

"What else?" I mumbled, wondering when I had last done that. If ever.

Sonny grinned and continued. "He and Mary chatted a minute and then she went out of the kitchen to put the book away. At that moment, Pete saw the meat thermometer lying on the counter, looking sort of like a skewer, he said, and something 'just told him' he had to take it with him. Using his handkerchief, he picked it up and slipped it in his jacket pocket. He said he left shortly thereafter. With all the stuff out on the counter, Mary didn't notice the thermometer's absence."

"When was this?" I took the last bite of the sandwich and wondered if I could convince him to bring me crab cakes for dinner.

"Not sure. About three days before the murder. It's weird, Alex, he said it made him feel 'secure' to know the thermometer, or skewer, he called it, was always in his pocket. He carried it around with him. And he said he began to get the idea or feeling that it was up to him to see that Jack got to the law school he wanted to attend, and that he be able to specialize in whatever type of law he wanted. Pete said he began to think of Jack's predicament all the time."

"He was obsessed," I suggested.

"He was sure as hell something!" Sonny nodded. "On that Friday evening, he was at the hospital visiting Juvenal, who had that ankle surgery. On his way out, he spotted a linen cart in the corridor. He 'got a feeling' he was going to need it for something, although he didn't know what. No one was around, so he pushed it out the loading exit, put it in his pickup and tossed a tarp over it. He said the fact he was stealing never entered his mind. It was like it had been put there for him to find. Now he felt even more 'secure,' knowing it was at hand."

"This is getting really strange." Nobly, I offered Sonny the last two fries. Nobly, he took only one.

"Crazy is more like it. He decided to give Grace one more try, to talk her into coming up with the money. Leaving the hospital, he went up to her house. She was in the library eating from a tray, watching the news. Pete said she seemed very 'up,' almost giddy and girlish over something. He got the subject around to Jack and money somehow or other and she just kept smiling at him, telling him she had great plans for the future and didn't need his input.

Finally she just laughed and told him to be a good boy and run along. I guess that was the last straw."

I snagged the last fry and then stopped with it halfway to my mouth. "Oh, God, Sonny, if she had just told him about those great plans, she'd be alive today!" I paused. "Or maybe not." I told him of Maureen's theory that Pete wanted to be a "hero" to Jack.

"And," I added, "Maureen knew nothing of the jewelry and cash. But if Pete got Grace out of the way for the future, and then came home from Europe with the money Jack needed right away . . . he'd have been a hero big time."

"Ye-es," Sonny mused. "And Jack would have been indebted to him forever. Oh, Pete would have been repaid, by a trust fund, or Richard or whatever, but Jack would still always 'owe' him for the original gesture. I think Pete would have liked that. Pete used to talk sometimes about all the favors he owed Jack. For picking up a tab, or covering a motel bill if they had dates, stuff like that. Pete used to say that someday Jack would need him and he'd be there. I just thought he meant personally. You know, like he was 'there' for Grace's funeral. But obviously he meant more."

Sonny drained his soda and tossed the can in the trash. "Oh, that reminds me. I guess after the funeral, the rector, or maybe the vicar, shook hands with Pete and told him how lucky Jack was to have a cousin like him to help him through these tough times. Pete said he then was sure he'd done the right thing if a priest said so. You know what I mean."

"Pete sounds a little hung up on Jack. I wonder if he would ever have told Jack of the wonderful gift he had given him? You know, when they were both very old, or maybe sometime if they were drunk together?"

Sonny bounced the front legs of his chair back onto the floor. "Wonderful gift? What the hell do you mean?"

"A life. What greater gift can you give somebody than a life?" I asked. "It is immeasurable. In value, in money, in importance or love. A gift beyond anything else you can even dream of. And he gave it to Jack. Jack must have been worth a great deal to Pete."

"Oh, yes. Jack was definitely his shining star. Sometimes I wondered if there might have been deeper feelings than just hero worship, but it really doesn't matter. Anyway, that Friday evening, Grace finished her dinner and announced she was going to go 'take a peek at the sky,' meaning she was going out to look through that big old telescope of hers. Pete walked her out to the bluff, said goodbye, kissed her and killed her." Sonny's voice was harsh, as if he were making sure it didn't quaver.

"He *kissed* her? That's sick." I balled up the wreckage from my lunch and fired it into the nearby wastebasket.

"It's certainly melodramatic. Almost as if he likes to tell you he did that. I mean, it really has no bearing on anything. It's just a little frill on the story. Whatever. He put her in the truck, in the cart. He went upstairs and took the jewelry and cash. You know, Alex, I should have known something was off when Lillian's jewelry wasn't touched."

"Probably," I agreed. I got up and walked around a little. The tiles felt cool and refreshing on my bare feet. "Actually, Aunt Mae was the first to sniff in the right direction when she said the killer left Grace's wedding ring and locket behind because he felt they were sacrosanct to her. Remember?"

"Yes. Now I do. Well, just to wrap it up, he parked the cart in your garage, as you well know. I asked him why. He said he knew you were away, and it was a good way to make sure the body wasn't found for a while . . . more time for trails to grow cold and confusing. That is probably true, but he *was* still miffed at you for being accusatory of Jack. He mentioned it several times to various people. I think that was part of it."

"Hell, Sonny, I wasn't nasty to Jack. We got quite friendly. Surely Pete knows sometimes you have to ask unpleasant questions. Anyway, doesn't he give me credit for 'saving' Grace from Mary's little fit in front of the restaurant?" I sat back down on the side of my bed, slightly lightheaded but definitely on the mend.

"On the contrary." Sonny shook his finger. "He was angry because you were there to do it. When I told him, he first got mad at me. Said if I hadn't had him out in the West End about a stolen bike, he might have been going to lunch himself and been in the area to break up the attack. Then he decided to be mad at you for 'show-boating.'"

"He must have been pretty mad. Enough to want to kill me."

Sonny gave an angry little laugh. "He referred to you and Fargo as collateral damage."

"That son of a bitch."

"He said he knew he had to find that book so he could make it disappear and he could deny it ever existed, so that certainly there would be no proof he ever saw or touched it. When Maureen left and you stayed in the house, he didn't have time to wait for you to leave and let him either find the book and take it or torch the house. He had a plane to catch, so unfortunately, you had to go with the house right then. Tough for Fargo and you, but necessary."

"That little prick!" I felt a great desire to give Pete a good hard kick. But not in the head.

"Get back into bed and stop yelling or you won't be going home tomorrow." Lainey's voice cut through my thoughts of what I'd like to do to Pete Santos. "Alex! Do I smell *pastrami*?"

"Er, ah, Sonny had a sandwich for . . . for a late lunch," I stammered. "Didn't you?" I asked. "Sonny?"

But Sonny was gone.

Chapter 31

Cindy picked me up early afternoon Saturday, and once home I settled happily into a chaise in the backyard. It was great to breathe unprocessed air. Fargo arrived with Sonny and Trish a short while later.

Our reunion was fervid, with loud whimpers and growls by both parties. He showed me his paw, which I kissed and made well. I showed him my bruised head, which he whuffled around and gave a soft lick, while the other three humans looked on with parental indulgence. Fargo walked over to his water bowl with the slightest of limps and had a good, long slurp, returning to my side with a look that said nobody had better try to move him.

Sonny had brought hamburgers and hotdogs and rolls and wandered off to start the grill. Fargo didn't even follow the trail of the meat.

Trish had brought a salad. Mom and Aunt Mae arrived with a great platter of fried chicken and a bowl of potato salad. Trained investigator that I am, I was beginning to see a pattern here. We wouldn't have to shop or cook for a week.

I thought of what I would be eating if I were still in the hospital. Then my thoughts jumped to what Mary was doubtless eating in jail.

"Sonny," I called, "When is Mary going to be released? Maybe we could get some of this food down to her."

"She's out," he replied. "As of this morning."

"Oh, my God, where is she? That house is unlivable and will be for months. She can't afford a motel for all that time even if her insurance covers part of it. We have to find her."

Mom placed a soothing hand on my shoulder. "Easy, darling, Mary is just fine. Her neighbor, Ann Cartwright, has an extra room and bath, and by now Mary is comfortably settled. Ann is a lovely woman. Mary will be well cared for."

"Does she have a cat?" I asked.

That got me a bunch of concerned looks. Fortunately the arrival of Lillian and Richard Sanhope spared me an explanation. They were bearing a case of chilled champagne and a dozen yellow roses, and were followed by Lainey and Cassie lugging about a dozen kinds of pickles and mustards and chips.

Lainey looked around the rapidly filling yard and shook her head. Her last words to me at the hospital had been, "Now you and Cindy run along and have a *very* quiet weekend. Rest is the best medicine—the only medicine—for a concussion." I laughed, remembering, and she shook her finger at me across the yard, calling, "Watch the champagne, Alex."

"I am watching it carefully," I agreed. "Isn't it beautiful?"

Lillian stopped by my chair to let me sniff the roses before she followed Cindy inside to locate our largest vase. "How are things?" I asked conspiratorially.

"St. Patrick's Day may have a whole new meaning." She grinned and gave me a thumbs up.

Richard said something conventional and then scurried to Sonny's side. I don't know if he felt outnumbered by women in general or lesbians in particular. But he didn't look a great deal more at ease when Peter and the Wolf arrived with Dan and Vance, bearing desserts by the pound.

"Dar-r-rling!" Peter caroled, giving me a brain-rattling hug and smooch on the cheek. "Our brave, *brave* Alex! Heroically wounded in the line of duty! And dearest Fargo! Trying to save you from that horrid man!" He stroked Fargo, who smiled graciously, but didn't move.

"Fargo *did* save me," I corrected. "If he hadn't awakened me, we wouldn't be here. He's the hero, not me. I just stood there and let Santos bop me one."

"Well," Wolf put in, "We'd have given you a party anyway. You just wouldn't be here to enjoy it."

The other three men gave him looks of deep despair and Vance said quickly, "These things need to be kept cool. We'll go put them in the fridge." I wondered how they were going to fit, but today that was not my problem. He dragged Wolf toward the back door, while Peter and Dan excused themselves to head for the makeshift bar Sonny and Richard had set up near the grill.

Trish and Cindy pulled chairs up close to me. "I'm relieved about Mary," Trish remarked. "I was going to talk with John about a place for her, but this sounds perfect. I wonder where the *casus belli* is keeping herself?"

Unthinking, I answered. "Oh, she's with her old roomies for awhile, but she'll be transferring back to Boston. She's going into some corporate training program. I hope she gets into some sort of sales job, she'd be good at that."

"Indeed, she would," Cindy agreed. "How did you hear about this, locked up in a hospital, darling?"

"Well, ah, she came by the other morning. You know, kind of to say goodbye and that she was sorry about all that had happened."

Trish drained her glass. "Probably sorrier about what didn't happen."

"At least, we *assume* it was what didn't happen," Cindy said sweetly. I was delighted to point out the arrival of Jeanine and her

219

husband, bearing a large casserole, and Cindy had no choice but to go and greet them. Trish followed. Maybe Cindy would forget this conversation. Maybe I would win the lottery.

Fargo and I found ourselves alone for the moment, and I don't think either of us minded. I sipped at my excellent Krug. I *was* watching my intake. I was admiring my tomatoes and peppers from afar, when I heard a raspy, "Hiya, Alex," and looked up to see Harmon standing beside me, attired in clean overalls and a fresh, blue work shirt.

He gave me a horny handshake and then proffered a somewhat ratty looking red geranium in a pot wrapped in foil of violent purple. "Uh, Alex, me and the boys down to the Rat all kicked in, Joe too, to get you this flower and hope you're feelin' better. We was sorry you got hurt."

"Harmon, how lovely! And how nice of all of you to think of me!" I had a great desire to cry. The yellow roses were gorgeous, the Krug champagne was a delectable elegance, but I would treasure that geranium.

Sonny had come over when he saw Harmon arrive and saved me from making a fool of myself. "Harmon! Glad you stopped by. Come on over here with Richard and me and let's get a beer."

"That's good, Sonny. We'll let Alex get her rest. I heard that when you get them concushions, you're s'posed to get lots of rest."

"Indeed." Sonny was trying not to giggle as he steered Harmon toward the bar. I wondered what the very proper Richard would think of our latest guest.

I looked around the yard, and took another small sip of my drink. I was alone again, but not really. I was extremely lucky in the assemblage gathered here. I let my hand drop to my side, where it encountered a sleek black pelt. Fargo—especially, always—Fargo.

Publications from
BELLA BOOKS, INC.
The best in contemporary lesbian fiction

P.O. Box 10543, Tallahassee, FL 32302
Phone: 800-729-4992
www.bellabooks.com

THE KILLING ROOM by Gerri Hill. 392 pp. How can two women forget and go their
separate ways? 1-59493-050-3 $12.95

PASSIONATE KISSES by Megan Carter. 240 pp. Will two old friends run from love?
1-59493-051-1 $12.95

ALWAYS AND FOREVER by Lyn Denison. 224 pp. The girl next door turns Shannon's
world upside down. 1-59493-049-X $12.95

BACK TALK by Saxon Bennett. 200 pp. Can a talk show host find love after heartbreak?
1-59493-028-7 $12.95

THE PERFECT VALENTINE: EROTIC LESBIAN VALENTINE STORIES edited by
Barbara Johnson and Therese Szymanski—from Bella After Dark. 328 pp. Stories from the
hottest writers around. 1-59493-061-9 $14.95

MURDER AT RANDOM by Claire McNab. 200 pp. The Sixth Denise Cleever Thriller.
Denise realizes the fate of thousands is in her hands. 1-59493-047-3 $12.95

THE TIDES OF PASSION by Diana Tremain Braund. 240 pp. Will Susan be able to hold
it all together and find the one woman who touches her soul? 1-59493-048-1 $12.95

JUST LIKE THAT by Karin Kallmaker. 240 pp. Disliking each other—and everything they
stand for—even before they meet, Toni and Syrah find feelings can change, just like that.
1-59493-025-2 $12.95

WHEN FIRST WE PRACTICE by Therese Szymanski. 200 pp. Brett and Allie are once
again caught in the middle of murder and intrigue. 1-59493-045-7 $12.95

REUNION by Jane Frances. 240 pp. Cathy Braithwaite seems to have it all: good looks,
money and a thriving accounting practice . . . 1-59493-046-5 $12.95

BELL, BOOK & DYKE: NEW EXPLOITS OF MAGICAL LESBIANS by Kallmaker,
Watts, Johnson and Szymanski. 360 pp. Reluctant witches, tempting spells and skyclad beau-
ties—delve into the mysteries of love, lust and power in this quartet of novellas.
1-59493-023-6 $14.95

ARTIST'S DREAM by Gerri Hill. 320 pp.When Cassie meets Luke Winston, she can no
longer deny her attraction to women . . . 1-59493-042-2 $12.95

NO EVIDENCE by Nancy Sanra. 240 pp. Private Investigator Tally McGinnis once again
returns to the horror-filled world of a serial killer. 1-59493-043-04 $12.95

WHEN LOVE FINDS A HOME by Megan Carter. 280 pp. What will it take for Anna and Rona to find their way back to each other again? 1-59493-041-4 $12.95

MEMORIES TO DIE FOR by Adrian Gold. 240 pp. Rachel attempts to avoid her attraction to the charms of Anna Sigurdson . . . 1-59493-038-4 $12.95

SILENT HEART by Claire McNab. 280 pp. Exotic lesbian romance.
1-59493-044-9 $12.95

MIDNIGHT RAIN by Peggy J. Herring. 240 pp. Bridget McBee is determined to find the woman who saved her life. 1-59493-021-X $12.95

THE MISSING PAGE A Brenda Strange Mystery by Patty G. Henderson. 240 pp. Brenda investigates her client's murder . . . 1-59493-004-X $12.95

WHISPERS ON THE WIND by Frankie J. Jones. 240 pp. Dixon thinks she and her best friend, Elizabeth Colter, would make the perfect couple . . . 1-59493-037-6 $12.95

CALL OF THE DARK: EROTIC LESBIAN TALES OF THE SUPERNATURAL edited by Therese Szymanski—from Bella After Dark. 320 pp. 1-59493-040-6 $14.95

A TIME TO CAST AWAY A Helen Black Mystery by Pat Welch. 240 pp. Helen stops by Alice's apartment—only to find the woman dead . . . 1-59493-036-8 $12.95

DESERT OF THE HEART by Jane Rule. 224 pp. The book that launched the most popular lesbian movie of all time is back. 1-1-59493-035-X $12.95

THE NEXT WORLD by Ursula Steck. 240 pp. Anna's friend Mido is threatened and eventually disappears . . . 1-59493-024-4 $12.95

CALL SHOTGUN by Jaime Clevenger. 240 pp. Kelly gets pulled back into the world of private investigation . . . 1-59493-016-3 $12.95

52 PICKUP by Bonnie J. Morris and E.B. Casey. 240 pp. 52 hot, romantic tales—one for every Saturday night of the year. 1-59493-026-0 $12.95

GOLD FEVER by Lyn Denison. 240 pp. Kate's first love, Ashley, returns to their home town, where Kate now lives . . . 1-1-59493-039-2 $12.95

RISKY INVESTMENT by Beth Moore. 240 pp. Lynn's best friend and roommate needs her to pretend Chris is his fiancé. But nothing is ever easy. 1-59493-019-8 $12.95

HUNTER'S WAY by Gerri Hill. 240 pp. Homicide detective Tori Hunter is forced to team up with the hot-tempered Samantha Kennedy. 1-59493-018-X $12.95

CAR POOL by Karin Kallmaker. 240 pp. Soft shoulders, merging traffic and slippery when wet . . . Anthea and Shay find love in the car pool. 1-59493-013-9 $12.95

NO SISTER OF MINE by Jeanne G'Fellers. 240 pp. Telepathic women fight to coexist with a patriarchal society that wishes their eradication. ISBN 1-59493-017-1 $12.95

ON THE WINGS OF LOVE by Megan Carter. 240 pp. Stacie's reporting career is on the rocks. She has to interview bestselling author Cheryl, or else! ISBN 1-59493-027-9 $12.95

WICKED GOOD TIME by Diana Tremain Braund. 224 pp. Does Christina need Miki as a protector . . . or want her as a lover? ISBN 1-59493-031-7 $12.95

THOSE WHO WAIT by Peggy J. Herring. 240 pp. Two brilliant sisters—in love with the same woman! ISBN 1-59493-032-5 $12.95

ABBY'S PASSION by Jackie Calhoun. 240 pp. Abby's bipolar sister helps turn her world upside down, so she must decide what's most important. ISBN 1-59493-014-7 $12.95

PICTURE PERFECT by Jane Vollbrecht. 240 pp. Kate is reintroduced to Casey, the daughter of an old friend. Can they withstand Kate's career?   ISBN 1-59493-015-5 $12.95

PAPERBACK ROMANCE by Karin Kallmaker. 240 pp. Carolyn falls for tall, dark and . . . female . . . in this classic lesbian romance.   ISBN 1-59493-033-3 $12.95

DAWN OF CHANGE by Gerri Hill. 240 pp. Susan ran away to find peace in remote Kings Canyon—then she met Shawn . . .   ISBN 1-59493-011-2 $12.95

DOWN THE RABBIT HOLE by Lynne Jamneck. 240 pp. Is a killer holding a grudge against FBI Agent Samantha Skellar?   ISBN 1-59493-012-0 $12.95

SEASONS OF THE HEART by Jackie Calhoun. 240 pp. Overwhelmed, Sara saw only one way out—leaving . . .   ISBN 1-59493-030-9 $12.95

TURNING THE TABLES by Jessica Thomas. 240 pp. The 2nd Alex Peres Mystery. *From ghosties and ghoulies and long leggity beasties* . . .   ISBN 1-59493-009-0 $12.95

FOR EVERY SEASON by Frankie Jones. 240 pp. Andi, who is investigating a 65-year-old murder, meets Janice, a charming district attorney . . .   ISBN 1-59493-010-4 $12.95

LOVE ON THE LINE by Laura DeHart Young. 240 pp. Kay leaves a younger woman behind to go on a mission to Alaska . . . will she regret it?   ISBN 1-59493-008-2 $12.95

UNDER THE SOUTHERN CROSS by Claire McNab. 200 pp. Lee, an American travel agent, goes down under and meets Australian Alex, and the sparks fly under the Southern Cross.   ISBN 1-59493-029-5 $12.95

SUGAR by Karin Kallmaker. 240 pp. Three women want sugar from Sugar, who can't make up her mind.   ISBN 1-59493-001-5 $12.95

FALL GUY by Claire McNab. 200 pp. 16th Detective Inspector Carol Ashton Mystery.   ISBN 1-59493-000-7 $12.95

ONE SUMMER NIGHT by Gerri Hill. 232 pp. Johanna swore to never fall in love again— but then she met the charming Kelly . . .   ISBN 1-59493-007-4 $12.95

TALK OF THE TOWN TOO by Saxon Bennett. 181 pp. Second in the series about wild and fun loving friends.   ISBN 1-931513-77-5 $12.95

LOVE SPEAKS HER NAME by Laura DeHart Young. 170 pp. Love and friendship, desire and intrigue, spark this exciting sequel to *Forever and the Night*.   ISBN 1-59493-002-3 $12.95

TO HAVE AND TO HOLD by Peggy J. Herring. 184 pp. By finally letting down her defenses, will Dorian be opening herself to a devastating betrayal?   ISBN 1-59493-005-8 $12.95

WILD THINGS by Karin Kallmaker. 228 pp. Dutiful daughter Faith has met the perfect man. There's just one problem: she's in love with his sister.   ISBN 1-931513-64-3 $12.95

SHARED WINDS by Kenna White. 216 pp. Can Emma rebuild more than just Lanny's marina?   ISBN 1-59493-006-6 $12.95

THE UNKNOWN MILE by Jaime Clevenger. 253 pp. Kelly's world is getting more and more complicated every moment.   ISBN 1-931513-57-0 $12.95

TREASURED PAST by Linda Hill. 189 pp. A shared passion for antiques leads to love.   ISBN 1-59493-003-1 $12.95

SIERRA CITY by Gerri Hill. 284 pp. Chris and Jesse cannot deny their growing attraction . . .   ISBN 1-931513-98-8 $12.95

ALL THE WRONG PLACES by Karin Kallmaker. 174 pp. Sex and the single girl—Brandy is looking for love and usually she finds it. Karin Kallmaker's first *After Dark* erotic novel.
ISBN 1-931513-76-7 $12.95

WHEN THE CORPSE LIES A Motor City Thriller by Therese Szymanski. 328 pp. Butch bad-girl Brett Higgins is used to waking up next to beautiful women she hardly knows. Problem is, this one's dead.
ISBN 1-931513-74-0 $12.95

GUARDED HEARTS by Hannah Rickard. 240 pp. Someone's reminding Alyssa about her secret past, and then she becomes the suspect in a series of burglaries.
ISBN 1-931513-99-6 $12.95

ONCE MORE WITH FEELING by Peggy J. Herring. 184 pp. Lighthearted, loving, romantic adventure.
ISBN 1-931513-60-0 $12.95

TANGLED AND DARK A Brenda Strange Mystery by Patty G. Henderson. 240 pp. When investigating a local death, Brenda finds two possible killers—one diagnosed with Multiple Personality Disorder.
ISBN 1-931513-75-9 $12.95

WHITE LACE AND PROMISES by Peggy J. Herring. 240 pp. Maxine and Betina realize sex may not be the most important thing in their lives.
ISBN 1-931513-73-2 $12.95

UNFORGETTABLE by Karin Kallmaker. 288 pp. Can Rett find love with the cheerleader who broke her heart so many years ago?
ISBN 1-931513-63-5 $12.95

HIGHER GROUND by Saxon Bennett. 280 pp. A delightfully complex reflection of the successful, high society lives of a small group of women.
ISBN 1-931513-69-4 $12.95

LAST CALL A Detective Franco Mystery by Baxter Clare. 240 pp. Frank overlooks all else to try to solve a cold case of two murdered children . . .
ISBN 1-931513-70-8 $12.95

ONCE UPON A DYKE: NEW EXPLOITS OF FAIRY-TALE LESBIANS by Karin Kallmaker, Julia Watts, Barbara Johnson & Therese Szymanski. 320 pp. You've never read fairy tales like these before! From Bella After Dark.
ISBN 1-931513-71-6 $14.95

FINEST KIND OF LOVE by Diana Tremain Braund. 224 pp. Can Molly and Carolyn stop clashing long enough to see beyond their differences?
ISBN 1-931513-68-6 $12.95

DREAM LOVER by Lyn Denison. 188 pp. A soft, sensuous, romantic fantasy.
ISBN 1-931513-96-1 $12.95

NEVER SAY NEVER by Linda Hill. 224 pp. A classic love story . . . where rules aren't the only things broken.
ISBN 1-931513-67-8 $12.95

PAINTED MOON by Karin Kallmaker. 214 pp. Stranded together in a snowbound cabin, Jackie and Leah's lives will never be the same.
ISBN 1-931513-53-8 $12.95

WIZARD OF ISIS by Jean Stewart. 240 pp. Fifth in the exciting Isis series.
ISBN 1-931513-71-4 $12.95

WOMAN IN THE MIRROR by Jackie Calhoun. 216 pp. Josey learns to love again, while her niece is learning to love women for the first time.
ISBN 1-931513-78-3 $12.95

SUBSTITUTE FOR LOVE by Karin Kallmaker. 200 pp. When Holly and Reyna meet the combination adds up to pure passion. But what about tomorrow?
ISBN 1-931513-62-7 $12.95

GULF BREEZE by Gerri Hill. 288 pp. Could Carly really be the woman Pat has always been searching for?
ISBN 1-931513-97-X $12.95

THE TOMSTOWN INCIDENT by Penny Hayes. 184 pp. Caught between two worlds, Eloise must make a decision that will change her life forever. ISBN 1-931513-56-2 $12.95

MAKING UP FOR LOST TIME by Karin Kallmaker. 240 pp. Discover delicious recipes for romance by the undisputed mistress. ISBN 1-931513-61-9 $12.95

THE WAY LIFE SHOULD BE by Diana Tremain Braund. 173 pp. With which woman will Jennifer find the true meaning of love? ISBN 1-931513-66-X $12.95

BACK TO BASICS: A BUTCH/FEMME ANTHOLOGY edited by Therese Szymanski— from Bella After Dark. 324 pp. ISBN 1-931513-35-X $14.95

SURVIVAL OF LOVE by Frankie J. Jones. 236 pp. What will Jody do when she falls in love with her best friend's daughter? ISBN 1-931513-55-4 $12.95

LESSONS IN MURDER by Claire McNab. 184 pp. 1st Detective Inspector Carol Ashton Mystery. ISBN 1-931513-65-1 $12.95

DEATH BY DEATH by Claire McNab. 167 pp. 5th Denise Cleever Thriller.
ISBN 1-931513-34-1 $12.95

CAUGHT IN THE NET by Jessica Thomas. 188 pp. A wickedly observant story of mystery, danger, and love in Provincetown. ISBN 1-931513-54-6 $12.95

DREAMS FOUND by Lyn Denison. Australian Riley embarks on a journey to meet her birth mother . . . and gains not just a family, but the love of her life. ISBN 1-931513-58-9 $12.95

A MOMENT'S INDISCRETION by Peggy J. Herring. 154 pp. Jackie is torn between her better judgment and the overwhelming attraction she feels for Valerie.
ISBN 1-931513-59-7 $12.95

IN EVERY PORT by Karin Kallmaker. 224 pp. Jessica has a woman in every port. Will meeting Cat change all that? ISBN 1-931513-36-8 $12.95

TOUCHWOOD by Karin Kallmaker. 240 pp. Rayann loves Louisa. Louisa loves Rayann. Can the decades between their ages keep them apart? ISBN 1-931513-37-6 $12.95

WATERMARK by Karin Kallmaker. 248 pp. Teresa wants a future with a woman whose heart has been frozen by loss. Sequel to *Touchwood*. ISBN 1-931513-38-4 $12.95

EMBRACE IN MOTION by Karin Kallmaker. 240 pp. Has Sarah found lust or love?
ISBN 1-931513-39-2 $12.95

ONE DEGREE OF SEPARATION by Karin Kallmaker. 232 pp. Sizzling small town romance between Marian, the town librarian, and the new girl from the big city.
ISBN 1-931513-30-9 $12.95

CRY HAVOC A Detective Franco Mystery by Baxter Clare. 240 pp. A dead hustler with a headless rooster in his lap sends Lt. L.A. Franco headfirst against Mother Love.
ISBN 1-931513931-7 $12.95

DISTANT THUNDER by Peggy J. Herring. 294 pp. Bankrobbing drifter Cordy awakens strange new feelings in Leo in this romantic tale set in the Old West.
ISBN 1-931513-28-7 $12.95

COP OUT by Claire McNab. 216 pp. 4th Detective Inspector Carol Ashton Mystery.
ISBN 1-931513-29-5 $12.95

BLOOD LINK by Claire McNab. 159 pp. 15th Detective Inspector Carol Ashton Mystery. Is Carol unwittingly playing into a deadly plan? ISBN 1-931513-27-9 $12.95

TALK OF THE TOWN by Saxon Bennett. 239 pp. With enough beer, barbecue and B.S., anything is possible! ISBN 1-931513-18-X $12.95

TO HAVE AND TO HOLD by Peggy J. Herring. 184 pp. By finally letting down her defenses, will Dorian be opening herself to a devastating betrayal?
ISBN 1-59493-005-8 $12.95

WILD THINGS by Karin Kallmaker. 228 pp. Dutiful daughter Faith has met the perfect man. There's just one problem: she's in love with his sister. ISBN 1-931513-64-3 $12.95

SHARED WINDS by Kenna White. 216 pp. Can Emma rebuild more than just Lanny's marina? ISBN 1-59493-006-6 $12.95

THE UNKNOWN MILE by Jaime Clevenger. 253 pp. Kelly's world is getting more and more complicated every moment. ISBN 1-931513-57-0 $12.95

TREASURED PAST by Linda Hill. 189 pp. A shared passion for antiques leads to love.
ISBN 1-59493-003-1 $12.95

SIERRA CITY by Gerri Hill. 284 pp. Chris and Jesse cannot deny their growing attraction . . . ISBN 1-931513-98-8 $12.95

ALL THE WRONG PLACES by Karin Kallmaker. 174 pp. Sex and the single girl—Brandy is looking for love and usually she finds it. Karin Kallmaker's first *After Dark* erotic novel.
ISBN 1-931513-76-7 $12.95

WHEN THE CORPSE LIES A Motor City Thriller by Therese Szymanski. 328 pp. Butch bad-girl Brett Higgins is used to waking up next to beautiful women she hardly knows. Problem is, this one's dead. ISBN 1-931513-74-0 $12.95

GUARDED HEARTS by Hannah Rickard. 240 pp. Someone's reminding Alyssa about her secret past, and then she becomes the suspect in a series of burglaries.
ISBN 1-931513-99-6 $12.95

ONCE MORE WITH FEELING by Peggy J. Herring. 184 pp. Lighthearted, loving, romantic adventure. ISBN 1-931513-60-0 $12.95

TANGLED AND DARK A Brenda Strange Mystery by Patty G. Henderson. 240 pp. When investigating a local death, Brenda finds two possible killers—one diagnosed with Multiple Personality Disorder. ISBN 1-931513-75-9 $12.95

WHITE LACE AND PROMISES by Peggy J. Herring. 240 pp. Maxine and Betina realize sex may not be the most important thing in their lives. ISBN 1-931513-73-2 $12.95

UNFORGETTABLE by Karin Kallmaker. 288 pp. Can Rett find love with the cheerleader who broke her heart so many years ago? ISBN 1-931513-63-5 $12.95

HIGHER GROUND by Saxon Bennett. 280 pp. A delightfully complex reflection of the successful, high society lives of a small group of women. ISBN 1-931513-69-4 $12.95

LAST CALL A Detective Franco Mystery by Baxter Clare. 240 pp. Frank overlooks all else to try to solve a cold case of two murdered children . . . ISBN 1-931513-70-8 $12.95

ONCE UPON A DYKE: NEW EXPLOITS OF FAIRY-TALE LESBIANS by Karin Kallmaker, Julia Watts, Barbara Johnson & Therese Szymanski. 320 pp. You've never read fairy tales like these before! From Bella After Dark. ISBN 1-931513-71-6 $14.95

FINEST KIND OF LOVE by Diana Tremain Braund. 224 pp. Can Molly and Carolyn stop clashing long enough to see beyond their differences? ISBN 1-931513-68-6 $12.95

DREAM LOVER by Lyn Denison. 188 pp. A soft, sensuous, romantic fantasy.
ISBN 1-931513-96-1 $12.95